COMPANY OF DECEIT

Bobby Green

Greenlight Publishers, Inc.
Ridgeland, Mississippi

Book design by Bryan Rogers

Manufactured in the United States of America

Greenlight Publishers, Inc.
P.O. Box 1617
Ridgeland, Mississippi 39158-1617

Printed by Hederman Brothers
Ridgeland, Mississippi

ISBN 0-9713974-7-3

Acknowledgements

Although an enjoyable challenge, this novel was not a solo effort. Credit must and will be given to those whose dedication and positive influence gave encouragement.

To my wife Jane for her long hours and literary excellence who always had a positive word of encouragement as we labored in this endeavor.

A sincere appreciation to Andrew Branscome to whom befell the task of grim reaper as he candidly edited the text with guidance, criticism, and direction.

To my son Timothy whose youthful intrusions were fresh and stimulating.

A special thanks to Pat Ross whose sound advice was a beacon in a storm of inexperience and also Jeanie Tadlock at Hederman Brothers for her efforts and support.

Bryan Rogers for his outstanding art work on the cover and the many others who shared in this total effort.

CONTENTS

1 Lure of Easy Money

In the near blackness of the Honduran jungle, the night seemed to press against him. This constant chatter from the soldiers camped along the edge of the trees a hundred or so yards south of the hastily constructed dirt airstrip was a constant reminder of where he was and what he was doing.

Rob Marshall needed the quiet break he was getting. He stood with his right hand on the propeller blade of the old cargo DC-3, her metallic finish shining dully in the moonlight as it streaked from between the low clouds. Lifting his deeply tanned arm, he peered out of a weathered and wrinkled face at his watch. Just past ten. The last eight hours had been a living taste of hell. It would be another five hours before they could leave this place.

A moist, tropical breeze from the south brought the fragrance of the late summer flowers mingled with marijuana smoke from the revolutionaries' camp. Kicking the large, black tire on the main landing gear in frustration, he mumbled to himself, son of a bitch. Twisting his muscular body around, he sat down on the moist ground in front of the tire and leaned his shoulder and head back. With his right hand in a habitual motion, he grasped the bill of his baseball cap and pulled it up from his head and with his left hand, combed the thick, streaky gray hair, pulling his cap back on. A muffled snore off to his right told him his buddy Mike wasn't missing any sleep, jacket rolled up in a misshapen pillow under his head. His cap was pulled down over his eyes, long blue jean clad legs crossed, left arm over his face, sound asleep. One little revolutionary war was far down on the list of things that Mike would stay awake for.

Huddled around the aged jeep, the Latino soldiers were passing around a marijuana joint. Again, the smell drifted over to Rob as he tried vainly to relax. The damp warm jungle breeze blew across him and made him even more aware that his clothes were soaked through with the sweat. The breeze did temporarily dim the buzzing of the millions of mosquitoes flying around his head looking for a snack. God, he needed to sleep; he needed to be sharp if they were to be off the ground by three a.m. They had to wait until then. If they were back at the island airport any sooner, fast-talking might not do any good.

A shadowy shape appeared. Rob would have known Juan Pablo's form anywhere. He was half Chinese and half Hispanic. His oriental half dominated and he walked with a slow, deliberate pace that matched his speech. His stocky form moved toward the old DC-3. He was the interpreter that Jacobson sent with them. Whether he could be trusted or not was beside the point. He was in the same situation as they were. A crackle from the radio, and two soldiers leaped from the jeep and rushed toward the plane. "You must go; you must hurry!" they said in broken English.

Rob looked up at them with a puzzled expression. And then he heard the important part. "Our border post has spotted a helicopter coming up the coast," said the other soldier. "Someone has reported you to the Sandinistas."

"Well, that's just perfect," Rob said jumping to his feet, "Mike, Mike, wake up." Mike rolled over, grumbled, and then went back to sleep. "Get up you lazy coon ass, we gotta get the hell out of here."

His soft Cajun accent coming through even in his sleep, Mike lifted his head and then looked at his watch. "What the hell are you talkin' about, it's only ten fifteen."

"There is a Sandinista gunship coming up the coast to blow us to bits. If you want to stick around till it gets here, fine by me, but I'm leaving." To suit his words he turned down the side of the airplane and ran for the cargo door. He sprinted up the slanted floor of the cargo compartment of the plane and sprang into the cockpit, soon hearing the thud of Mike's and Juan's following footsteps. Rob knew the old DC-3 was no match for a modern Russian helicopter gunship flown by experienced Cuban pilots. His DC-3 was not armed and it was on the ground-a sitting duck.

Damn, what else was going to go wrong? Now they were tangling with a Russian gunship. This definitely wasn't part of the deal Rob had made with Jacobson. These last three weeks had been like a bad dream; their asses were out of one crack and into another. Man, what am I doing here? But he knew the answer to that—-it was the lure of easy money. At least, that was the story this great inspirational leader Jacobson had given him. Really easy, the easiest money he would ever make in a short period of time. Now it looked as if they were going to earn every penny of it the hard way. The man he was working for was a "company" man. They called it the company, but he knew what it was. It meant he had the authority to recruit idiots to do the dirty work, ones who would risk their lives while he, Mr. Jacobson, was back in his home in Florida or anywhere that was safe.

The number two engine came to life with some coaxing, as Mike took his place in the copilot's seat. "Number one giving you trouble again?" Mike asked as he looked to Rob with as close to terror as Mike could manage. "This is a bad time for her to be acting up."

"Tell me about it," Rob said to Mike as he reached his hand out and rubbed the instrument panel. "C'mon baby, start for me. I know you want to." With that the number one engine sprang to life billowing thick black smoke. "Good girl."

Rob looked out of the dirty cockpit windows, watching the Latinos run from oil pot to oil pot, lighting the runway for take off; they were running way too slow for Rob's taste. Yelling above the engine roar, "Lets go, lets go!" Rob pushed on the throttle and began to swing the old bird around. "The borders only a few miles away. I hope we can make it before that helicopter shows and rips us a new one. They don't know our exact location, or they would be here by now. In the darkness the crew of the helicopter will have to spend some time searching for this airstrip, and those damn lights will make that easier," Rob added.

"You don't have to tell me twice, man. It's your bird, but it's my ass." Mike's emphatic reply came as they swung the big old bird around and lined up with the lights. Mike locked the tailwheel. That was the extent of the run-up. They pushed the throttles, prop controls, and mixture controls full forward. The plane lunged once as the brakes were released, then lumbered off, slowly at first, gradually gaining speed. The time it took to get airborne seemed like eternity, when in reality, it was only seconds. Now the silver DC-3 lifted off the ground, straining as it made a right turn to the north, just clearing the treetops. If they were lucky, the helicopter hadn't spotted them. "Avoiding that gunship is our only way out of this mess so keep the lights off. We'll use our flashlights, turn them on just to check our heading and airspeed," Rob said.

The airplane rattled and shook as he pushed the throttle to climb power but kept the heading straight as an arrow, bringing her to her maximum speed. Hugging the trees and staying under the sparse cloud cover, they held their breath as they raced for the coast. If they stayed close to the ground and avoided the radar tracking systems on the chopper, they had a chance. Still they were easy prey for the rockets and machine guns of the attack helicopter. The crew had a small prayer of a chance.

"Hey, God, are you listening?" Rob said to himself as he peered every way at once searching for any sign of the helicopter.

The bright moon in the east was sometimes covered by clouds, causing moments of total darkness. "We need to keep the airplane out of the trees and hug the ground. Maybe the radar won't pick us up," Rob said.

Now they were only five minutes from the east coast of Honduras. Both men were beginning to relax and took time to put on their headsets. There was still very little talking. They were both busy scanning both sides and ahead of the airplane.

"Maybe, just maybe, that long turn to the north has put enough distance between us and the border to discourage the sons of bitches," Mike said. Then suddenly over to the south at two o'clock, the chopper's main rotor blades were flashing in the moonlight. Mike whispered into the intercom as if he thought they could hear. "God, please! Don't see us. We're not any faster than they are and for damn sure can't outrun those rockets." His heart pounded in his throat. Then suddenly they were swallowed by darkness as another cloud obscured the moon. If they could hug the treetops, maintain their heading, and get over the next little rise, they would be safely out over the ocean.

During all the excitement, Juan Pablo Ming observed the two men and remained completely silent.

With a flash they were back out of the cloud's shadows and into the moonlight. Mike gazed to the south through the narrow stained side windshield of the airplane, straining to see the helicopter. There it was making a slow turn to the west. Suddenly, he jerked straight up and leaned close to the glass. The helicopter had stopped its turn and was heading directly towards them. There was a burst of orange light and the helicopter was no longer a faint shadow but a bright glowing image.

"Oh shit." Mike exclaimed as he caught sight of a glint from the main rotors of the Sandanista gunship. "They fired on us," Mike shouted and slammed the control yoke forward.

"Down," he yelled. Their only chance was to break the radar contact, and to do that, they had to get behind the ridge they were now crossing and stay out of the trees.

"Hang on," Rob cried as the old airplane shuddered and shook from the desperate dive. With a flash of light, the rocket whistled past them by only a few feet. Seconds later it exploded into a fireball between them and the ocean. No one spoke as the airplane was buffeted by the turbulence of the explosion. "Those bastards!" Rob shouted as his adrenaline pulsed through his body with a tingling sensation.

They were still skimming treetops. The gleaming moonlight on the ocean waves was a welcome sight. Looking to the south, Mike exclaimed, "I can't see the helicopter. They think they've got us and have turned back."

"Man, I guess we squeaked by one more time," said Rob. "These last twenty-four hours have been a nightmare. In forty years I've faced a lot of crap, but I don't remember ever letting myself get in a screw-up like this." He wiped sweat beads off his face.

"I let them load us up with enough arms and ammunition to start World War III and send us off into the Caribbean in the middle of a storm. Bad weather made the flight too long, and we almost ran out of fuel. Then when we got to dirt international in the middle of this damn Honduran hellhole, those part-time jungle fighters had decided to go home for the day. Luckily for us, that local was out horseback riding, saw us land, and alerted Caberallos and his people. Now we've become target practice for the Sandinistas. That about the way it's gone?"

"Yeah, but where do we go from here?" Mike asked. "Our original plans called for us to be back at the island by dawn. Now that's screwed up. We'll be getting back in the middle of the night with no one around to greet us except maybe the local law."

"You're right," Rob said. "If we land at the International Airport in the middle of the night without a flight plan, there will be all kinds of questions that we can't answer. We're on our own. Jacobson made that clear from the beginning. There'll be no help from him. 'You deliver; we pay. No delivery, no pay. You get your ass in trouble; you get your ass out of trouble. That's the way the system works.' At least, Jacobson made me think that."

They were flying with no identification and no registration on the airplane. If they were to go to the Caribbean island airport, who could they call or get to help them through customs? There was also the small problem of the cargo that the soldiers loaded for the return trip, the locked, canvas bags that Caberallos said Jacobson knew about and would take care of. They both knew it was contraband drugs, but they had to play dumb. There were certain things that were done to protect the relationship between the company and the freedom fighters.

The money made from the sale of this special merchandise would end up in a secret Swiss account along with any other funds that couldn't be traced.

Rob knew if he lost the special cargo, the company had the excuse for not paying the sixty thousand dollars owed to them for making this ill-conceived and disorganized flight.

"Well, are we going back to the island?" Mike asked.

"Looks like that's the only thing we can do," Rob answered. He took a deep breath and looked at Mike.

"Yep, I guess you're right. A damp, dirty jail is better than a wet Caribbean Sea, and right now, those are our only options." Sometimes shit happens was all Mike could think.

When the DC-3 reached seven thousand feet, Rob trimmed it up and set the power for a slow cruise. They were on an easterly heading and had about four hours to decide on a plan of action.

They were definitely not government employees by anyone's definition. If they were arrested when they landed in the islands, they couldn't count on Jacobson and his group getting them out of jail. There was one other alternative, a seldom used, dirt airstrip out in the country about forty miles east of the International Airport. In the darkness, with no one expecting them before seven a.m., they would have to land from over the ocean between trees and up a mountainside, which was a difficult task even in the daylight. After weighing the odds, Rob decided not to go for it. The International Airport was it. They would just have to take their chances with the authorities.

Rob pushed the intercom button and looked over at Mike, "You take over. Maintain this heading and altitude. I want to take a look at something."

"I've got it," said Mike. Rob released the yoke, and his partner took over.

Rob pulled the release handle and pushed his seat back. Fumbling around in the darkness, he located his flashlight and began mulling over the flight charts. Studying the maps, he knew they had made the right decision.

2 THE PRICE IS RIGHT

The events of the last four or was it five days-he couldn't remember- were a real bitch. They'd gotten themselves into a struggle dominated by powerful people, constantly pressing them to compromise their learned values of a lifetime. It had sounded so good in the beginning. Now he remembered something his mother once said, "Wrong choices limit future options." This had been a bitch of a wrong choice.

It had begun almost a year earlier when he had purchased an old DC-3. He planned to expand his flying business by getting into the air freight delivery of car parts to auto assembly plants in Georgia and Tennessee. He was to deliver parts for several local manufacturers in southern Virginia and North Carolina. Things had not worked out; it wasn't what the companies originally promised him. He had gone into debt to the local bank to buy the airplane, the note was due, and now they wanted to be paid.

He remembered sitting in his small, two-roomed office, looking out the window at the crumbling asphalt with grass breaking through in clusters here and there. The old, deteriorating airport was a former World War II training facility with years of weathering and wear. It now showed its age. It was owned by the county, and they refused to make any improvements. Staring with a fixed gaze at the DC-3 sitting on the ramp, he made a decision. Much to his regret, the big toy had to go. Rob placed his ad in *Trade-a-Plane*, which was circulated world-wide: "Douglas aircraft cargo DC-3, all inspections and airworthy directives current, ready for immediate delivery, sell to best offer." He'd had several inquiries by phone, but only one man had committed and made an appointment to actually see the plane, a man who identified himself only as Jacobson.

Jacobson arrived by car on a steamy, hot August day shortly after lunch. When he came through the sagging door with the cracked windowpanes, Rob was across the room, leaning over the old, noisy, window air conditioner, trying to cool himself off. Another man accompanied Jacobson. They both came into the office. "Good afternoon," Jacobson said.

Rob turned to greet an impressive man with a strong, military presence. Although he was wearing a white starched Panama shirt, tan slacks with shiny dark brown plain-toed shoes, he was military. Not a big man, he was about average height with large, square shoulders and strong facial features. Dark hair with flecks of silver around the temples framed his face, adding a somewhat distinguished touch. Reaching up, he removed his sunglasses and introduced himself in a deep, subdued voice. "I'm J.B. Jacobson; this is Al," as he reached out with a solid grasp and shook Rob's hand.

"That's the old bird across the ramp," Rob said. He picked up the large manila envelopes that contained the aircraft logs and handed them to Al, dressed in khakis, whom he assumed was the mechanic.

"We'll go have a look," Rob said as he stepped to one side and pulled the old faded office door open and allowed the two strangers to exit first. The soggy humidity and the searing mid-summer sun high overhead greeted them.

On the way out to the airplane across the hot, reflective blacktop surface, it became apparent that Jacobson was not accustomed to such conditions. Perspiration popped out across his forehead and arms. The front of his starched shirt was beginning to change to a darkened shade as his perspiration soaked through along the neckline and out to each sleeve. He was constantly blotting his face with a folded white handkerchief. As they walked around the exterior, visually checking the airplane, Rob became concerned for Jacobson as his forehead and cheeks were turning bright red.

"Let's go back into the office and let Al complete his inspection," Rob said as they walked around the tail of the airplane and faced the small two-roomed frame building, sitting snugly beside the faded white hangar.

"This looks like mostly farmland," remarked Jacobson as they strolled back.

"Yes, it is," replied Rob. "We operate a small agricultural flying business. Years ago they would have called us cropdusters. We have just one old Grumman Ag-cat. The season's about four months in the spring and early summer. We spray mostly fungicides and pesticides on the crops for the farmers."

"Well, how did a little ag-flying outfit come to own a cargo DC-3?" Jacobson asked.

"At the time I thought I could make money in the air freight business, but it didn't work out."

"Then you have a crew that can fly this plane?"

Rob paused a minute, then answered, "Well, I guess you could call us a crew. It's just me and a friend of mine. We did get a few jobs hauling cargo."

"If we buy the airplane, would you be interested in flying for us?" Jacobson asked.

Rob thought a minute. "Depends."

"Depends on what?" countered Jacobson.

"I guess it depends on when and where and how much flying."

"It won't be a lot," explained Jacobson, "maybe two trips a month, three or four days each."

"I'd have to think about it and talk it over with my friend, Mike," said Rob.

About that time the mechanic, soaked with perspiration, bounded through the office door. "It's hotter than hell up in that plane. It's got to be 150 degrees in there," he panted as he stepped over and placed the large manila bags, containing the logs, along with two small bottles of engine oil he had drawn for analysis to determine the condition of the aircraft engines, on Rob's desk.

"Well, what do you think?" Jacobson asked.

"I'd say the thing is in excellent shape for its age. No doubt it will fly. If you need a cargo DC-3 and want my opinion, this is as good as any- maybe better than most."

"We've gotten the plane ready to go to work. The maintenance requirements are current, and now all she needs is a good home," Rob said, smiling.

Jacobson wiped the sweat from his brow again and sat silently for a moment. "That price we discussed, is it negotiable?"

"No," said Rob rather emphatically with his hopes beginning to fade. "I think we both agree the appraised value is at least two hundred thousand dollars, and the price I quoted is the best I can do."

Jacobson was on a fishing expedition, trying to see just how desperate Rob was to sell and he had gotten his answer. This fly-boy was not going to give an inch. "We'll take it. I'll give you twenty-five thousand as a deposit and the balance when you deliver the plane to me in Florida."

"We didn't discuss delivery," said Rob. "That's not part of the sale."

"Well, can you deliver?"

"Sure, but there will be added delivery costs."

"How much?" Jacobson asked.

"Where to?" Rob asked. "Florida's a big state."

"Orlando Executive," Jacobson answered, dabbing at the perspiration.

Rob thought a minute, "Two thousand will cover the fuel and our return airfare."

"It's a deal," Jacobson said as he stood up and extended his hand across the desk to Rob.

"You just bought yourself a good airplane," Rob said, standing to shake on the deal.

"Where do I sign?" asked Jacobson.

Anne, Rob's secretary, had been listening to the conversation from her small office in back. She came out quickly and handed Rob a sales agreement with all the numbers in the right place. Rob looked at the paper then placed it in front of Jacobson.

Jacobson scanned the figures, pulled a pen from his pocket, and signed. "Okay," he said, "I'll wire the twenty-five thousand plus the two for expenses to your bank in the next three days."

"Thank you," Rob said.

"My pleasure," replied Jacobson as he slipped on his sunglasses and the mechanic picked up the oil samples. "Now, we've got to get going. The car's got to be cooler than this office. No offense, Mr. Marshall."

"You're probably right, Mr. Jacobson," said Rob.

On Tuesday after Friday's visit by Jacobson and his mechanic, Rob got the call he had been waiting for. They wanted him to fly the aircraft to Orlando Executive Airport. Jacobson would be there to meet them. The money would be wired and in the bank no later than Wednesday morning.

"Okay," said Rob to Anne with a boisterous voice, "Call Mike and tell him to pack a bag. We're going to Florida for a couple of days. We have to leave from here Thursday morning," Rob continued with an excited voice, "and it'll be the usual two hundred and fifty plus expenses for the trip."

Robert Verdey Marshall was a six-foot, one hundred ninety-five-pound, a stocky build with broad shoulders, thin, dark brown hair with touches of gray, sprinkled at the temples and forehead. His complexion was rugged and worn by years of being outside in the natural elements. He was college educated and from a middle-class working family. Most of his life was one continuous struggle mixed with limited success and spotted with moments of failure as noted by his recent divorce.

Wednesday afternoon was an exception. Rob sat in the office going over the outstanding bills he had to pay with the proceeds of the recent sale of the airplane. He would get one hundred seventy-eight thousand dollars, and the bank would get most of that. That would leave a few grand to pay on some of his other debts. No time to think about that now. He had to concentrate on getting the thing delivered and collecting the balance, then he would see how far the money would stretch.

The office door opened and Mike's six-foot four lanky body leaned into the room. "Come on in," Rob said with a big smile.

"How's it going?" Mike asked with his Cajun drawl, as he took a seat in the old, tattered brown chair.

"Doing better now that I found a buyer for the DC-3."

Mike was one of the good guys, a close friend who went back a long way. They would do almost anything for each other. He was there to help Rob deliver the airplane. It was one of those understood things; if one needed help, the other was always there to give it. This was a routine delivery of an old DC-3. At least, that was the way it started out, just another routine flight.

3 The Orange Blossom Special

Rob made it to the airport before six a.m. Thursday morning. He brewed the coffee, walked over to his desk, and looked at the bank slip verifying that the money had come in and was credited to his account. So far, so good. Now to get the airplane delivered without a hitch and get the balance of the money. He checked over the papers to be sure that they were all in order. The bank had signed the release form, which was to be delivered to Jacobson when the balance was collected as they had agreed.

Rob stood up slowly, stretched, and yawned. A life of hard work weathered his face and eyes. He ran his hand through dark brown hair, now receding into a high forehead. Mentally checklisting his flight to Orlando, he put on his baseball cap and went over to the coffeepot. As he filled his cup, he heard a car on the gravel road to his office. Rob looked out the window in time to see Mike getting out of his Ford Bronco. Mike was the out-of-doors type. He didn't spend a lot of time cleaning a vehicle, and it showed. The truck was two years old and still had all of the original mud and dirt caked on it. That was definitely Mike. To him, a truck was for work or play, not for show. He didn't spend a lot of time on the appearance.

"That coffee sho' do smell 'bout right," he said as he entered the room and reached for a cup, "and jes the way I lak it; strong and black." Mike was originally from south Louisiana below Baton Rouge and a little to the west. In that part of the state, most folks are "Cajuns" and real proud of it. They drink Dixie Beer, eat crawfish, make music, mind their own business, and make damn sure no one sticks his nose in places where it's not wanted.

As a lad, Michael Bodron Ricau always dreamed of flying. After two years in a local community college, he was given an opportunity to enter the military and be trained to fly both fixed wing and rotary wing aircraft. After training, Mike spent two tours in the latter part of the Vietnam Conflict, flying Huey helicopter gunships. He and his crew were shot down twice, but both times, Mike managed to survive. The only thing upon his return to civilian life that came close to emulating the adrenaline rush of his combat experience was cropdusting, flying close to the ground and in and out of the trees.

As young crop dusters in south Louisiana, Rob and Mike had met years ago and shared good times. Both had a love for adventure. This was to be one of those fun, "routine" flights, or so they thought.

"I've checked the weather," Mike said. "Everything looks good except for a little activity around Myrtle Beach and on down south to Charleston. Nothing serious, just a little ol' mushroom thunderstorm. Don't see any major problems. I got all the flight charts from here and on down to Orlando."

They walked out the front door and stopped to look at the silver DC-3 sitting, glistening with dew in the early morning sunlight. The tail sat on the ground with the nose gracefully pointed up toward the horizon. It appeared ready to lift into flight at a moment's notice. It was an old airplane, designed in the '30's and produced in the '30's and '40's. It was simple and dependable, an easy airplane to fly, but slow by jet standards. With big, main landing gear tires, it was ideal for landing and taking off from unimproved dirt airstrips. That made it very popular in most of the third world countries. Rob and Mike were removing the control locks when Anne drove up. She came out to where they were standing with a sad look on her thin face.

"I'm going to miss this old girl sitting out here. We've had her for almost a year, and she sort of feels like family," she said, then paused. "I've got you two a room with two beds. I didn't want to get separate rooms; you might get into trouble," she added jokingly and smiled at Mike. "It's all written down here on this sheet of paper. Just call the hotel, and they will come out and pick you up."

"All right," said Rob. "We're looking good. Put that sheet with all the other papers inside the flight bag."

Rob read out the checklist. "Got the gear pins, the pito covers, the control locks, the sumps drained, fuel visually checked, the oil checked. We're ready to go flying, man!"

They walked back into the office and picked up their bags. Anne had prepared a fresh thermos of steaming hot coffee for the trip and placed it beside the bags with the papers and records for the DC-3. They had gathered up everything and were walking out to the plane when the phone rang. Anne came to the door and called for Rob, "You have a long distance phone call."

Rob returned to the office and picked up the phone in time to hear Jacobson say, "No, it's important that I speak only to Mr. Marshall."

"Operator, this is Mr. Marshall."

"Go ahead," the operator said.

Jacobson started talking, "How is everything?"

"Fine, we were just leaving," Rob said. He was a little uneasy, wondering what was going on.

"Rob, something has come up. It will be Friday before I can meet you in Orlando."

"All right, we've made all of our arrangements, so I guess we'll head on down today as planned. We'll see you on Friday," Rob said slowly with a question in his voice.

"Okay," said Jacobson, "we'll see you then and thanks for understanding."

Rob hung up the phone. Maybe things weren't going to work out as smoothly as he had originally hoped. Then again, one more day couldn't be too bad. There was nothing really pressing here at the office, and Orlando was a pretty good place. He had been there before and enjoyed it.

Mike climbed into the right seat as Rob buckled himself into the left. Rob turned on the battery switch, then the inverter switch, set the fuel selector for the main tanks, then turned on the boost pumps. He checked the fuel pressure gauge for pressure. Rob pushed the starter button on the left engine, then counted six blades as the engine turned, flipped on the mag switches, pressed and held the primer switch. The engine whined, strained, then roared to life with a puff of blue smoke. He pushed the mixture lever full rich, released the primer, and checked the oil pressure. It was in the green. Moving the throttle forward, he set the idle at one thousand r.p.m.'s and repeated the procedure on the right engine with little difficulty. The engine sputtered and coughed but did not start. Mike asked, "What's the problem?"

"You know the thing is just hard to start sometime. I think the induction vibrator on the ignition is weak. We'll let it sit for a few minutes and try again."

They unfolded some of the flight charts and looked at them while they waited. The other engine was rumbling, making it difficult to talk.

"Okay," said Rob, "let's give it another try."

He turned the boost pumps back on, cracked the throttle with the mixture closed, pushed the starter button, and the engine began to turn slowly at first; then after several revolutions, it caught. Rob pushed the mixture in and released the primer. It began to pick up speed. Smoke puffed out the exhaust stacks. He did a visual check of the gauges; everything looked good. He allowed the engines time to warm up, then taxied down to the end of the runway and did a complete run-up. Everything checked out good.

As they taxied into place for take-off, Mike and Rob talked over the procedure to be sure they were in sync and understood their responsibilities as they made their lift-off. Mike would have the flaps and landing gear, and Rob would have the engine throttles and check the gauges. Flaps were set, landing gear down and locked, and tail wheel was locked into position. On breaking ground, Mike was to get the gear up and locked.

Everything was going well. As they started their roll, Rob did a second check to make sure that the tail wheel was locked as he slowly added power, being careful not to over boost the engines. The take-off was easy and uneventful. The throttles were pulled back to climb power, and the engine r.p.m. was set. Rob checked, Mike had the gear and flaps up. Everything was operating smoothly, and there were no warning lights. All was nice and orderly, the way it was supposed to be. Despite twenty years of takeoffs, Rob never took the miracle for granted. They climbed to six thousand feet and then leveled off. The old engines purred, and the big prop blades flashed in the early morning sunlight. The wings were shining silver against a sky that was a pure soothing blue. It was beautiful this time of the day, Rob thought to himself.

Mike filed the flight plan with the air traffic control center. "We're on our way," Mike said as he set the assigned frequency into the transponder, then started singing, "It's that Orange Blossom Special, rolling down that Seaboard Coast Line!"

The flight was routine with the exception of some light rain and turbulence along the coast of South Carolina. After three hours of flying, they were cleared for final approach into Orlando Executive Airport.

They finished running the checklist: gear down and locked, flaps set, boost pumps on, gauges scanned; everything was set. The airspeed bled off slowly and the wheels touched down.

"Another good landing," shouted Mike with a thumbs up gesture.

On rollout, the tower advised, "Douglas November One Niner Niner Eight, contact ground on One Two One Niner and a good day to you."

Rob answered, "One Niner Niner Eight, affirmative."

Switching the frequency, Mike spoke into the microphone, "Orlando ground, this is November One Niner Niner Eight, we would like clearance to taxi to the general aviation ramp north."

Orlando tower returned, "Niner Niner Eight, clear to north ramp. Be advised there is a Cherokee taxiing out for take-off."

4 A COMPANY MAN

J ames Bright Jacobson, Colonel, U.S. Marine Corp, retired, sat fumbling through the papers on his desk. The answer wasn't there, only the problem. On his flight back to Fort Lauderdale, he had done some serious thinking and his thoughts roamed back to his youth.

At the age of four, young James realized something was not right. He would listen as his dad spent night after night, coughing and wheezing. It didn't take many years before James knew that the dark, damp mines, laden with coal dust, were a slow, agonizing death trip. He would decide to escape and by the only means he knew- hard work and a good education.

At eighteen, four months after his father's death, he walked onto the stage at his high school graduation and gave the Valedictory Speech. With excellent grades the opportunity of scholarships to several colleges and universities became available. Escaping the coal mines of West Virginia was no longer a probability, but now a fact.

At the University of West Virginia James joined the local Marine Corps ROTC program. At first it was for the extra cash, then he was hooked. The military with its strong discipline and high moral values became home. For twenty-seven years, he was married only to the Corps and worked his way up through the ranks to Lieutenant Colonel in intelligence. Then he was asked to take this position. It was a decision that he hoped he would not regret, since it had required resignation from his beloved Corps.

Things weren't going the way they had promised when he let them talk him into resigning his commission. Now he was contract working for the

Company, as it was called, in a "civilian" capacity. It started right, but just as things were beginning to get organized, those liberal bleeding hearts in Congress had voted to cut off the funding. All his scrounging efforts were having minimal results, and that was being optimistic. Less than fifty thousand dollars was left in his operating fund, and most of that had been promised to a man as the down payment on an old DC-3.

All of his staff had been relieved of duty except for one woman who was critical to the mission, that of keeping a war going with only promises. With the indoctrination of career military, he did his duty without questioning the powers above, but now sometimes doubted that wisdom. For weeks he had been promised the funding needed for his mission. So far it had not arrived.

The powers in Washington were always urging him to be very careful. No one was to know about this mission, not even the people in his own network. He understood his orders came directly from the top and bypassed the usual channels. Deep down inside he knew he was out there dangling on a string. If something went wrong, one snip and he would disappear. That's the way they wanted it: no ties, no tails, and no trails. He understood that. It was power politics; cover your ass at all times. These people did not get where they were by being sloppy. That's why now all the funding was in cash, no bank records to follow them home. "Plausible deniability" for everyone above him.

"Do what you have to do to make things work" were the Colonel's exact words. Jacobson had found the airplane needed to make those few runs into Central America, and the timing of these flights was critical. The arms and supplies were coming into the Caribbean, and it was his responsibility to get them to the freedom fighters so they could put them to good use. With all the noise in the press, he wondered how it was going to affect his work.

He had requested five hundred thousand dollars U.S. to get the supplies delivered. The money had not arrived, and he had to put those old country boys off another day. He was sitting waiting for a call from the man in Washington. He desperately needed the courier to bring the funds for the aircraft purchase, and he needed it today. Those old boys didn't look the type who had much patience or staying power, but they had committed and were now moving the airplane with just the deposit up front. What he needed now was that call confirming that the money was on the way. Jacobson pushed back in his chair, closed his eyes, and clasped his hands behind his head.

A tall, attractive Latin woman softly opened the office door and walked in. Lourdes Gil was his aide, assistant, interpreter, and all-round. His academic Spanish was okay, but lacked subtlety. It totally missed the country-to-country nuances of usage. That's where Lourdes came in.

Lourdes Gil Velasquez was born in Cuba, and in the spring of 1959, was eight years old. On an overcast rainy day, her father appeared at her private

Catholic school. Senor Gil, a high ranking bank official in the government of Batista, had received a phone call from his wife, who pleaded with him to hurry and get Lourdes from school and take her to safety. Castro's revolutionaries had overrun their upper middle class neighborhood. All the affluent people were being rounded up and loaded into trucks. That was the last time Lourdes' father spoke with his wife. He later learned through rumors that she either perished in jail from sickness and starvation or was placed before a firing squad.

Senor Gil, along with his daughter Lourdes, found refuge on an outgoing fishing vessel, owned by a loyal friend. He and Lourdes with several others fled to Nicaragua, leaving all their possessions behind. In Nicaragua, with his experience in banking and finance, he quickly moved up the ladder and into the elite and prominent social circles of President Anastasio Somoza.

Along with her father's success, Lourdes found acceptance and a lifestyle of luxury. Educated in Europe and the United States, she possessed a classic Latin beauty. Five feet four inches, one hundred and fifteen pounds with olive skin and sparkling brown eyes, she was always a smiling face. With a sharp wit and a deep trusting personality, she was loved by the men and envied by all the women.

After school, she accepted a position with a national Nicaraguan airline as a flight attendant, then rose with her usual grace through the ranks to be the department head.

There was always the agonizing hatred that sometimes broke to the surface and spilled over her controlled emotions. She had long repressed her rage for the Communists who had taken her mother's life and deprived her adolescent years of the mother's love she had so desired.

In May of 1978, she married Gabriel Luis Velasquez, son of the Minister of Defense and captain in the Nicaraguan National Guard. Their blissful happiness was short-lived when in the summer of 1979, the Sandinistas ambushed a patrol, led by Captain Velasquez, where he, along with four others, was killed.

The Sandinistas thrust became extremely violent. In a matter of days, she, along with several officers of Somoza's government, took flight to the United States. In Miami, Florida, they were granted political asylum.

In the mid-eighties, she became very active in the Contra movement and was recruited to work alongside Colonel James Bright Jacobson as an advisor. She knew the people; she knew how they thought. She was Jacobson's ace. And now her rage had an outlet.

Jacobson picked up the phone on the first ring, and immediately recognized the Colonel on the other end. There was that tone which generally meant that things were not going as they had originally planned. The Colonel's voice was deep, well-controlled, confident. The words rolled out—the very words Jacobson didn't want to hear. "Jake," as the Colonel called him, "there has been a slight change with that airplane you wanted to buy. We need to lease it. The funds are slow coming in," the Colonel continued, "so get the plane moved into the Caribbean where we will have a little bargaining strength. You know how to handle it. Just get their pants down around their ankles, and they'll come around. Jake, you know I hate to do this to some of our civilians, but desperate times call for desperate measures. We will make it up to them when the funds do arrive. That shipment will be in the south in four days, and we need to be prepared to move as quickly as possible. We've come too far to let something go wrong, you understand?"

"Yes sir."

The Colonel began again, "I'll be damned if this is going to get screwed up. We are going to stay on schedule if I have to take these supplies to them in a rowboat. It's up to you now. We're counting on you. I'll be back in touch with you Sunday, before noon your time."

The shipment from Europe was coming in, and they needed the plane to get it to the Nicaraguans in Honduras. Yes sir, they were counting on him to use these old boys to maybe get their asses busted for a promise. Jacobson had to follow orders, and the rumors were that the Colonel took his orders from the very top. At least, other people in the Company had told him that on several occasions. You just don't say no to people with that kind of power.

Jacobson turned and looked at Lourdes, "Get a ticket and go to Orlando. There are two guys down there who need entertaining, and you've just been elected to the entertainment committee," he said with a weak grin.

He pulled out the lock box and opened it, giving Lourdes five thousand dollars. Then he returned the box to his desk drawer. Jacobson explained his plan to Lourdes, and she was off to Orlando. Jake pushed back in his chair and stared at the ceiling. Who would have believed the old jarhead would be a Company man?

5 A Mickey Mouse Welcome to Orlando

Rob and Mike taxied the aircraft up to the back of the ramp. They knew that the old leaking radial engines did not get the best reception when parked out in front where all the executive jets carrying the Fortune 500 crowd usually park. The people running these executive airports liked to roll out the red carpet, and they didn't like getting black engine oil on it. They shut down the engines and finished the rest of the checklist when they noticed that the boy on the golf cart hadn't stayed around long after parking the DC-3.

"Maybe we aren't exactly a Cessna Citation Three, but you'd think they would at least talk to us," said Mike.

"Don't give us too much respect and maybe we won't come back," said Rob. "Maybe that is their policy toward DC-3's." They both stepped down on the concrete. The August weather was sultry. The humidity was at least ninety percent and the temperature close to the 100 degree mark. Both men were beginning to sweat heavily. It looked as if they were not going to get any help from the ground crew, who were over by a Lear jet and a King Air, helping the passengers with their luggage.

Mike and Rob took the long trek from the airplane to the office on foot. As they entered the door, a sharp, tan blonde in tight, white shorts and a halter-top, working behind the desk, spoke first. "Hi, welcome to Orlando Executive." She flashed a warm smile.

"Thanks," said Rob as he and Mike strolled over to the desk. "I guess you want us to fill out something on the airplane?" he asked.

21

"Yes, sir," answered the blonde. They could read Susan on her strategically placed nametag.

"Susan," Mike said, "where is the best place to stay around here? We've got reservations at the Holiday Inn on I-4, but that can change."

"That is a really good place. There is also the Regency," she said with a pause. "It's a little on the formal side, and you don't strike me as that type." She grinned, looking at Rob's boots and jeans.

"Yeah," said Rob with a grin, "and I bet the Holiday Inn has a nice lounge where the people get really friendly. Would you mind giving them a call and telling them Rob Marshall and party are here."

Susan called the Holiday Inn. The green and yellow van was there to pick them up before both men could relieve themselves of the coffee they had drunk on the flight that morning.

"Man, I am beginning to like this place," stated Mike as the driver of the van, an attractive young woman, also with a dark tan, stepped out wearing a Tux top over her tight shorts. Both men were throwing their bags into the rear of the van when a white patrol car with the green stripes and lettering of the Orange County Sheriff's Department drove up. As the car slowed to a stop, a heavyset, middle-aged deputy opened the door and stepped out. With a rather solemn look he asked, "You boys the ones who flew that old DC-3 in here?"

"Yeah, I guess we are," said Rob, not looking up from loading the bags into the back of the van.

"Boys, I hope you don't take offense, but I need to take a look inside," the deputy continued. "Just doing my job, you understand. It's our policy to check these things when they land in our jurisdiction."

"No problem," said Mike, "we know that sometimes these old birds are used by the wrong people for the wrong reasons, like maybe hauling things that aren't legal."

"Do you mind waiting a few minutes while we let this man look inside the plane?" Rob asked the van's driver.

"Hey, no big deal! Get in and I'll drive you over there. By the way, my name is Jennifer, and I'm here to help, anyway I can." As she leaned forward and turned toward the men, the wind from the open driver's window swirled her shoulder-length auburn hair about her face.

"Do all guests to Orlando get welcomed by the local sheriff's department?" asked Rob as they were driving over to the parked airplane. Jennifer didn't respond. When they drove up, Rob got out and unlocked the aircraft door. He stood outside as the deputy crawled in, stood up and looked around. Rob knew the DC-3 was getting very hot sitting in the sun with the door closed. If the deputy wanted to sweat some, that was his privilege, just as long as he didn't expect a guided tour. Shortly, the deputy reappeared at the back door with sweat flowing down his face and showing through the front of his shirt. He was breathing hard; it was apparent that this was more exercise than the deputy was accustomed to getting.

"Everything looks okay," said the deputy, "but we like to keep tabs on anything like this when it's in our area. Never know when it will leave and come slipping back late at night. Get my drift, boys? I want ya'll to know we're always watching. Now ya'll have a good time and take care. Hope ya'll understand what I'm saying," the deputy said. His lips smiled but his eyes did not. He walked over to his patrol car, opened the door, stopped and took a long look at the two men, got in, and drove off.

"This is Mickey Mouse bullshit," mumbled Mike. Riding along in the van to the Holiday Inn, he asked Jennifer, "Are the cops always that concerned about the welfare of the tourists, or was I missing something I didn't want to hear?"

"Oh, there's always something going on in a place this size with as many people coming and going, so the police are looking to jump on someone's case." Jennifer started to laugh, "Guys, it looks like today it's your turn." With a smile and her best mock hotel greeting voice she added, "Welcome to Orlando and Daytona Beach, Florida. We have a few beaches and a lot of bitches, and they're all beautiful." Then in her normal soft southern voice, "So don't let that ole sheriff's department get ya'll down. We want you all to have a good time in our fair state." They drove past the Holiday Inn sign and into the hotel parking lot.

Mike and Rob checked in, dropped off their bags, and headed for the lounge. They walked in and looked around, giving the place a good once-over.

"Must be early," said Rob, "we're the only ones here."

"Except for that pretty thing behind the bar," Mike said.

A well-endowed woman in a low-cut blouse with tiny freckles across her chest greeted them. "My name is Tesa," she said. "Now what'll you two have?" she asked, giving Mike a big smile.

"Two cold long necks," said Mike. The beer arrived cold and inviting. Rob and Mike sat with their elbows resting on the bar, more than a little tired. "Oh, how that cold beer sure does taste good!" said Rob.

"Hey, Tesa," Mike said with a big smile and a little emphasis on his Cajun accent, "Dat first un went down so good, I tink will have 'nother one." Now Mike, being a good old boy from down south Louisiana way had been practicing for a long time puttin' dat beer away, sometimes maybe a little too fast; and again the people from south Louisiana have a reputation to uphold. Mike was no exception. He did his part and knew how to let the good times roll when the time was right. Tonight, he felt right.

Tesa stopped slicing lemons and limes, brought two more long necks, set them down in front of Mike, slid Rob's over to him, and leaned over the bar. "Now big boy, where you from?" Obviously, Mike's smile and Cajun accent had gotten her attention.

"I'm from down sort of southwest of Lafayette, Louisiana, the bayou country. Good food, good drinks, and good neighbors, dat's us," Mike answered.

Still chuckling at Mike, Rob took a hefty swig of beer. "Damn, I nearly forgot. Tesa, I'm expecting a phone call. Can I get the desk to ring me in here?"

"Sure, why not?" said Tesa as she handed the phone from under the bar to Rob. "Just dial '0'."

Rob called the front desk and left a message that he and Mike were in the lounge, and he was expecting a call. Then they went back to drinking and talking about the hospitality of the Orlando Sheriff's Department.

"Why and how do you think they knew we were at the Executive Airport?" Mike asked Rob, holding his beer up to the light checking the level.

Rob answered, "They have a tendency to keep tabs on those old DC-3's; at least, I've been told that, and I guess we just found out for ourselves. The control tower must have called the sheriff's department and announced our arrival. Sure didn't take them long to find us, and find us they did."

"Damn, those sons-of-bitches; probably know when we fart. I wonder if they keep that in their computer. They seem to have everything else," Mike said.

Tesa walked up, and as she did, Mike reached in his shirt pocket and pulled out some loose bills and handed them to her. "How about playing us something to liven up this joint? Not heavy metal or acid rock, or whatever they call it, just some good rock and roll or country, know what I'm saying?" Tesa picked up the bills and went over to the jukebox. She knew which buttons to push, in more ways than one. Soon the music that she had chosen, not really country but good old rock and roll, spilled from the speakers as streaks of multi-colored lights played across the tiny dance floor, driving away the late afternoon shadows. "A little music, some cold beer, and good company; that is what makes life a lot smoother, and smoother is the order of the day," said Mike, "and no one is gonna change dat."

They were now working on their third beer. Each one seemed to be better than the last. Rob got up and walked across the dance floor to the side door leading to the restrooms. Thinking he and Mike were the only ones in the bar, Rob was mildly surprised to see a man sitting in the corner booth. Something about that man looked vaguely familiar; or maybe, it was just those beers. Maybe that sheriff's deputy had him a little paranoid. What was there to be paranoid about anyway? Everything they were doing was above board and legal, but just the same, that man in the gray knit shirt made him a little uncomfortable. "Mike," whispered Rob as he returned to the bar, "that man sitting over in the corner, have you noticed him? He looks familiar to me."

"Yeah," said Mike, "I think I saw him at the airport when we were unloading the luggage. He walked by so I don't think there is any reason to worry. He probably flew in like us and is staying here because of the free ride to the airport."

"Probably right," said Rob, "that must be where I saw him. He just looked familiar and seeing him sitting by himself over in the corner in the dark made me uncomfortable." They walked around the corridor to the front desk. There standing by the front door was Jennifer with her long legs, that auburn hair down to her shoulders. She sure did look better than this afternoon, or maybe it was the beer. Mike walked over to Jennifer. "Say, Cher, you 'spectin' somebody?" Mike asked with his slow Cajun drawl.

"No," was a quick reply from Jennifer, "just a little bored. Things are kinda slow, I guess, for a Thursday, but that's okay with me since I have one more day, then the weekend off, and the beach is calling me."

Mike said, "Sounds like you have your weekend all planned out."

"Not really," Jennifer answered, "I'm planning to go out with some friends."

"And what time is that?" asked Mike with a grin.

"I'm usually out of here by five-thirty, at the latest six," she stated with a warm smile, "but it's company policy we aren't supposed to associate with the guests on our off time," she said still smiling.

"If we just happen to run into you somewhere after you are off, there's not much they can say. Like, where do you usually go?" Mike continued with a big smile.

Jennifer thought for a minute. "There's a place called 'Jim's Sports Page' about two miles from here. I'll be there around seven." Then, almost as an afterthought and a glance toward Rob, she said, "I'll bring a girl friend."

6 THE OTHER ETERNAL TRIANGLE

Shimar was leaning over the rail of the mini-freighter looking into the cold black waters of the Atlantic. The moon was just beginning to show through the clouds. He reached out over the rail and flicked the ashes from his cigarette. The light from the moon flashed on the diamonds in his ornate pinky ring as he drew his arm back. He took a long drag, letting the smoke out slowly, then tried to relax, but he couldn't. The last few months had been very tense. He and his associate had made the largest arms deal in the history of their company. Vlasenko, his partner, using his Israeli friends and his contacts in Iran, had sold two cargo plane loads of SAM, surface-to-air missiles, with a value of forty-five million dollars to the Iranian military. The Iranians had paid a premium price for the SAMS. They were desperate. With little or no air power, they needed the SAMS to neutralize the Iraqi helicopters and fighter airplanes. It was rumored the Iranians had also agreed to a side deal which included releasing all hostages who had been taken in Beirut over the last five years.

The United States was in the midst of an official boycott of Iran and as such could not deal directly. That's where Vlasenko entered the picture. Vlasenko had strong ties to the arms business. His mother was from the northern part of Iran with Caucasian influence. His father was a Russian Jew who had immigrated to Israel in the early seventies. With these connections, he could travel freely between Tel Aviv and Tehran, turning that to his advantage in his entrepreneurial pursuits of anything so long as it made money. Over the years he had done well plying his trade.

The United States needed help with the continued annoyance of having free world patrons being kidnapped in and around Beirut. Intelligence knew that Iranian extremists were the root cause. Vlasenko, always looking for a lucrative opportunity, made several inquiries, matched up certain intelligence persons, and a deal was worked out. The Iranians desperately needed the SAMS, something small and portable; and the United States had an abundant supply of such a missile. Both sides' needs were met. Vlasenko, the middle man, needed only to sort out all the details of such a trade and then make the arrangements to close the deal of his life.

The United States' cargo planes delivered the SAMS to the Israeli military in Tel Aviv. Once the missiles were in Tel Aviv, they were loaded into trucks and moved to the border of Syria. At the border under heavy guard by Israeli soldiers, an inspection team from Iran came across the border. After the inspection was completed and everyone was satisfied, the funds were transferred to Vlasenko's account. Vlasenko then wired the funds less his two million-dollar fee, to a prearranged Swiss account. When all the wire transfers were completed, the Iranians moved the trucks with the missiles across the border. That was the last time Shimar saw the trucks and their cargo.

Shimar and his partners had a quiet ride back to Tel Aviv. Early the following morning Vlasenko called; he wanted him in the office as soon as possible. When Shimar arrived, Vlasenko was sitting in a chair talking to an American, a very clean cut, rather soft-spoken man with the look of iron resolve in his eyes. Vlasenko spoke first, "I want you to meet the Colonel. Colonel, this is my associate, Shimar." Shimar walked across the room, the Colonel stood up, and they shook hands.

"The Colonel needs some help," Vlasenko continued. "He needs infantry supplies, hand guns, assault rifles, anti-personnel mines, grenades, and ammunition. He wants this transaction all done on the quiet side. No one must know, not even the Israelis." Vlasenko handed the list to Shimar who slowly scanned it. The numbers were in the thousands.

"Colonel," Shimar asked, "please forgive me for questioning your credibility, but this is, as you Americans say, a tall order. Where in the free world could you buy this much firepower without it coming to the attention of the intelligence of any major country?"

The room was silent for the moment as Vlasenko walked to the window overlooking the busy street below. "You're a Colonel from the strongest country in the world with an unlimited supply; why ask us?" Vlasenko said.

"There are certain people in our government who don't exactly agree with what we're doing," replied the Colonel. "You've helped us on the missile thing, and it was kept quiet; so I thought I would give you a shot at helping us with this. We must have total secrecy. Not one person is to know what we are doing."

Vlasenko looked at Shimar, then at the Colonel, then back to Shimar again, "Where could we get this much military supplies, and no one know?" Vlasenko asked. They all knew the answer: the Chinese. The Chinese didn't care where it was going, or who was going to use it, as long as it wasn't used against them. The Chinese were tight-lipped; no one would ever know. "Okay, Colonel, give us some time to make some inquiries. We will get back to you in two days," Vlasenko said. With that the Colonel stood up, shook hands with each man, and departed.

A few days later Vlasenko had made all the necessary arrangements to ship the arms. In the middle, as in all of history, the Mideast traders formed a triangle of trade with the East and Europe. Now another triangle: Mideast, East, and West. Shimar joined the shipment as it passed through the Mediterranean. Vlasenko laid down the law; this shipment was to be delivered on time, or it could cost his life. He didn't know the people to whom he was taking the shipment, but they were powerful, to say the least. Shimar's instructions were to stay with the shipment; his life depended on it being delivered and delivered on schedule. This was the first time he had made a massive delivery of arms into this part of the world, especially communist made AK-47's, rocket launchers, grenades, all types of explosives, and ammunition. This was enough to start a war or, for damn sure, keep one going. There was much to this that he was not told, but he felt he had guessed most of it. The United States government was the biggie that made Vlasenko so nervous. Vlasenko was becoming one of the largest independent arms dealers in North Africa. Now things were going as planned. They would arrive at their destination late Sunday night, or early Monday. Hopefully, that wouldn't be a problem. When he did arrive, he had a code name he was to use when he called his contact. That was the extent of his information. This was not unusual in this business. You were given only the information needed to complete the mission. That was the way Shimar liked it. The less he knew, the better off he was. Now just two more days and he would be on his way back to Tel Aviv. He had a wife and two sons, one was four years old and the other one six. He really wanted to see them again. It had been almost two weeks since he last talked to them and almost a month since he had seen them. Those boys were growing up in a hurry, most of the time without him. Two more days and he would make the delivery and be heading home. The feeling of going home sent a warm feeling deep down inside. Just a few more days. He could handle that.

7 THE BRASS RING

The Colonel sorted his papers precisely into three neat stacks on his office desk in the basement of the Big House on Pennsylvania Avenue. He had a six a.m. meeting with a ranking staff officer, General Eugene "Big Mac" McKenzie. McKenzie was one of the elite inner circle who was rumored to have direct access to the oval office. The general's name was on a short list of people he was instructed to call on when the normal, slow, methodical grind of the military and government bureaucracy wasn't working. On this mission, using normal channels was too slow and definitely too compromising.

The Colonel wanted help to expedite a matter of utmost urgency. Earlier ventures with the general had gone smoothly and without any flaws. Weeks earlier the company had set up a numbered account in Switzerland under the guise of an international development corporation. In their earlier transactions this was ideal, but now they needed money. They had to get this large sum of cash from the account back to the U.S. without arousing suspicion.

Normally, moving large sums out of the country was done with ease; now bringing it back into the United States was a different matter. It could create unwanted attention, and they didn't need that. The several million dollars in a Swiss account wasn't doing anyone any good over there. It had been very convenient when they had been using it to purchase arms in Europe, but now they needed the funds back here in the States to complete a sensitive operation. The group working in south Florida was committed to getting the shipment of arms to the freedom fighters. The key element to completing this mission was the promised cash arriving in a timely fashion.

There was a knock on the door. As the door slowly opened, Joseph from housekeeping stepped in. He was an older, thin black man whose white hair matched his white jacket. In his hands was a large, silver tray with a coffee pot and cups. Stepping over and placing the tray on a corner table, "Anything I can get you this morning, Sir?" he asked.

"No thanks, Joseph. I think this is all I need," the Colonel said with a tight smile as he looked up from his work. Joseph walked out and quietly pulled the door closed behind him.

It was now seven a.m. The General was late. They had agreed to meet between six-thirty and seven to avoid any interruptions. The Colonel was an early riser, up every morning and into his office by six-thirty at the latest. His secretary usually came in between seven-thirty and eight. If the General was much later, their time to discuss this matter without interruptions was going to be limited. The Colonel was beginning to get a little anxious. He walked over to the coffeepot and poured a cup of fresh, hot coffee. As he went back to his desk, he weighed all the options that the General would have and tried to evaluate them. Staying one step ahead of him was always a priority. The General was a man of action and got things done, sometimes without giving due consideration to the complete picture. He knew that his solution would be to pack an overnight bag and take an Air Force jet to Switzerland, load the money in duffel bags, and bring it back to Andrews Air Force Base. Who would question what they were doing? They were working for the top brass, and that meant they had executive privileges. Yes, that would definitely be the General's plan.

There was a slight knock on the door. As it opened, the General came in. "I got caught on the bridge," he said as he shook the Colonel's hand.

"Good seeing you this morning, would you care for some coffee?" asked the Colonel.

"Yes, about half a cup. I'm trying to cut back on the caffeine. I need to get my blood pressure down," he answered. The Colonel poured the coffee, and they both sat down.

The Colonel began, "General, I need some help. You have spent more time in Europe than I have, and I feel you have a better understanding of the total picture than I do. We need the balance of those funds we have in Switzerland back over here in the States so we can complete this mission. Can you help me?"

The General responded, "I'll do what I can. How much time do we have?"

"This is Thursday; we need the funds or at least a good part of them here no later than Sunday afternoon. I'm open for any suggestions," the Colonel said, looking intently at the General.

"Why not have a courier pick up the package on a company jet and fly into Andrews Air Force Base here in Washington? You or I could meet them, so there would be no questions asked," spoke the General, "seems rather uncomplicated to me."

"Have you thought about how bulky eight million in hundred dollar bills will be?" the Colonel asked.

"Yes, it will be a good truck load," he added, "but we can keep it under wraps by calling it confidential cargo. We'll put the department stamp on it, and let it go. No one will ever question what we're doing."

"General Mac, that all sounds good, but I don't think we need to see a headline in the Post, 'Security commission ships large containers of cash into Andrews Air Base'. If one person talked," the Colonel left the rest unsaid. "That much money will start rumors, then someone will have too much to drink and say something. And then certain news people will be poking around and asking questions. That could bring us all down. No, I feel that Andrews Air Force Base is too high profile."

"Well, you've got a point," the General said.

"We need something a little less conspicuous, and we should be extremely cautious. Only the few who are directly in the loop should know the details. I have gone over and over all the scenarios, and only one keeps coming back as the best solution to this problem. Will your schedule allow you to go to Europe yourself and bring back half the funds in cash? That will be four million. We can handle that, maybe come back into the U.S. at Homestead in south Florida. No one will ask any questions down there. There won't be any press hanging around and paying off the locals for information." The Colonel paused, "What's your opinion?"

The General sat for a moment, sipping his coffee, and thinking over what the Colonel had presented. "That sounds like a plan that will work. Yes, I'll clear my schedule and go. You're right, there won't be anyone hanging around asking questions," he stated rather shortly. "We'll have the money where it's needed, right there in Florida. I'll leave most of it there; they'll fly the balance up here." Then the General said slowly as he was thinking. "Yes, Colonel, you've given it some thought; you've planned this well. I'll check with logistics over at the Pentagon on their flight schedules. If we use an aircraft that's already on the board, we'll be as inconspicuous as possible. Since this will seem like just another routine operation, no one will be the wiser. Okay, let me work out all the details. I'll have some answers for you by this afternoon," he was saying as he rose. He took one more sip out of his coffee cup and placed it on the corner of the desk. He shook the Colonel's hand. "Good job," he said as he grabbed his braided parade hat, tucked it under his arm, and strode out the door.

The Colonel felt some relief after the General's visit, but he was still in the hot seat. He had gone out on a limb as ringleader on this project and done a great many things on his own. He had kept the operation out of the hands of the bureaucracy, a bureaucracy that could choke a whale with its paperwork. He was determined that they were not going to kill this program. The Colonel had worked far too long and far too hard. After so many months the bits and pieces of the puzzle were finally beginning to come together. It felt really good.

General McKenzie had to get the funds to Florida in the next seventy-two hours. They now had their plan. The problem was to make sure that it was timed to fit into the overall schedule. This was a military operation; they had to get it right. Everyone had to be on schedule and do his part on time.

The phone buzzed. It was the Colonel's secretary reminding him that he had several calls waiting and his calendar was full. Now on to some of the other projects. There was always something that was pressing, staff meetings or someone from the State Department wanting a progress report. The endless chain of paperwork never seemed to end. These things he had learned to handle with virtual ease. It was the priority projects from the top that caused the sleepless nights. The Colonel was an Academy graduate and a career man whose life was spent serving his country. He was now working on the most important assignment of his life and for damn sure, it was going to get the right priority, yes, top priority. He was dedicated to doing his best. That was his life, a career military man and damn well proud of it. If nobody screwed up, he was about to grab the brass ring.

8 Paso Doble

Rob rolled up on his left elbow. There it was again, that ringing sound. The room was in total darkness except for faint rays of light casting shadows around the closed drapes over the windows. Where was he? He fumbled for the switch on the lamp. With a soft click, the room was brightly illuminated. Rob sat up on the side of the bed, shading his burning eyes from the light with his left hand and reaching for the phone with his right. Now the phone had stopped ringing, but his head still had an echo. He was trying to remember last night. Why was he feeling so bad? Then he began to remember Orlando, the girls, the nightclub, and the booze. At least, that was the nice way of putting it. Rob sat holding the phone. A glance at his watch told him it was seven a.m. He looked for Mike; the big guy hadn't made it in, or at least his bed was still made. The voice on the telephone kept saying hello. As he tried to speak with a dry mouth, his words came out in a squeaky, nasal way. He cleared his throat, then rubbed his nose and face. Now maybe he could talk he thought. "Hello," he began again. The female voice on the other end asked for Rob Marshall. "Speaking," he replied rather gruffly, "what can I do for you?"

The voice was businesslike with only a slight trace of Spanish accent. "My name is Lourdes, from Mr. Jacobson's office. I am calling to schedule a meeting as soon as possible."

"Oh, yes," Rob replied, "You will have to give me a minute. I'm having trouble getting awake. Didn't expect to hear from you so soon. Is Jacobson with you?" he asked.

"No, he was delayed. He'll be in sometime today."

"Okay," returned Rob. "Give me about forty-five minutes. I'll meet you in the dining room for coffee and breakfast."

"All right," Lourdes replied. "Let's make it eight o'clock."

"Even better. See you at eight," Rob replied as he hung up the phone.

His thoughts turned to Mike and last night. Where was that big boy? Well, the police hadn't called, so that was a good sign. Guess he had just camped out; at least, that's the way Mike would explain it. Through the haze, he began to remember from the night before that Jennifer, the van driver, was a really nice looking girl. He felt sure that Mike had smoothed his way into her bed for the night, or what was left of the night. He was trying to remember what time he had left the bar. It must have been between one and two. Now it was beginning to come back to him. It was around one-thirty when he returned to the room.

He also remembered the man, the one with the big nose, who had been following them. At least, it seemed that way when he had appeared at the sports bar last night. Maybe the man was following them, maybe not. The way his head was pounding, it didn't really matter now. He was scratching around in his bag for some instant relief for a king size headache. He grabbed a bottle of aspirin, took three, and swallowed a big gulp of water. Either the water tasted terrible, or something had used his mouth for a sewer. Rob dug down in his shaving bag again and came up with a toothbrush and toothpaste. Maybe, just maybe, that would make his mouth decent. He brushed his teeth and drank a glass of water. Brushing his teeth hadn't changed the taste of the water much.

He lay across the bed and covered his eyes with the pillow and relaxed. He had to give the aspirin time to work on the headache. He lay there, trying not to move. His head was beginning to feel better. Rob knew he had to get up, shave, take a shower, and get a move on. He was really pissed at himself for getting drunk, especially with a chance to close the deal on his old airplane, which he desperately needed to sell. Now he was going to meet someone and finalize the sale with a hangover. That wasn't very smart, and he knew it. He was lying there thinking he had really screwed up. Now he needed to make the best of the situation. He rolled out of bed and stumbled to the relief of a hot shower and some fresh clothes.

Fifty minutes later, Rob turned the corner and headed to the door of the restaurant, not really knowing what to expect. Who was this Lourdes? Why was she here and not Jacobson? He was beginning to feel half-human again. Some coffee would definitely help clear his head. As he stepped through the door of the restaurant, the morning aroma of coffee and food greeted him as he surveyed the room. A waitress approached and asked if he was Rob Marshall. With a weak half-smile, he nodded. The waitress asked him to follow her, and she led him to a corner table. Rob saw Lourdes as she sat elegantly in her chair. The lady was very attractive; and even in his state of mind, her presence was overwhelming. At least, he was going to assume she was a lady.

Lourdes spoke first, "Good morning."

"And a good morning to you," replied Rob, too hungover to pull off the intended cuteness. "I expected Jacobson to be here this morning."

"I know," she began, "Jacobson has a conflict. That is, Mr. Jacobson has a conflict. He is on a tight schedule. We are to go ahead with the paper work on the sale of the airplane, and he will be along to finalize it this afternoon."

"Well, there isn't much to do," Rob began. "The bank has signed off on all of the releases. All we need to do is have a bank check made out to them and my company. I will sign all of the F.A.A. bills of sale. You'll take the buyer's copy, and there is a current title search to verify the one lien that is in my bank's name."

About that time the waitress came over and asked, "How are you this morning?" By the way he looked, she shouldn't have to ask that question. Hopefully, his appearance wasn't as bad as he felt. "What can I get for you?" she continued. "How about some coffee for starters?"

Lourdes looked up with a smile and said, "That's a good idea. We're in no hurry, so the coffee is fine. Give us a little time, then we'll order breakfast." She seemed a little amused at Rob's condition.

Rob was beginning to come around. The caffeine of two cups of coffee helped to revive his dead and dying brain cells. His mind began to work. They had talked for over thirty minutes, but he wasn't getting any useful information from this woman. Either she was really smart, or he was really slowed by his hangover. He usually had the ability to maneuver people a bit, at least to get enough information to know what was going on. Not this time. This chick was smart; she slipped every question. It was clear that Jacobson had sent her to keep them busy until he could get to Orlando. She could talk all day and not say a thing.

Rob heard a good morning from over his shoulder and turned just as Mike, sunglasses and all, approached the table. Rob felt a little relief with the reinforcement. Mike looked like he'd had a good time, or the tale of a bad one. His condition was questionable. Mike sat down after being introduced to Lourdes. The waitress walked up. He ordered a cup of coffee and a glass of tomato juice. No breakfast for me they heard him mumble rather weakly.

"Gentlemen, I think I'll pass on breakfast. Please excuse me. Mr. Jacobson will call a little later this morning. I'll get his schedule and call you," Lourdes said as she stood up.

"We will be in our rooms," Rob added as she was leaving. "Have Mr. Jacobson call us and give us an estimated time of arrival, or as we say in flying, ETA, so we can make our reservations for our flight home."

Lourdes smiled to herself. She knew it was very unlikely that these two guys would be needing reservations. If everything worked the way it was laid out, the two men she had just met would be flying the airplane on a covert operation. At least, that was the way Jacobson had planned it. It would be a classic two step, and step one was getting them out of Orlando.

Back in their room, Rob and Mike tried to sleep off the effects of the night before. Much too soon, the phone rang; it was Jacobson. After the usual greetings, he said, "I apologize for not meeting you in Orlando as we originally planned, but I had a problem with my business partner. He is the one who is putting up most of the money for the airplane." Jacobson paused. This set-up had to be done right. He resumed with confidence, "The bottom line is he wants to see the plane before he will cut the check so I can finalize the sale."

"Well, tell him the son of a bitch is sitting at Orlando Executive Airport. If he wants to see it, come up and we'll give him a damn guided tour," Rob said, still hungover and more than a little peeved.

"No, I hate to ask this, but he wants the airplane brought to his place of business in the Bahamas. Then he'll approve the money to close the sale," Jacobson said. "I have discussed the matter with Lourdes. She is making arrangements for the extra funds you'll need to move the airplane, plus a little bonus for your trouble. She has all the details."

Rob listened patiently. "Mr. Jacobson, this is not the arrangement we made for delivery of the airplane," he said tiredly.

"I know," Jacobson went on, using his best persuasive voice. "I didn't foresee this problem with my business partner. I am truly sorry about this."

Rob paused for a minute. "This is going to be a real problem. My insurance prohibits flights out of the continental United States, and the Bahamas is definitely out of the country," he said. There was a long silence.

"All right," he said finally to Jacobson. "Let me talk to my co-pilot. I'll need him to help me fly the plane. I'll get back to you after we've discussed this."

"Okay," Jacobson replied, "just talk to Lourdes. She knows how to get in touch with me. She can handle all of the details," Jacobson went on to say, "but we need to move the airplane as soon as possible this afternoon and no later than Saturday morning." Step one in our paso doble, he thought.

Rob was getting himself into a real tight spot, and he knew it. Taking the airplane to the Bahamas without insurance left him wide open. Well, he was committed if Mike agreed to go along and help move the airplane to the Bahamas as Jacobson wanted, but to Mike the Bahamas just added a little spice to the trip. They would leave at first light Saturday morning. The flight over to the Bahamas from Orlando would take about two hours. Then they could get their business transacted and be home Saturday afternoon. Hell, what's one more step anyhow, Rob thought.

9 The Twilight Zone

The flight had been almost too smooth. Early morning flights usually were the best. In the afternoon the heat of the day made it a little bumpy, and there were afternoon showers. They were going to a place called Eleuthera. The chart that had been given to them by Lourdes showed the airport on the north side running along parallel to the beach. There was an island off in the distance. Yes, it looked like the one on the chart. Now to locate the airport. Rob unfolded the chart some more. There, that gave him a better view. There was a little rise; then the bay was to the north. Yes, that was the right island. Now he could see the airport. Even though there was a slight haze, the runway was visible. Strangely, there were no other planes, no other vehicles on the ground. The wind was out of the south; the whitecaps on the waves were drifting to the north.

Rob spoke into the intercom, "Mike, you scan for traffic. When I get us on final, you get the gear down and give me about twenty degrees of flaps." Everything went well on approach. They were touching down. No problem. Rob had taken a real chance flying to the islands without insurance. His banker would have stroked had he known about this flight out of the country, not knowing where they were going or who for. They completed the rollout.

There still wasn't any sign of ground activity; things looked really quiet. They taxied up on to the ramp, swung the bird around, and pulled the mixtures. The old engines slowed, then stopped. Still there was no sign of life. Things were a little spooky. The island was green with short, bushy vegetation growing down to the beaches and around the perimeter of the airport. Up a narrow path to the north was a small, faded white frame building with a sign on which "customs" was printed in sun-faded black letters. They threw their bags on the ground and looked around for a customs official or anyone who could tell them if they were at the right place. There had to be someone to talk to; they had just flown into another country, not the twilight zone.

Rob and Mike picked up their bags and started walking up the hill when two men stepped around the building. They were wearing uniforms, not unlike our regular army thought Rob. Both men were carrying rifles and had side arms. At the same time both of them dropped the rifles to their waists from over their shoulders and shouted, "You two, don't move! This is the Bahamian Defense Force." Rob and Mike began to look around. There must be some mistake. "Drop your bags, and put your hands over your heads," the big black sergeant demanded. The men dropped their bags simultaneously. They had a problem, and they knew it. There was more of the welcoming party up on the hill behind the airplane. This had to be a mistake. The big sergeant demanded that they spread eagle on the ground. "You are under arrest," the sergeant went on.

"What have we done?" Rob asked.

"Don't play dumb with me," the sergeant went on with a heavy Bahamian accent. "We've been waiting for you. We know what you have done. You have been hauling dope into the Bahama Islands and corrupting our good people. You are going to spend a long time in our jail as a guest of the Bahamian authorities. That airplane is now the property of the government; it has been confiscated for being used illegally."

"There must be a mistake," Rob said. "We just flew in from Florida."

"Yeah, yeah, that is what they all say when we catch them, just flying around in the night seeing the sights. What do you white honkeys think we are, just a bunch of dumb island n......?"

The sergeant and his soldiers marched the two into the office and sat them down and began questioning them. The first question was where is your flight plan if you just flew into here from Florida? A cold chill ran up Rob's spine. Taking a chance, they had slipped out of the airport in Orlando. Knowing the proper procedure was to file if they were going from Florida to the Bahamas, especially flying a big old cargo plane like this DC-3, they were in trouble. No phone number, address, or anything, assuming that Jacobson would be here to meet them, definitely not the Bahamian Defense Force. Man, what a way to start off the day. They needed to find Jacobson and have him straighten the entire thing out now, before these soldiers filed charges against them.

"This is a big mistake," Rob said for the third time. Now was the time to settle down and get his composure. He was beginning to sound desperate; it showed in his voice. Don't panic; just be calm. Hell, he was just kidding himself. Their asses were in real trouble. These soldiers really thought they were drugrunners and were treating them as such, and he had his good friend up in the middle of this mess. Damn, it was time to panic, but don't let those soldiers know. The thoughts kept running through his head. It was time for a game plan. Boy, had he been a fool to be so trusting and to leave without getting phone numbers and addresses. That was his fault. No, he had an address and phone number for Jacobson somewhere on the sales agreement. It was in his case in the airplane. The big sergeant, speaking with the heavy accent, walked over and pulled up a chair to the table. He didn't sit down but put one foot in the chair seat, crossed his arms over his leg, and leaned over, "You gentlemen ready to tell us the whole story about last night. Where you come from and where you were going when you landed here? Now who is in this with you? There has to be a ground crew. Where did you land last night before coming in here?"

Mike, who had been silent for some time spoke, "We were just bringing this plane to be delivered to the buyers."

"That's right," followed Rob, "if you will take me to the airplane, I can furnish you with a name and an address that will verify all this."

"Sure," the sergeant spoke. Then one of the soldiers, who had been standing across the room, added, "We have airplanes delivered at night all the time. You are delivering, but not airplanes," he continued.

The sergeant loaded both Rob and Mike into a jeep and took them three miles from the airport to a tiny village clustered on a hillside along a winding, pot-holed, tree-shaded road. The faded stucco home blended into the hillside foliage on the left; and on the seaside was a small store beside an ancient weathered structure. Out front hung a small tattered sign, Beach Hotel. The jeep slowed and came to a brake-squealing halt.

"Get out," the sergeant growled from the backseat. Rob, Mike, and the young soldier, who had been driving, all stepped out onto the shell-covered parking area.

"Through there," the sergeant demanded, pointing his rifle toward the opening of the hotel door. Sitting patiently inside in a high backed, weathered wicker chair was an elderly white-haired man, legs crossed and hands clasped on his lap, gazing as the troop rumbled through the door.

"We have guests," the sergeant added as he prodded Mike and Rob with the butt of his rifle, forcing them through the lobby and to their left along a shadowy corridor into a small, dark room with one bed and a wooden chair. Hanging crookedly on the wall opposite the bed was a framed mirror. A tree shaded, mildew streaked window admitted only a few shadowy rays of light, casting shadows throughout the drab cubicle.

"You two are under house arrest," he explained. "There will be armed guards outside this room. I have sent for transportation to take you two to

Nassau. There you will see a judge, and he will determine what to charge the two of you with." Maybe this is the twilight zone after all, Rob decided.

It was ten-thirty; time was passing in a hurry. Rob needed to get to a phone, and there was none in the room, of course. The young soldier outside of the door seemed like a nice enough person. Maybe, just maybe, he could talk him into giving them a break and letting him use the phone that he had seen on the outside of a nearby building on the way into the hotel.

"Mike," said Rob, "what do you think our chances are of getting to a telephone? We need to get a call to Anne back at the office and have her get in touch with Jacobson."

"It's Saturday. She won't be in the office," Mike replied.

Mike was right. "Maybe this early she will still be at home. God, I sure hope so," said Rob.

The door of the hotel room was standing half-open. The guard was sitting in a chair with his rifle lying across his lap. Mike walked to the door. The soldier looked up at him. The big imposing Mike towered over the guard, especially with him sitting. It was obvious that the guard was nervous. "Just want to talk," said Mike in his soft Cajun lilt, holding his open hands up shoulder high in submission, "Seems we have gotten ourselves in a tight spot." The young, black soldier nodded with a grin, relaxing his military bearing a little. Mike went on, "Have you ever had a situation where you need a favor from a complete stranger?" The black soldier shrugged his shoulders, trying not to commit.

"Well," said Mike, "I don't exactly know how to do this, but I need- we need- you to do something for us. We need to make a phone call. You can help us; just give us five minutes on the phone."

The soldier replied in a heavy accent, "Like, why should I help you and risk myself and my job? Mon, I have a family and need to keep this job to take care of them."

" I know what you are saying. I won't ask you to take a chance for nothing," Mike continued. "What you say I do something that will help your family? See, I have a hundred dollar bill, greenback, U.S. I don't need it if I can use the phone for five minutes, and we won't give you any trouble."

"I will make it two," added Rob from behind Mike. The soldier was giving it some serious thought.

"Okay," he said, "just five minutes and don't give me any trouble. I will shoot. Mon, I mean it," he added. "Both of you stay here," the soldier said as he got up and started to the hotel lobby. The room was on the bottom floor only two doors from the front of the hotel. They could hear the soldier talking to the clerk but could not understand what was being said. They didn't talk long. The soldier returned. He was a little nervous; he knew he could get into a lot of trouble for letting them make the call.

"Okay, mon, okay," he said, "only one can make the call. One will stay in the front lobby with me while I let the other one go and make the call."

"That's fine," said Mike. "Rob will make the call. I will wait in the lobby with you."

"The phone is across over there," he said, pointing as they walked up to the front of the hotel. Rob could see the phone hanging on the side of the building across the street. "Five minutes," he said, "and I will have that money now." Mike handed him the two bills. Rob walked across to the phone. He picked up the receiver and dialed the operator. He gave her Anne's phone number and waited. The phone rang several times; he was getting nervous. Come on, Anne, be at home. Answer the phone. After seven rings, she finally did.

"Oh, boy, I am glad to hear your voice," began Rob.

"Slow down," said Anne. "Where are you? What's the problem?"

"Anne, just listen to what I am about to tell you, and do exactly as I say. I don't have time to explain. We have problems, and you are the only one who can help us. Call that guy Jacobson and tell him we are in the Bahamas where we are supposed to be, and there is a misunderstanding. We need his help in straightening this matter out. I think he will know what you're talking about. Just remember, we are in the Bahaman Islands at the airport on Eleuthera."

"You are where?" Anne asked, still trying to grasp the situation.

"At the airport on Eleuthera in the Bahamas. Tell him."

"Don't ask questions. Just call Jacobson; he has an answering service if I remember right. He is either in Fort Lauderdale or in his office in Nassau in the Bahamas. Get in touch with him as soon as I hang up this phone. This is critical! Anne, I'm counting on you. Please don't let me down. Remember, get a message to Jacobson. Now! If you don't, I don't know how we'll get out of this."

10 A Fine Swiss Movement

The warm rays of the early morning summer sun cast a mirage of shadows as the traffic snaked its way along I-395 southwest at a pace resembling a slow-moving parking lot. General Eugene E. McKenzie gripped the steering wheel of his brown Ford sedan, staring blindly at the brake lights of a large white commercial van in front of him. Maintaining his composure and not giving into the tug of rage could redefine the expression, self-control. Over the van appeared the green and white road sign he was looking for: Pentagon, Jefferson Davis Highway, Exit one mile.

The General turned right onto Jefferson Davis, then onto an off ramp leading into the Pentagon Complex, then north along the perimeter to the entrance of the senior staff officers' parking lot. Slowing the brown Ford down, the General allowed the guard to eye his bumper decal, then salute. The car passed through the gate and around to his right and into a parking spot marked with two white stars on a sign with gray background with "General E.E. McKenzie" in small print at the bottom.

Entering through the first thick glass door, he paused and pulled his I.D. out and slipped it through the slot on the reader. As a green light came on with a low buzz, he then pushed the second door open and proceeded along a well-lit austere corridor to two massive dark oak doors with a numbered code on a plaque overhead. As he passed through the door into an office complex, he was greeted by a lieutenant colonel in his dress greens.

"Sir," Colonel Olvey stated, "how are you this morning?"

"Good," said General Mac. "Come on in my office. I have a project that needs immediate attention. We'll go over it before this morning's staff meeting."

"Yes, sir," the Colonel said as he followed the General through a door into an office with taupe carpet and soft gray walls sparsely clad with military memorabilia.

The General tossed his hat on the cadenza behind his curved, mahogany desk. They sat down. "I want you to clear my calendar for the next three days. Until Monday. Next I want to see a list of all military aircraft departing from Andrews Air Force Base to Europe, preferably Germany's Rhine Air Force Base to be exact. I'll need to be there twenty-four hours then back to south Florida late Saturday or early Sunday. Call James Barfield at the state department. Tell him you're calling for me and to remember California two years ago. He'll understand. I'm calling in that favor. I need a jet, something civilian like the corporate executives use, to pick me up in Germany then fly me to Zurich then back and I'll also need three or four Marines from the Embassy as guards. Now this can't be discussed outside this office, and be damn sure James understands. Tell him it's very sensitive, from the top."

As the Colonel was leaving the office, the General picked up the black phone from his desk and punched a speed dial. "Margaret," he said when the phone was answered, "get my hang-up bag out and put that dark blue suit and some underwear, socks, and two matching ties and two white shirts in it. Yes, I know you made dinner plans, but that'll have to wait. Call and tell them you're married to the military. When duty calls, I have to go. I'll make it up to you. It's only a few days." After eighteen years of marriage, his wife had learned to expect the unexpected.

As General McKenzie returned from his staff meeting, the colonel was waiting for him. "Come in," the General said as he walked past and into his office. Colonel Olvey stopped and pushed the large, brown oak door closed then followed General Mac across the room.

"Sit down," General Mac said as he himself sat down in a soft somewhat worn leather chair.

"Okay, Olvey, what do we have?" the General asked.

"There's a KC-10 in-flight refueler departing Andrews AFB, fourteen-thirty today, and after one stop in England, it will be arriving at Rhine AFB, Friday, sixteen-forty local time Germany. Then the state department will pick you up at the air force base and take you to a local airport where a charter jet provided by the state department, courtesy of James Barfield, will be waiting to take you to Zurich. Then it will be returning at your convenience back to Germany, where Saturday afternoon a C-141 departs at sixteen-thirty local time; and you will arrive at Homestead AFB Sunday at twelve-ten local time."

"Sounds good, but I can't transact my business Friday night, so schedule the charter flight from Germany to Zurich for early Saturday morning around six hundred hours then see if they can delay that KC-10 about ten hours. It'll leave, then arrive in Germany early Saturday morning."

"The Embassy in Zurich will provide an escort of Marines when you arrive there," the Colonel said.

"Okay, call someone and see if the KC-10 delay will cause a conflict. Don't make it a major issue. Find out why they're going. If it's a routine training flight, then make the change in their schedule. I don't want any special favors."

Two hours later, General McKenzie picked up his black phone and buzzed Colonel Olvey. "Olvey," he said, "I'm going home at sixteen hundred. Have a staff car pick me up there at twenty-one hundred hours and take me to Andrews AFB. Colonel, I don't need to remind you this mission is extremely sensitive. Let's keep it that way." General Mac hung up the phone.

Hours later at approximately thirty-four thousand feet, the dozing General McKenzie felt a gentle tug at his shoulder.

"Sir, we're approximately twenty minutes from touch down. You asked me to awaken you," the young thin sandy-haired navigator said with an expressionless face.

"Oh, thank you," General McKenzie said, brushing his blonde hair back with his right hand as he sat up on the side of the crew bunk. They had made one rendezvous with some jet fighters and had refueled, then after the exercise, General McKenzie had gone back in the crew quarters and gotten a couple of hours of sleep.

Now the race was on. After landing he went into the pilot's lounge at operations and changed into his civilian clothes. He then met with Jerry Allen, a state department employee, who drove him over to a small, private airport. Stepping from the black Mercedes sedan, General McKenzie turned and faced the corporate aircraft, a Grumman G4, standing tall on its sleek landing gear, not unlike Pegasus, the flying horse ready to spirit its riders off on an adventure into all parts of the world.

According to his watch, it was six-ten local time in Zurich. Putting his left hand on Jerry's shoulder, then reaching out his right hand with a strong grip clasping Jerry's hand, the General said, "It is a pleasure; again, thank you for providing the aircraft on such a short notice."

"Sir, that's my job," he turned, then walked over to his black Mercedes and stood watching as General Mac climbed up the softly padded steps into the plush interior of first class luxury. He was going first class but didn't have time to enjoy it.

"Good morning," General McKenzie said as he stuck his head into the cockpit of the G-4. The pilot turned in his seat and offered his hand to the General. General Mac eyed the softly lit instrument panel all in shades of gray, soft black instruments. "Well, Commander, things sure have changed," he said with a big smile, pointing to the sophisticated flight panel. "Back when I began, it was needle ball and airspeed, sometimes an old magnetic compass. Now look at this," he said, pointing to the panel trying to make conversation and be congenial.

Both young men smiled. "Yes, it gets a little easier every year," the co-pilot said.

"Well, gentlemen, do you know where we're going?"

"Sir, I was told Zurich by Jerry Allen, so that's what I filed for," the co-pilot said.

"Well, let's go," the General said as he backed out of the cockpit and turned to face a young, round-faced lady with soft blonde hair and a big warm smile.

"Good morning, sir," she said, stepping to one side.

"Good morning to you," the General answered.

"I'm your hostess. When you get seated, is there anything I can get for you?" she asked with a slight Bavarian accent.

"I believe I'll have some coffee," the General answered as he sat down in a soft, gray leather chair, trimmed in a dark burgundy with a gold eagle crest on each arm, and buckled the shiny clasp on his seat belt.

There was a soft whine as the air stair door was retracted and then a loud sound of engines as they taxied out and were airborne.

Precision. Everything was going like clockwork. Step by step, minute by minute, it clicked off.

In less than three hours, General McKenzie was in the hushed confines of the secured boardroom of one of Zurich's largest banks.

The General stood, looking over the shoulders of the two men double-counting U.S. currency. Then he looked at his watch. It was going to be a tight schedule. The last twenty-four hours had been a logistical nightmare, getting to Zurich and having the bank get everything ready. At first they said it was impossible to have four million in U.S. one hundred-dollar bills ready on a Saturday morning. When he called Thursday morning, it was afternoon in Switzerland. That in itself had created a real problem. When he reminded them of their worldwide reputation for just such transactions, and that he could and would compensate them for the extra time and trouble, the bankers agreed that they could accomplish the task the next day. The General had his way of refusing to take no for an answer.

"They should be through in another ten minutes," the bank senior vice president said. The General took another look at his watch. They were cutting things close. The chartered jet was at the airport. They had to go to Germany and had less than four hours before the Air Force C141 transport jet would be leaving for Homestead Air Force Base in Florida. He had to make that connection. It had bothered him having to lie stating that they were moving records from the bank to the United States as a part of an ongoing investigation when he had borrowed three marines from the

U.S.Embassy in Zurich for the movement of the money to the air base in Germany.

The money was placed in unmarked boxes. Then the large boxes were placed two each in large plain canvas pouches. The large, tan canvas pouches had rope handles on each end, similar to a small trunk. Two men could conveniently carry them one at a time. The General had insisted that the bank provide an armed van to take them to the airport.

General McKenzie had not taken time to call and confirm Sunday's schedule. He depended on the Colonel to make arrangements with Jacobson to meet him Sunday afternoon at Homestead Air Force Base. The plans were to leave part of the money with Jacobson so he could complete his mission and pay the freedom fighters. This group had gone several months without a payday. Now, as agreed, part of these funds was to be used to make a badly needed payroll. Many of the men fighting for freedom in Nicaragua were men with families either in Honduras or in the United States.

The flight from Switzerland to Germany had given him the opportunity to switch from street clothes back to his flight fatigues. The cargo was moved from the civilian airport to the airbase and then loaded onto the C141. Another thirty minutes the aircraft would be on its way, so he relaxed. General McKenzie hadn't realized how stressed he was until this very moment. Now it showed; a stubble of beard and aching shoulders reminded him that he hadn't stopped for the last twenty-four hours. He had a right to be tired, but once they were airborne, he would find an empty crew bunk and get a few hours of sleep before they landed in Florida. The Swiss movement was finished with jeweled precision.

11 Trapped In Paradise

At two o'clock in the afternoon, Jacobson called Nassau to speak to his old friend, Captain Lord Nelson Mann of the Bahamas Police Force. "Mann, this is Jacobson," he began, "how is everything going over there?"

"Just as we planned," Mann replied in his local Bahamian accent with the strong English influence. "Your crew and their airplane are all very secure. We need for you to come over and get this taken care of before some of these people start asking questions. As you know from past experience, there is always someone wanting to be paid for his services. When they find out what is happening, they feel they should be compensated, be part of the team. You understand what I am saying. The sooner we get this matter settled, the better it'll be for all of us," replied Mann.

"I'm at the airport now. We will be leaving here shortly. I'll pick you up in Nassau at say about three-thirty. Then we will go over to the other island and settle this."

"All right," said Mann, "I will be at the general aviation hangar in the customs office. I'll see you there."

Jacobson walked over and boarded the blue and white twin engine Piper Navajo. The flight from Opa-Locka to Nassau was about an hour's flying time. He had made the trip several times in the last few months. His pilot George owned this charter service, and Jacobson used him exclusively to minimize his exposure. George was a Cuban who had done well since coming to Florida from Cuba in the early sixties as a young man. He was violently anti-Communist, someone Jacobson had learned to count on. George and his other pilots made their services available around the clock. Because of the places they were always flying, the rumors of illegal activity were common place. Jacobson used George and his service to go to all of the Caribbean Islands. At least, it seemed that way. They were always going to Central America for a meeting or to take a leader of the freedom fighters back and forth. These flights had to remain confidential. George knew just how to do that.

Jacobson made the stop in Nassau and picked up Captain Mann. They were now approaching the airport in Eleuthera.

"Mann," spoke Jacobson, " let me handle this when we get there. I have an idea that our American friends will be angry," he continued. "I have to maintain some measure of control; and limiting their access to information is the best way." Jacobson was a professional, and he knew what he was doing. The captain knew Jacobson, but he did not know about him. Jacobson acted on a need to know basis, and that was the extent of the information provided to the captain. Mann did know that Jacobson had all the connections right up to the top. That was enough for Captain Lord Nelson Mann.

The airplane landed. George taxied up beside Rob's DC-3 and shut the engines off. All three men got out and went into the small customs office. They had cleared customs in Nassau, and with Mann along, there was no need to go through customs again. They just showed their visa and I.D.'s and walked on through with the captain of the police leading the way. Captain Mann called to one of the soldiers sitting on the bench in front of the office, "Where can I find Sergeant Sanders?"

"Sir, you must be Captain Mann," the soldier spoke standing up sharply.

"Yes, that's right," the Captain spoke.

"Sir," the soldier continued, "the sergeant has gone after the two Americans who were flying the DC-3, the ones we arrested this morning."

"Good," the Captain said. "How long will it take him?"

"Oh, no time at all," the soldier continued. "They are in the hotel just up the road about three miles. The sergeant left when he saw your plane coming."

Rob and Mike were lying on the bed. They had been very quiet for the last hour or so. Their earlier conversation had covered every aspect of the situation. They agreed that the matter would be resolved once Jacobson was made aware of what was going on, unless he was a part of the whole damn mess. If that was the case, anything could happen.

In the distance Rob heard an airplane. It sounded like it was making an approach to the airport. He rolled over and looked out the window. He couldn't see a thing. The bushes were grown over the side of the building. He listened intently. Yes, it was landing. "Hey, Mike," he said as he jumped to his feet, "did you hear it? That sounds like a plane landing."

"Yeah," said Mike, "it is about the third or fourth one today and still no Jacobson. I could sure use something to eat. That donut and coffee at five this morning was gone by nine. What time is it now?" he asked, half to himself. "Damn, it's after four-thirty and still no Jacobson. Maybe these people are just dope runners planning to frame us, shoot us, and take the plane. That does happen."

Rob kept his cool. Similar thoughts had gone through his mind several times over the last three or four hours, especially since the phone call to Anne produced no response from Jacobson. This was a really quiet out-of-the-way place. A good place to disappear. No, he thought, I can't let myself think like that. I have to be positive.

They could hear a car coming up the hill. As it got closer, it began to sound familiar. They looked at each other. It did sound like the jeep the sergeant was driving; and it was stopping at the hotel. They weren't sure if that was good or bad.

The sergeant kicked the half open door fully open and stepped in. "Let's go," he said in a rather loud voice making sure everyone knew that he was in charge. The two men didn't say a word, just looked at each other, got up, put on their baseball caps, and walked out in front of the sergeant. The young soldier followed. The sergeant pointed to the jeep. "Get in," he ordered.

They all climbed in and sat down. The driver started up the engine, backed out onto the road, retracing their early morning ride. The jeep slowly descended the hill to the airport. The sea emerged through the sparse foliage. It was really nice, a soft teal green; too bad they weren't in a mood to enjoy it. The sergeant hadn't spoken since the beginning of their ride back to the airport. At least they weren't taking them into the underbrush. No, they were on the way back to the airport.

Rob got a glance at his DC-3. It was still there and in one piece. That was some comfort.

As the jeep rounded the final curve and the customs building was in view, Rob saw a form he recognized. Yes, it was; it was Jacobson. "Do you see what I see?" he said.

"Yeah," said Mike, "I can't decide whether we need to kiss him or kick his ass."

As they drove up to the airport customs building, Jacobson was standing in front talking to an officer who was dressed differently from the soldiers. The driver stopped the jeep a few feet away from where they were standing. Without saying a word, the sergeant nodded for them to get out. Mike stepped out; and Rob followed. Jacobson was still talking to the officer with all the brass and braid. They could tell he was someone important. At least, that is the way it appeared to them, and the soldiers were maintaining a safe distance. Mike and Rob slowly approached Jacobson and the officer. As they got closer, Jacobson and the officer stopped talking and looked up at the two men.

Jacobson spoke first, "Understand you gentlemen are having a little trouble."

"Kind of seems that way," Rob spoke, "hopefully, a little matter of mistaken identity."

"Have you got a place we can talk in private?" Jacobson asked the captain.

"Sure," the captain followed, 'I think the customs officer will let you use his office."

The customs officer was standing by and nodded. "This way," he said as he swung one arm out in front and walked toward the office. They stepped into the office and closed the door behind themselves.

"What is going on?" asked Rob in a really angry but controlled voice. "They have arrested us, and they say that they are taking the airplane. We did just what we were told to do by you and Lourdes. Now you have got to straighten this damn mess out. We need it done now, not tomorrow."

"Okay, boys, I am doing the best I can," Jacobson said. "There was a mix-up. I wanted the airplane in Nassau, not over here," he went on. "The problem is I had everything cleared for Nassau. Lourdes got things mixed up." Then he paused. "I was going to bring the airplane over here after we got the sell finished. Now we have a real problem. Someone was seen landing a DC-3 on one of the islands last night. They think it was you. These people think you're involved in drug smuggling, and they want to take the airplane and put you two away." He went on, " But I am using all of my influence to get this matter resolved." Jacobson was lying, and knew he was lying. He just hoped they didn't. "I've got this captain, who is a very good friend of mine here, to talk to the locals and try to work out something that we can all live with," he continued. "Here's the way it looks now," Jacobson started again. "I want both of you to listen and listen closely. My partner will be hard to work with if he finds out that you have been arrested for this alleged involvement with drugs. Then it's all over for both of you. He is a very influential person in the Islands, so this will have to be handled very quietly or else."

"What do you mean or else?" asked Rob, visible shaken and annoyed.

"My partner is the one who handles the purse strings, and without funds to take care of these people over here, we are in real trouble. I was buying this airplane to do some contract flying for a group, and this group doesn't like people asking questions. I am limited on funds, and we will have to work together if we want to pull this off." He continued, "It'll take about thirty thousand dollars to get this mess corrected, and that's part of the funds I was going to use to pay you for the airplane. Now there is an alternative. I could pay the locals to let the plane go; you would have to work with me and sub-contract to do what I was going to do. That way all of us can get out of this mess with our shirts and our asses still in one piece."

Rob and Mike looked at each other. Both were thinking along the same lines. Their asses were in a crack, and they didn't know who to blame. Had they screwed up by not filing the proper flight plan, or did they smell a rat who was setting them up? If so, they were in trouble either way. They were hooked, really hooked. If they refused, they were headed to jail, maybe for a very long time. If they went along, they were possibly getting in even deeper.

"How long will this supposed contract take?" Mike asked.

"Less than a week," Jacobson said rather confidently.

"We've got to talk this over," said Rob. "I've gotten myself in this mess, but I don't have a right to drag my friend in with me. If he wants out, will you let him go, or at least see what you can do to get him back to Florida? I'll find someone else to help me fly this thing."

"I can do one better than that," said Jacobson. "I'll let you think about it until tomorrow. At least, the Captain said he thought he could stall the locals off until then." Jacobson was holding back. He didn't want to say too much.

"If we agree, and that is a big 'if'," said Rob, "how does this thing work? Where are we going? When do we leave, and how will it be worth our time?"

"You will be paid well for the use of your airplane, and both of you will be well compensated for your time. Probably the easiest money you will ever make for the time you spend."

"No dope deals," said Mike. "I might have smoked a joint once or twice in my life, but I am not going to be involved in hauling it to school kids. You do get my drift?" he said staring directly into Jacobson's eyes.

"This doesn't involve drugs. It is something you will be doing with the blessing of the United States government. That is all I can tell you at this time."

"All right, all right," said Rob, "can we get off this island, say maybe, to Nassau for the night?"

"I'll see if the Captain can arrange to get you out of here," Jacobson said as he was walking off.

As Jacobson strutted away confidently, the two men looked at each other. Mike spoke first, "What is that saying? When you have them by the balls, their hearts and minds will follow. I think they have a good grip, and I don't like it," he added.

Rob sat quietly thinking the situation over. They needed help, but he couldn't come up with another plan other than to go along with Jacobson's offer. For now, he didn't have a choice. Losing that old DC-3 and going to jail didn't appeal to him at all. They definitely had him by the balls, and there wasn't another way out. At least, not at this time.

Mike sat quietly. He had been in bad situations before, many times before. Those two tours as a helicopter pilot in Vietnam had put him in some desperate situations, and this looked like they were getting into something that possibly compared to the action in Vietnam. At least they didn't know what was happening, and that was how it was in Nam. You spent half your time trying to figure out what was going on and the other half wishing you didn't know.

Rob spoke, "Well, Mike, old boy, what do you think of the situation I've gotten you in this time?"

"I don't think you planned it. If you did, you screwed up because your ass is in here with me," said Mike with a grin.

Jacobson returned in a few minutes. "Okay, boys," he began with a slight pause, "if you will guarantee me that you will do as I say, I am taking personal responsibility for both of you. We can go over to Nassau for the night. I'll put you up in a hotel on Paradise Island. Now I have to have your word and no bullshit. These old black boys over here will put your ass in the jailhouse and throw away the key. Now I'm not trying to pressure you, but I have got to have an answer as soon as possible. There will have to be arrangements made, and this matter with the police put behind us," he said.

"Give us some time to think about this and discuss it. You're talking, but we don't understand," said Rob slowly. "First of all, I don't make decisions on an empty stomach, and it has been a while since we've had a decent meal."

"All right, let's go back to Nassau," Jacobson said.

"What about the airplane?" asked Rob as they were walking out of the customs office.

"I think it will be all right for now. These boys from the defense force won't let it out of their sight. This is a big catch for them. It's a chance to- let's say- better themselves personally. The plane will be here when we get back," Jacobson seemed to be speaking with real confidence. It looked as if he had pulled this little act off without a real hitch. Yes, really smooth, maybe too smooth. Rob and Mike got their bags from under the DC-3 as the five men went toward the Piper Navajo.

As they walked, Jacobson introduced them to each other. "Now ain't this real cozy," thought Mike. "Just one big happy family. And there is no doubt who is heading it up." Yes, he hadn't said much to Rob, but he was getting the feeling that they were going for a long ride, and they didn't have a real chance to decide for themselves if they wanted to. He knew that he couldn't leave his good friend in this mess to be screwed over and maybe shot and buried in some shallow grave down south when this bunch of bastards was finished with him. Rob was a good sort of person, sometimes too good. Now these assholes had him playing their game and in their ballpark and by their rules. Well, we'll know in a few days. Yes, we will know," he thought to himself.

The men all got into the Navajo. George looked around after he had started the engine asking if everyone was buckled up. The airplane taxied out onto the runway, and they were airborne. Rob sat looking out the window thinking how beautiful the islands really were, especially late afternoon. Too bad he couldn't enjoy it. There wasn't a thing he could do now. "Take a deep breath and relax, just relax," he repeated to himself under his breath. The sun was beginning to set. At this time of day things are really beautiful-the white sandy beaches, the emerald green water with the red and yellow sunset reflecting on the soft waves. Off in the distance there were several small islands whose white beaches blended into the green background of the landscape. It was a peaceful scene. Well, if you were going to be in trouble, this was as good a place as any.

The airplane landed and taxied into the parking ramp of the general aviation terminal in Nassau. The flight had been in virtual silence. No one spoke. Jacobson had made himself a drink and offered one to Mike and Rob, but both men had refused. They had some very important decisions to make. That is if it could be considered a decision: work for Jacobson or go to jail. Big choice. They were still going to give it some time before committing to Jacobson. Of course, Jacobson was sure that they were cornered. Given time they would realize that they had no choice, and time passes quickly in paradise.

12 Ming the Merciless

After leaving the aviation terminal, Rob and Mike retrieved their bags and walked toward the gate at the taxi stand. Mike looked to his right. There through the window in the customs office was the captain talking to the agent on duty and a policeman, pointing towards them. Mike was sure that the captain was warning the men to keep an eye out for Rob and him just in case they tried to leave.

Jacobson stepped forward and motioned. An overweight black Bahamian man slid under the wheel of his taxicab and pulled the car over to where the three men were standing. Mike opened the left rear door as Jacobson went around to the right front. The driver sat as if glued to his seat, making no effort to help. "Where to, Mon?" he said, looking back as Rob and Mike got into the backseat and dropped their bags on the floor. Mike only pointed to Jacobson.

"Paradise Island," Jacobson said as he pulled the door closed with a squeaky rattle.

The breeze fluttered softly through the open windows as the old Buick wound along the beach side road. The orange rays of the setting sun cast long shadows of the tropical foliage lining the scenic drive.

The taxi crossed the bridge over to Paradise Island and pulled up in front of a very elaborate hotel. The three men got out of the car with their bags in hand. Jacobson paid the taxi driver, then went into the lobby and up to the desk to make the necessary arrangements for the rooms. Rob and Mike followed at a distance, not saying much. Mike understood that Rob was feeling discouraged.

"Look, man," Mike said with a big grin and a slap on the shoulder. "We've been in bad situations before. We've got to get it together and teach these bastards who they're dealing with. Whatever you do, don't show any weakness. You make them come to us, and we'll have them playing by our rules. They'll think they're in the swamp with the 'gators before this is over with. Let's play along for now, and we'll have a chance to get these assholes. Now you need to relax and have a good time. There ain't nothing we can do tonight," Mike continued.

Mike was right. He needed to get himself under control. It was apparent by his subdued manner that he was losing it, and in this game, that could be fatal.

Jacobson walked up holding two keys and spoke, "You're both on the third floor, room three fourteen and room three sixteen. They're adjoining rooms. Why don't you go clean up, come back down, and have something to eat. I'll meet you back here, say around ten in the morning." With that Jacobson shook their hands and was out the front door. Rob and Mike picked up their bags and headed for the elevators.

They took the time to enjoy long showers, then a leisurely dinner in the dining room. "It's amazing how a good shower, some fresh clothes, and a hot meal can make you feel after the day we've had," Rob sighed.

"Yeah, that really hit the spot," said Mike as they were leaving the dining room. "How about a drink?" he asked Rob as they were strolling past the lounge.

"Sure thing," he replied, "Maybe that will get my mind off all this mess I've gotten us into."

The lounge sat off to one side of the casino. There was a divider of stained glass and dark-grained wood. The décor suggested subdued elegance. Most of the men were in eveningwear. Some were in tuxes and black tie, while others bowed to the climate and wore white dinner jackets. A few were dressed casually. Rob and Mike were conspicuously in the latter group as they entered and sat at a table by the door where the action in the casino was only an arm's length away. The bright lights and bells ringing as the slot machines paid off provided a pleasant diversion.

As they sat down, Rob spoke first, "Be sure to remind me to call Anne when we get back to the room. We need to let her know we're safe. I know after that last call she's worried sick about us."

The cocktail waitress in a short black dress, blond hair twisted into a knot on her head, painted face, and big smile stopped at the table. "What can I get for you, cowboys?" she said with a grin.

"I need something strong. I'll have a double Chivas with a splash of soda and a twist of lemon," said Rob with a smile. He was beginning to feel better.

"I'll have a bourbon and coke," Mike added, "and bring me a glass of water on the side; I'm seriously thirsty."

The waitress brought the drinks. They relaxed and their discussion always returned to their situation. There were several questions that lacked answers. These were questions that Jacobson would have to answer when he returned in the morning. Rob was sitting with his back to the casino and had to turn around at a slight angle to see all the hustle and excitement of the people gambling. Rob noticed a somewhat quizzical but serious expression pass over Mike's face. He looked in the same direction several times.

"What's the problem," asked Rob.

Mike's answer came very slowly and deliberately, "I'm not sure, but I think our visitor from Orlando is with us again. If this is the same man, it can't be just coincidence. I'm sure it's him. He keeps looking through the openings between the slot machines over to your left."

"It's time to get back to the room, so I'm going to get up and head toward the restroom. Then I'll stick my head around in the slots and see if I can spot whoever this bastard is. You get the tab," Rob said, leaning across the table to Mike.

Rob stood up and stepped quickly out of the lounge to the second row of slot machines then turned the corner, facing several people on both sides of the aisle playing the machines. Scanning up and down each side carefully, Rob looked for the man they had seen in Orlando, the one with the big nose and tan shirt. He wasn't in sight. This man had the uncanny ability to disappear. Rob walked around through the slot machines for several more minutes looking for their mystery man. There was no sign of the him.

Mike came up. "Did you see the guy?" he asked while looking around nervously.

"No," said Rob, "that guy, whoever he is, knows when he's been spotted. That was a fast disappearing act."

Both men strolled toward the elevator trying to appear casual, but checking the lobby as they went. Maybe, just maybe, they could get another glimpse of the strange man who had such an interest in them.

"I'll go by the desk and see if there are any messages," said Mike.

"You do that," said Rob. "I'll go out by the pool and have a look around."

Rob went down the corridor, past the front desk, and out the side door onto the patio. The patio around the pool was filled with ferns and small palm trees and landscaped with brightly colored tropical flowers. There was a light sea breeze blowing in, carrying the sound of the ocean waves breaking on the beach. The bright lights in the pool made the water sparkle. One couple was cuddled in a corner of the pool. Across to the right, several people stood in the shadows at a bar in the cabana, having drinks, and talking. Rob walked slowly up to the side of the pool and looked around. There was no big nose character in a tan shirt here. He then walked over to the cabana. The aroma of fresh fruits and liquor mingled in the sea air as the bartender mixed exotic tropical drinks. In big, colorful glasses, they were very appealing.

"What do you call that?" asked Rob, motioning his hand toward a large drink with fruit on top.

"That's the house special; we call it the Bahamian Paradise," the Oriental bartender said with a toothy smile. "Can I make you one?"

"Sure why not? I'll try anything once," Rob answered, still looking around. He knew this feeling of insecurity had to be controlled or his conscious sense of reality would go, and then he'd be in trouble. He had to keep a clear head; things were changing too fast.

The bartender put the drink in front of him as Mike walked up.

"What you got there?" asked Mike, pointing to Rob's drink.

"Oh, I'm not sure. I'll tell you in a minute," Rob said as he lifted the glass and took a big swallow. "Not bad. You've been thirsty all evening. You need to try one."

The bartender looked at Mike. Mike nodded, "Sure thing. I'll give it a try."

After the bartender left to mix Mike's drink, Mike turned to Rob and said, "No word from Jacobson. I left a message at the desk to let him know that we would be out by the pool or in the lounge. But somehow, I have the sneaky feeling that he knows where we are all the time."

The men finished their drinks, signed their tab, bid the bartender good night, and headed for the elevator. On the way up to their rooms, Rob felt an almost claustrophobic tightening in his chest. Time was short. Jacobson was pushing. He had to have a decision by tomorrow morning.

The elevator stopped on the third floor. They got off and walked down the hall toward their rooms. As Rob approached his door, he thought he heard noises coming from his room. Something was going on, and it sounded like a struggle, like furniture being turned over. He motioned to Mike to see if he had also heard the same sounds, who nodded a quick yes. A lamp crashed, then a loud groan, then silence. Rob had quietly slid the key into the lock during the struggle. Mike was standing to one side of the door while Rob turned the knob slowly. With one big hand, Mike slammed the door back. The big nose man in the tan shirt lay motionless on the floor. A pool of blood slowly spread under him, soaking the brown carpet. Standing over him was an Oriental man of compact build. About five-nine, maybe one hundred sixty pounds, he still held the knife as he turned to the doorway to face them. His black eyes, glistening with the intensity of his struggle for survival, fixed them in a stare as hard and cold as two polished stones. Other than that, his features were perfectly composed and expressionless. Both Mike and Rob stood frozen for a second. Then they stepped back into the hall through the still open door. The man very deliberately stooped to put the knife down, then slowly straightened. As he walked toward the two men, they instinctively backed up across the hall.

"My name is Juan Pablo Ming. I work for Jacobson. This man is no good. He was following you. You must trust me. Come back inside and close the door," he said in strongly accented English.

Rob and Mike looked at each other. They had just witnessed a killing. Neither of them was sure of anything, whether to call the police or run for their lives. Their bodies went to full alert-fight or flight.

Again the man spoke, "Please come inside. This man was very dangerous. He could have killed you both. Now you must trust me and come into the room and close the door. We will call Mr. Jacobson. He will know what to do."

The big-nosed man had been following them, and now he was dead. That much was clear. Rob looked at Mike. Mike nodded and motioned for Rob to go on into the room.

"It is most unfortunate that this has happened, especially in your room, Mr. Marshall. Yes, I know who you are. I have been assigned by Mr. Jacobson to watch over both of you and make sure nothing happens to you," said Juan.

The men walked cautiously into the room. Mike stood by the door. He pushed it partly closed making sure the latch did not catch, just in case they needed to make a quick exit. The room was a mess. Furnishings were strewn everywhere. Juan straightened an overturned chair to get to the telephone. He picked it up and called Jacobson. All he said was, "We have a problem. We need you to get here as soon as possible. We are at the hotel in Mr. Marshall's room which is three-fourteen." Juan Pablo then hung up the phone.

"I will let Mr. Jacobson explain all this to you," he said. "He is the man who makes all the decisions."

The big-nosed guy was still lying in the middle of the floor, curled up in an almost fetal position. The struggle had been swift and fatal, very professional. A single stab wound had gone directly into the heart.

Rob stood for a moment trying to control his emotions. He was feeling a little weak and nauseated. Mike, however, seemed all right. During his tours in Vietnam, he had seen enough dead bodies, both friends and enemies, but the old sick feeling was still there. You are never numb to the sight of violent death.

"Mr. Ming, or whatever your name is, we will be next door in my room when Mr. Jacobson gets here," said Mike getting Rob by the arm and leading him out the door.

Mike unlocked the door to his room and opened it. Rob walked in first, not saying a word. He approached the bed and sat down with a dazed stare. Both men sat for several minutes without talking.

Rob was the first to speak, "What in the hell have we gotten ourselves into?" he asked still looking at the floor, "and what in God's name is this Juan?"

"I don't know. But Juan Pablo Ming is one cold bastard. I do know that much. He put that guy down with his bare hands without making a sound or breaking a sweat. Then he asked us to sit down real polite until his keeper gets here. I think it's time for true confession. I mean, call the cops and get this thing out in the open. We're getting in deeper and deeper, and this hole we are digging will cave in on us," replied Mike. Rob shook his head in agreement, not saying a word, still staring at the floor.

Time passed in tense silence. After several minutes, there was a soft tap on the interconnecting door. Mike opened the door, and Jacobson stepped through looking at Mike first, then at Rob sitting on the bed. He walked over to the window and stood looking out, collecting his thoughts. He would try to minimize the impact of this situation on them. Jacobson turned slowly and began to explain. His voice was a little too calm, too deliberate.

"I know you have some questions that need answers," he paused. "I think you both need an explanation. You need to know what is happening. You deserve to know." He went on, "That man in the next room is a piece of a big puzzle. Well, both men are a part of the puzzle, the dead one and the live one. First, the dead man was an enemy. That's the short answer. His mission was to do us harm in anyway he could. He was a Cuban-trained agent, Carlos Macedo, sent here to find out what we are doing. Juan caught him going through your room. Macedo pulled a knife. The rest you saw. Secondly, Mr. Ming is an associate of mine. If you, Mr. Marshall, had walked in on Carlos in your room, that would be you lying in there on the floor. Carlos was a professional, so is Juan Pablo Ming. Let's leave it at that. Now let me explain and give you a little background on the flying we are going to do. Then you will understand the importance of getting Macedo out of our hair, even though we didn't plan to do it this way. We will fly supplies to the freedom fighters in Nicaragua by way of Honduras. We will be picking up supplies in the Caribbean and taking them to Honduras. Secrecy is critical. Our success depends on it. Our lives depend on it. Macedo created a possible threat to that secrecy. It's best we caught him before he gained access to information that could compromise our mission. I'm sorry gentlemen, but both of you are now committed. There is no turning back." Jacobson continued, "We are in a foreign country. What Juan did, just forget. This act was committed in your room, Mr. Marshall. If we bring the local authorities in, there will be all kinds of questions that we would have trouble answering. Your airplane, for instance, how would we explain that situation? We have to clean this mess up, handle this ourselves. You and Mr. Ricau stay here in this room. I have a key to your room, Mr. Marshall. We will bring your things over here. Juan will take care of everything. Leave this to him. He will clean this up. I will see both of you tomorrow afternoon." Jacobson finished talking and turned and walked through the interconnecting door into Rob's room. They heard him speaking quietly to Juan. He came back shortly with Rob's bags, handed them to Mike, and closed the door between the two rooms.

They sat in silence for a few minutes. Mike spoke first, "You think the son of a bitch would at least give us a chance to voice our opinion. What he said was, we are committed and don't have a choice. I don't like it."

Rob sat staring, not saying a word. Still in shock, he tried to take in what Jacobson had told them. He felt the noose tighten around his neck. His choices had just run out. He was in the middle with no way out. Mr. Ming, who was busying himself in the next room, would see to that.

13 The Chinese Laundryman

Juan Pablo Ming pulled the sheet off the bed and used it to wrap the body like a mummy, rolling it over and over until the sheets were completely wound up. He took both pillowcases and pulled one over the head and down as far as it would go, then put the other one over the feet. He then took some wet towels from the bathroom and placed them over the blood. He had to keep the area wet to try to prevent a stain.

Juan Pablo left the room, pulling the door closed behind him, shaking the doorknob to make sure it was locked securely. He walked down the hall, entered the elevator, and checked to make sure that it would go all the way to the basement. It did, and he pushed the button marked basement. He wanted to find the laundry room to get a laundry cart and some housekeeping clothes for himself. The laundry cart would be used to transport the body down to the loading ramp. At this time of night there would be only a few people working in housekeeping. As the door opened, he could see to the back of the long corridor where two women were talking. They were paying no attention to what he was doing. He walked on down the corridor to large double doors. The doors were open; it was the laundry room. No one was around. Over in the corner was a group of laundry carts, and stacked in the back of the room on large white shelves were the clean linens and work uniforms.

He shuffled through the shelves and found what he was looking for, a white housekeeping jacket and pants. He then pulled the uniform on over his clothes. Juan rolled the laundry cart over to the linen shelves and began pulling down the towels and fresh sheets he would need to clean up the mess. Taking several quick steps, he pulled the cart over by the door and left it. Now he must find a way to get his car around to the service entrance without drawing too much attention. There was at least one security guard. As Juan walked out onto the loading ramp, he spotted the guard returning from his rounds. Juan lit a cigarette to make it look like he was out taking a smoke break. He finished his cigarette and went back into the laundry room and pulled off his uniform. In his regular clothes now, he went up to the first floor, out the front door, got in his old Chevrolet, and drove around to the street next to the guard house. He opened his trunk and took out a roll of duct tape and pulled off a small strip. He pushed the trunk lid down but not all the way so the lock wouldn't catch. Then he put the small strip of tape from the trunk lid to the back bumper of the car. This held the trunk in a closed position and would allow him to open the trunk without using his keys. That way his car could remain running when he pulled into the loading ramp, and the trunk would open quickly, no fumbling with keys or trying to start the car.

He got in his car and drove around the hotel to a parking area a few feet from the loading ramp, then turned out his lights and waited. If he was right, the security guard would be coming by on his rounds shortly. A few minutes passed. The guard appeared right on schedule. He looked at his watch and confirmed it was now five past the hour. He had thirty minutes to get everything done. Quickly he exited his car and went down the walkway beside the loading ramp. It appeared the walkway was wide enough to accommodate the cleaning cart. With a few quick steps, he was through the door and into the corridor leading to the laundry room. The door to the laundry was closed, but he hoped, unlocked. As he turned the knob, he felt a sigh of relief as the door opened easily. Letting out his breath slowly, he fully opened the door, looked around, and saw that no one was there. Picking up the jacket, he put one arm in, grabbed the cart, and started pushing it to the door as he finished putting on the jacket. Juan checked to be sure the sheets and towels were still on the cart as he headed for the elevator. In a short time, he was on the elevator and up to the third floor. It was very quiet this time of night. Most of the guests were in the casino gambling. He approached one couple in the hall. They were slightly intoxicated, carrying stemmed wine glasses. Neither paid any attention to him as they passed. He was now nearing the room, so he slowed and listened intently. All was quiet. He pushed the cart past the door, reached into his shirt pocket, pulled out the card key, slipped it into the slot, removed the key, and the green light came on. With smooth rapid moves, he opened the door with one hand and entered, pulling the cart behind him with the other hand.

Quietly, Juan closed the door and began removing the linens, then he folded the body and placed it in the lower part of the cart. He had to move fast.

The blood on the carpet was beginning to clot and dry in some spots. Grabbing the towels from the spot on the floor, he rushed into the bathroom, placed them in the tub, and began running cold water on them. Returning quickly to the room, he removed fresh towels from the cart, hurriedly going to the bathroom and wetting them with cold water. He then returned and placed them over the blood stains. He got down on his knees and began to scrub. The carpet was dark brown. This should mask some of the stains. After making several trips to the bathroom, washing out the towels, and repeating the cleaning process on the floor, he felt things were looking better. By now, most of the blood was up. The carpet was wet, and it was difficult to tell if it had come clean. He looked at his watch. The time was passing fast. It was now fifteen minutes past the hour. He needed to leave shortly to get past the security guard before he made his round. Juan decided to place some wet towels over the stains until he could return. Quickly, he unfolded several sheets and draped them over the sides of the cart to hide the body. Then he stacked the remaining dry towels on top of the cart to cover the top of the sheets. This made the cart appear normal, somewhat.

He opened the door, looked left and then right. It was clear. He backed out of the room, pulling the cart behind him, then reached past the cart and caught the door as it was closing to keep it from slamming shut. With brisk strides, he was down the hall and to the elevator. He punched the button and waited. He needed the left elevator; it was the one that went all the way to the basement. As he waited, he checked his watch. It was now twenty-two past one. He had approximately ten minutes. Then he heard the rattling of the elevator as it came to a stop. This was the elevator to the right, and it did not go to the basement, so he stepped inside, pressed the lobby button, and jumped back off the elevator and watched as the door closed and the elevator with a slight rumble was gone. Maybe, just maybe, if he waited. Again, he pressed the elevator button as he stood patiently in the hall and waited. Looking at his watch, he saw that it was now twenty-four past one. Time was running out. Again, he heard the elevator coming up. It stopped, and the doors opened. It was the left elevator, the one he needed. An elderly man was standing in the rear of the elevator car. Juan paused. The man motioned for him to come on in, and said in a low voice, "I don't mind company. I couldn't sleep. I am going down and try my luck in the casino." Juan nodded with a shallow smile and pushed the cart into the elevator. The old man continued talking, "You're working a little late."

Juan nodded, "Yes, a spill. You know how people are when they have had too much to drink." He wasn't comfortable with this. The elevator would now stop at the lobby level. Carefully, he positioned himself and the cart so he would have the least amount of exposure, and could see out without drawing much attention to him and the cart. The elevator stopped at the lobby, and the door opened. Juan stood sideways looking over his shoulders out the elevator doors. The lobby was deserted. The old man exited without speaking. Juan pressed the "door closed" button. In a few moments the doors opened to the basement level.

Juan backed out of the elevator, stopped, looking first right, then left. The two women, who earlier were stacking linens, were now gone. No one was in sight. As he pulled the cart from the elevator, he looked down. There was blood on the elevator floor, a small patch the size of his hand. In a flash, he grabbed a towel and wiped it up. Had the old man seen this? He now moved more hurriedly. He went down the corridor, past the laundry room, and out to the loading ramp, stopping the cart inside of the doors, and with fast steps walked toward his car. He unlocked the old Chevrolet and slid under the steering wheel. Turning the key, he heard the engine sputter and come to life. Putting the car in drive, he then pulled over to the loading ramp and placed the gear selector in park. Leaving the engine running, he made twenty or so steps to the door in record time, pulled the door open, grabbed the cart, and pushed it to the rear of the Chevrolet. With one quick move, he opened the trunk lid, pulled the body from the cart, and loaded it into the trunk. He closed the lid and removed the strip of duct tape, then pushed the cart back down the side of the loading ramp and through the door of the laundry room. Grabbing some towels, he wiped the cart clean, removing the bloodstains and his fingerprints, then ran to the door and pulled it open. This was cutting it close. The guard could be appearing at any moment. It was now one-thirty. If the guard was on time, he had, at the most, five minutes. With cat-like moves, he slid into the driver's seat, the car still running. He pulled away from the loading ramp, past the guard-house, and into the street, making a left turn and crossing over the small channel from Paradise Island to the main island, waving at the guard as he exited. The tolls were collected as you entered Paradise Island, so he had no need to stop. Juan swung to his left and onto the main road leading away from the busy area and along the coast. In his pocket were the keys to a friend's Boston whaler. He made a brief stop at a construction site and placed four large cement blocks in the rear floor of the Chevrolet.

Juan Pablo Ming drove up to the dock, glancing at his watch as he opened the door; it was now two-ten. He unlocked the chain securing the boat, climbed on board, inserted the key in the switch and checked the fuel gauge. There was over a half a tank of gas, more than enough for the trip he needed to make. He returned to the car twice and picked up two blocks each time, then paused for a minute and looked around before opening the trunk. This was a critical time; hopefully, no one would see him and think he was stealing the boat. He had to be fast once he opened the trunk. The key clicked and the trunk lid of the old Chevrolet opened. He grabbed a hand-ful of towels and placed them on his shoulders, being careful not to stain his clothing with blood. Then he slung the body over his shoulder, closed the trunk lid, and went to the boat. In no time he was cranking the engine. The 160 outboard motor came to life with a subtle roar. There was enough moonlight to navigate without using the lights of the boat. Running without lights was illegal and if he was caught, the lights were the least of his problems. He pushed the throttle open about 1/3 and eased around the key, heading out to the deep water. The locals called it the Black Water. This was the deep channel, about thirty minutes out. You drop something in here, and it didn't come back.

Juan Pablo navigated by using the light of the islands. He had fished out here many times. Now it was time to do something he didn't like. Reaching into his pocket, he took out and lit a cigarette. As he rode along, it was calm; the waves were light, making the ride smooth for the twenty-five foot whaler. When the boat reached the deep water and stopped, he took the blocks and tied them to the limp body with some nylon cord. Leaving approximately four feet between the body and the blocks, he could ease the body over the side into the black water and then toss the blocks two at a time.

All went well; Juan had finished the task. He thought idly about the man he had killed. This was all a part of a very serious game, one involving life and death. He had to stop thinking this way. It was the job, and someone had to do it. Letting the boat motor run about a quarter throttle, he did a quick clean up using a piece of one of the bedsheets. Then he took the hand-held flood light and did a final check. All seemed okay. He would come back after daylight and check again.

The boat maneuvered into the small channel and eased up to the mooring. He jumped from the boat to the small dock, then grabbed the chain, wrapped it through the metal loop, and locked it, then walked to his car, opened the door, and sat down with his feet dangling to the ground. He looked at his watch; it was now 3:45. He could relax for the first time in over six hours. He took out a cigarette, lit it, and took a long draw, letting it out with a slow breath.

Swinging his feet into the car, he pulled the door closed, started the engine of the old Chevrolet, and drove off. He turned his lights on as he entered the main road. Now back to the hotel and finish his cleaning task. Juan drove around and parked the car in the front parking lot, then headed up to the third floor.

Rob was lying on the bed; his feet were on the floor, boots on. He was fully clothed. Mike was in a chair. His boots were off, and his feet were in another chair. Neither had had much sleep. It had been several hours since they had heard any noise coming from the adjoining room. Both wondered what was happening. At least the police hadn't knocked on their door. Rob had dozed off. He woke up when he heard something. It was someone knocking on the adjoining room door. He sat motionless for a period of time; then, the knock came again, a little louder. He sat up on the bedside, then stood up, and took the four steps to the door and opened it. There stood Juan Pablo Ming, a 5'9", one hundred sixty-pound, half Latino and half Chinese. Early on, there wasn't time for introductions. Now Juan Pablo asked simply, "You two all right?" Rob shrugged. He heard Mike from behind him asking who was there as he unfolded his 6'4" frame and stood up.

Rob answered, "It's Juan." Mike stiffened.

Juan asked if it was all right if he came in. Rob nodded, but Mike didn't say anything. Juan stepped into the room. It was evident he had not had any sleep.

Rob walked over to the window and looked out. The morning light was just beginning to show in the east. He could see it around the corner of the hotel, which partly blocked his view.

Mike had been quiet all night. He had only spoken a few times as he stood looking at Juan Pablo; it was now time for some answers. "Juan," he began, "what the hell is going on? I am very tired, Rob's tired, we've had very little sleep. Now someone is going to tell us what is going on and now. You get that Jacobson, or whatever the lying bastard's name is, over here. He is the one who caused this whole damn mess, and I have had it. You've screwed over my friend. They have his airplane, and we're virtually prisoners; some-one tried to kill us. Now we've had enough of this bullshit." Mike was nor-mally very quiet and easy-going. Now he was hot. "Get the lying bastard over here. We want to talk and right now," he said in a strong and deliber-ate voice.

Juan regarded him impassionately, his black eyes shining and unblinking. He said, "I must leave you for a while, but you will be all right here. Mr. Marshall's room is clean now."

14 SEND FOUR MILLION DOLLARS BY GENERAL DELIVERY

General McKenzie opened his eyes. A young sergeant in a flight suit was tapping his arm. "Sir," the sergeant said, "we are approximately thirty minutes out and will begin our descent soon. You had asked to be told."

General McKenzie nodded and thanked the sergeant. Remembering the four million dollar cargo, he immediately got up, pulled on his boots and zipped them, walked across the flight deck, and went down a ladder to the cargo compartment. The two large canvas bags were still strapped under the cargo net. Relaxing somewhat, he climbed back up the ladder to the crew compartment, went into the latrine, and relieved himself. Washing his hands, he looked at the reflection in the mirror to see a tired man in his late 50's who had puffy, red eyes and thick blond hair that was oily and unruly. He washed his face in cold water and passed a comb through his wet hair. Stepping from the latrine, he put on a headset and listened to the crew talking, preparing for letdown and approach into Homestead Air Force Base, just outside Miami.

So far, all was going as planned. In a few minutes they had landed and taxied onto the parking ramp. The crew shut down the airplane engines and went through their post-flight routine. Now came the critical moment, getting through customs. He filed his declaration, claiming nothing of value, then gave it to the loadmaster. The loadmaster turned it into Flight Ops. Hopefully, no one would ask about the two large canvas bags. He had listed them as classified NATO documents. Surely no one would question a general staff officer doing his duty.

73

General McKenzie turned to the young man, "Sergeant Milligan," he said, "I need a big favor. I need those records in the boxes off- loaded first."

"No problem, sir," the sergeant replied. "We'll get a cart and have someone bring them to you in Ops."

"Okay," the General replied. The General walked off the airplane, carrying his flight bag. He had his casual clothes with him and needed to change as soon as possible. As he neared Ops, he looked around. Jacobson was supposed to be here with an agency car to receive the boxes. As he opened the door of Ops, he saw Jacobson standing just inside. He was dressed unobtrusively in a brown, tailored suit. There were two other men with him. McKenzie had not seen him in several months. Jacobson usually worked with the Colonel, not McKenzie, so there had been no need to communicate. As he stepped inside the open door, Jacobson approached.

"General McKenzie, sir, how was your flight?" Jacobson asked.

"Very good, very good," the General answered, shaking Jacobson's hand.

"Sir, I have a car for you. It's parked out back," Jacobson explained.

"Right," the General said. "They are bringing some baggage from the aircraft now. Catch the sergeant and show him where the car is parked."

The General looked around. No one seemed to be paying attention to them. At least, if they were, they didn't want a two-star general to notice. The flight crew began drifting into the Ops building. General McKenzie walked over to the aircraft commander who snapped off a salute to greet the General. The General returned the salute casually and then put out his hand to shake the captain's hand and thank him personally. He then turned, picked up his flight bag, and went out the side door. Just then the sergeant and a ground crew member passed by on a small tug, pulling a cart with the four million in one hundred dollar bills.

"Wouldn't they stroke?" the General was thinking to himself. "If they only knew."

General McKenzie walked out and followed the sergeant, who was being led to the van by Jacobson and his men. So far, so good. There was no one else in the parking lot as they were loading the boxes into the back of the minivan Jacobson had secured from the agency pool.

With no complications, they were soon out the gate and on their way. Jacobson and McKenzie were the only ones who knew what was in the canvas bags. The two other men had not spoken. One sat quietly while the other drove the van. Jacobson had them along for security only.

There was little conversation as they rode. Jacobson had learned a long time ago not to say anything about the operation unless he was asked. He took his orders from the Colonel, unless he was told otherwise.

The driver pulled the green van into the driveway beside Jacobson's office. It was brown stucco with a red tile roof, an inconspicuous building.

The two men helped unload the canvas bags. They moved them in through the side door and into Jacobson's back office.

"Okay, you two," Jacobson said, "go out to the van and wait. We need some privacy so keep your eyes open. We don't want to be disturbed," he said, patting one man on the shoulder and opening the door with the other hand.

As both men exited, Jacobson closed and locked the door behind them. When Jacobson turned back around, the General was unlocking the first canvas bag. He unzipped the cover and removed the first of two boxes.

"Okay, Jake," he said, "I'm leaving three million of this with you. You are to take five hundred thousand for your flying operation, and the rest is to be used to finance the freedom fighters. You understand we are to get it to the leaders to be used to pay the soldiers. My suggestion is do it at, say maybe, three hundred thousand to five hundred thousand a month. That way you can keep them going for several months."

Jacobson nodded. He and the Colonel had already discussed the payment to the freedom fighters. The General was talking, but Jacobson knew it was the Colonel's plan.

The General placed the one million in one hundred dollar bills into a smaller, blue bag that Jacobson had provided. Jacobson then opened a wall panel, revealing his large safe. Quickly, he punched in a security code and then dialed the combination, opened the door, then placed the three bank boxes inside. He then closed the door and spun the lock, pushing the code button again, setting the alarm.

"Okay, General, it is now one-thirty. We need to get you cleaned up and changed into your casual clothes. I have a Learjet waiting at the Opa-Locka Airport to take you to Washington National."

"I need a place to shave, shower, and change," the General said.

"Down the hall, first door on your right," Jacobson answered.

With the General gone, Jacobson reopened the safe, removed one hundred thousand dollars, reached beneath his desk, and pulled up a black leather briefcase. He rolled the combination to the correct code, popped the case open, and tossed in the wrapped bundles of one hundred-dollar bills. He pulled it closed and thumbed the combination lock back over, then slid the case back under his desk. Some cold cash would warm the attitude of his nervous flight crew and get things going.

He closed the safe and reset the alarm just as the General came down the hall and back into the office. They were quickly on their way south to Opa-Locka. It was a thirty minute drive along I-95.

Jacobson put the General on the Lear and watched as it taxied out. In just minutes, it shot down the runway, made its take-off roll, and disappeared to the east.

Jacobson got back into the van and rode around the hangar to where George was waiting with the airplane fueled and ready.

He got out of the van, spoke briefly to his two men, and watched them drive off. Jacobson walked into the office trailer. George was sitting behind his desk. He looked up and said, "You ready, Mr. Jacobson?" Jacobson nodded. "Then, let's go."

They walked out to the blue and white Navajo. Jacobson boarded first, sat down, and threw his case in a seat across the aisle. George closed the door, walked past Jacobson, climbed into the left seat, started the engines, and they were off-back to Nassau.

"Maybe this carrot will quiet the caged critters," Jacobson thought to himself with a chuckle. "It usually does."

15 The Man's Plan

Stressed and distraught after witnessing the death of a stranger and having a harrowing near-death experience themselves, the two men knew by their passiveness that they too were now trapped as surely as the knife had trapped the life of Big Nose. Their hours of conversation were likened unto a circle, round and round, with no solution and no end. During the early morning hours, they repeatedly tried to call home, an attempted stretch to reach back to something of comfort with always the same reply. The operator would try to pacify them with "I'm trying, but the lines are all busy," she would say.

The clock had now wound around to the late morning hour of eleven a.m. Rob broke the subtle quiet of several minutes of silence. "Mike, I'm getting hungry. Maybe we can go down and get something to eat. That is, if the babysitters don't mind."

"To hell with them," Mike said, "I'm getting cabin fever. We need a change of scenery."

Both men picked up their baseball caps and started out the door. Rob paused as they were leaving the room. "What if they get through to Anne? I'll call the desk and tell them that we will be in the restaurant." Rob went back into the room, picked up the phone, and punched "O". The operator answered. He left a message, and they were down the elevator and to the restaurant in five minutes. They had ordered and were eating when Mike looked up and said under his breath, "Here comes our babysitter." Sure enough, Juan was headed straight for their table. He looked a little better.

He had showered, shaved, and changed clothes. Unlike Rob and Mike, he even looked somewhat rested.

Neither Rob nor Mike looked up. Juan Pablo walked up to the table and placed his hands on the back of an empty chair between Rob and Mike. He didn't speak at first. A short time passed as Rob and Mike continued to eat. Juan finally spoke "Good morning," he said rather quietly with a slight nod.

Rob acknowledged him first, "Have a seat." Juan Pablo paused; he could feel the tension and sensed hostility from both men. Without speaking, he pulled out the chair in front of him and eased down into it.

He hesitated a moment, then spoke, "Mr. Jacobson is taking care of some business he had previously scheduled and will be back here at the hotel at four o'clock. He wanted me to tell you to be a little patient. The arrangements are being made to get us all out of here, and that includes your airplane." Rob finished eating without speaking. All three men sat quietly as the tension subsided somewhat.

Rob again broke the silence. "I need to call home. Do you think there is a chance to get a call off this damn island?'

Juan Pablo sat a minute. "I think I can arrange that." He pushed back his chair. "Please wait for my telephone call when Mr. Jacobson returns." He was out of the restaurant and into the crowd.

Mike spoke, "You think he'll tell them to let us make a call?"

"Sure hope so," Rob said.

Both men finished, signed their food tabs, and went back to their rooms. Mike opened the door. The message light on the phone was on. Rob picked up the phone and dialed the operator. "Sir, I can now place that call," she said.

"Yes, if you would, please." Rob waited. There were a few clicks, then the phone on the other end began to ring. He could feel his heart beating; he was getting excited. The phone rang three times, then Rob heard Anne's voice.

"Hello," she answered.

"How are you doing?" Rob said. "It's good to hear your voice."

Anne began, "Where in the world are you? I called Orlando, and they said that you had checked out. I called the airport, and they said the plane was gone. They didn't know where. Then you called and said you were in the Bahamas. I have been worried sick."

"Slow down," Rob began. "We're okay. Just a little miscommunication. I can't go into detail now, but I'll call you back at the office tomorrow morning at eight-thirty. There are some numbers in my Rolodex I want you to look up. Remember Jim Wilson who owns Superior Air Parts in Miami? I need his and David Harris' number. David is a mechanic in Miami. Have those numbers ready when either Mike or I call you in the morning. Then I want you to call Jim and David. Tell them I need a big favor, okay?"

Anne started to ask questions. Rob stopped her. "Now call Katherine. Tell her I'll be gone a few days longer than expected. When I get back, I'll come by; it's my weekend to have the kids. I was to pick them up and take them fishing. We may have to postpone it until next week. Okay, now you will have to hold down the fort until we get back. I'll try and call as often as I can, and don't worry. Oh, by the way, Mike says hello."

Anne started to talk, "What's going on?"

"I'll explain it all when I get back. Be sure to get their name, address, and phone number, please. It is very important. Tomorrow, eight-thirty, Okay? Don't forget."

"I won't," Anne said. She paused, then added, "Both of you promise to be careful, okay?"

"You got it," said Rob, and somewhat reluctantly, hung up the phone.

Mike and Rob exchanged a glance. The telephone call to Anne had given them their first contact with their world of normalcy since leaving Orlando. That seemed a lifetime ago.

That contact and their full stomachs broke through the stress adrenaline that had pushed them. Now both fell into the deep sleep of physical and emotional exhaustion. The body's natural drugs took them down into a temporary darkness past caring.

Mr. Ming, however, was very much awake, tidying up the loose ends of Senor Macedo's sudden departure. Anyone who wished to pick up clues to Macedo's last activities must simply find a single irreducible finality: He had vanished without a trace as if he had never even been there.

Carlos Macedo's total disappearance was completed by three-forty-five, and Juan was standing outside the custom's office as the blue and white Navajo taxied up and shut down the engines. Jacobson slowly crawled down from the small aircraft, carrying his small, black briefcase. He walked over to Juan and the two men spoke briefly. Jacobson continued into the front of the custom's office, showed his I.D. and walked on through to the outside. The two men got into Juan Pablo's old blue Chevy and drove off at a deliberate cruise.

Juan was quiet, as usual; didn't speak unless spoken to. Jacobson began, "Now fill me in," he stated.

Juan answered, "Everything's all right. It never happened. The men are a little upset about your absence. I checked on them this morning. They have been quiet this afternoon. They'll be all right. I let them call home, then they settled down some. I had our girl at the desk tape the call. Nothing much, just some airplane talk."

They made the turn onto the Paradise Island Road. The guardhouse was just ahead. Jacobson pulled out two one pound notes. He was on the side next to the guard. In the Bahamas, as in England, driving is on the left side of the road. In the old Chevrolet, the driver was on the side next to the curb.

Jacobson paid the toll. They passed into the small resort island, turned right, and entered the crowded parking lot.

Jacobson had Juan call the room to see if Rob and Mike were in. He hung up the house phone and then stated, "They're in." The two men went across the lobby to the elevator and up to the third floor. Jacobson knocked on the door. Mike responded by opening the door cautiously.

"Well, boys," Jacobson said with a smile as he entered the room, "we have most of our problems solved. They have agreed to drop the charges related to the improper entry of the DC-3 into Bahamian territory if we will leave within forty-eight hours."

Mike and Rob looked at each other. Rob spoke first, "Leave for where?" he asked.

"I believe I have a plan that works everything out. Mr. Marshall, it's your aircraft. What do you say we discuss this in private? I think it's a plan you will like. Juan, you and Mr. Ricau, please excuse us."

Mike looked at Rob. Rob said, "It's okay."

"Well then, I'm going down to the lounge and have a cold beer," Mike said.

"I'll join you in a few minutes; this can't take too long," Rob replied.

Jacobson didn't speak. He waited patiently as the two men left the room. As the door closed, Jacobson picked up his small case, opened it, and threw three bundles of hundred dollar bills on the bed. Rob stared briefly, "Okay, what's this for?"

"Let's call it a down payment-earnest money," Jacobson said. "There is thirty thousand dollars-ten thousand in each bundle. I am in a position to pay you your expenses plus twice that much to make a cargo haul. The details of the plan will be explained if you accept this offer."

"One haul?" Rob asked.

"If it works out, there are three, maybe four trips from an island airport to Honduras on the Nicaraguan border. The same applies, sixty thousand dollars for each trip, and you get to keep your airplane."

Rob sat for a minute, staring at the money and taking it all in, thinking four times sixty thousand. That's two hundred forty thousand dollars. "You will pay all our expenses?"

"Now we won't maintain the airplane. That will be your responsibility. We will pay for fuel, oil, and minor expenses, and you will have to deliver to get paid. You will be flying as a private contractor. Basically, we will take care of all the details, but you will be on your own with the actual flying."

Rob thought a minute. Two trips and I'll have my money out of the old DC-3. It was a big gamble. He couldn't do it without Mike. "All right, Jacobson, I'll talk to Mike. If he will help, I'll do it. If he says no, I guess our asses will be in a crack," Rob said slowly. "I can't talk him into something like this. It must be his decision and his alone. I know he won't be involved in any illegal activity, especially hauling drugs. I feel the same way.

We need to have that understood from the beginning," Rob continued.

"This has nothing to do with drugs. I give you my personal assurance," Jacobson said. "Now you keep the money. If you change your mind, well, we'll get to that when we have a need to. But I do need to know tonight. This is something that won't wait," Jacobson continued. "Let's just say it's past due."

"All right," Rob said, "I'll talk to him. You'll get your answer tonight."

Jacobson knew they didn't have a choice, but he wanted them to feel committed, like they had made the decision. It was either take the deal and make money, or lose the airplane and possibly go to jail. He knew they didn't have a real choice. Jacobson stood up, excused himself, shook Rob's hand, and left.

Rob sat for a few minutes looking at the money. He knew what Jacobson was doing. He also knew it was working. He had never had his hands on that much money and a chance to make much, much more. He was getting hooked and a little excited. No, hell, he was getting really excited. He felt a little like celebrating as he picked up the money in both hands. He sat holding the money for a few minutes. He had to figure out where thirty thousand dollars in cash could be hidden. He knew he couldn't leave it in the room. Pulling up his jean's legs, he put two of the bundles of hundred dollar bills in his left boot and one in his right. As he stood up and walked to the dresser, the left was a little tight. He picked up the card key and headed for the lounge. He needed to talk to Mike before Mike had more to drink than he should.

On his way down, his thoughts were on his big Cajun friend. He didn't want them getting in over their heads. These people were really sons of bitches and he and Mike were being used. He had to remember that. They needed them now, but what would happen when the missions were complete? He had a bad feeling deep in his gut.

Before the elevator door opened on the ground floor, Rob knew only two things for dead damn certain: he did not trust Jacobson or his plan, and he needed a plan of his own for himself and Mike.

Rob stepped off the elevator and crossed the lobby to the lounge. It was easy to spot Mike and Juan Pablo. They were sitting at a table a few steps inside the lounge entrance. Rob eased up to their table and pulled out a chair. Both looked up as he sat down.

"I'd have ordered you a beer if I had known you were coming," Mike said with a grin. Rob spotted the cocktail waitress and motioned for her to come over to the table as she approached and asked, "How we doing?"

"I need a cold beer," Rob said quietly.

"How you guys doing?" she asked, looking at Juan Pablo Ming and Mike.

"I'm okay," Mike spoke. Juan sat quietly and didn't answer. With that the little blonde waitress walked to the bar and returned with Rob's beer. Mike sat staring at Rob. He had a hundred questions but didn't want to ask them with Juan present. Juan sensed that they needed to talk. He took one last sip of his absolut neat, stood up with a faint smile, and excused himself.

Rob looked at Mike for a moment in silence. Then he took a long pull on his beer and began, "This man's got a plan. A quarter-million dollar plan."

16 THE MICE PLAN

"There are some things we need to discuss," Rob began, "but this is not the place. I don't think the room is the place either."

The two men finished their beers while making small talk and watched the people out in the casino gambling and having a good time.

Mike went over to the waitress and paid the tab. Both men then walked across the lobby and out to the swimming pool. Rob checked his watch. It was six thirty-five, and the pool was quiet with the exception of a young couple sitting at a far corner table, talking.

Mike and Rob sat down as Rob began earnestly, "Mike, we've been friends a long time, and what I am about to tell you has nothing to do with friendship. It's business, and I want you to make a logical decision, based on what is best for you."

Mike sat without speaking. He knew deep down there was no way he could make a decision concerning Rob without being influenced by their friendship.

Rob continued, "The offer is for us to make three or four cargo runs from an island to Honduras. We will be paid well. The way I figure it is, we will be taking a big chance, but we will be paid sixty thousand dollars per trip for our services and the use of the airplane. Each trip will be a two-day round robin, down one day, back the next. We'll time it so we won't be over water at night or at least try to keep it to a minimum. We'll split the payment up this way- thirty thousand for the airplane lease and thirty thousand for the crew. That is fifteen thousand dollars per trip for four trips or sixty thousand for each of us."

Mike continued to sit without saying anything. Rob continued, "I don't think we can trust these people as far as we can throw them, so if we do this, we'll need a plan. One that will cover us when we are through. I feel once we complete this, they won't need us, and we'll become expendable." Mike sat motionless looking into Rob's eyes. Rob continued, "I don't have much of a choice. If I lose that airplane with no insurance, my business will be gone. I think Jacobson knows that, so I'm committed. Now, you are another story. I think I know a way to get you out of this if you want out, so don't feel pressured."

Mike sat staring over Rob's shoulder out over the beach and looking at the blue sea. He knew if he thought only of himself what his choice would be, but could he live with the fact that he had deserted a friend? He knew Rob didn't stand much of a chance facing these people alone, but if he were to tag along, the odds would definitely improve. Deep down inside, he didn't like this feeling of being trapped, and he definitely felt trapped. The money was great, but money never meant that much to him. Being comfortable was enough, and having his freedom and his friends were the most important things in his life. He knew Rob needed him, and he would be there as always. Rob had two kids. How could he face them and know he left his friend stuck between a rock and a hard place to fend for himself? No, he was in. There wasn't much of a choice. He finally spoke, "Oh hell, sounds good. I need a new truck anyway. This will take us- what- a week, and we'll be back home. Easy money."

As they got up and stood with locked stares, they both smiled, then walked back toward the lobby. Walking along, Rob nudged Mike. "I've got something to show you when we get to the room." Mike responded with a nod.

Walking down the hall to the room, Rob was thinking about all the arrangements he had to make and how to guarantee payment for their services and a way to prevent them from being used or ripped off or maybe in the end being disposed of like junk mail. It was quite evident Jacobson's people knew how to handle unwanted problems. The dead man in his room was a prime example. These people were pros, and he and Mike were mere amateurs. Deep down inside he knew this was all a big mistake. God, he sure prayed he was wrong.

Rob slid the key card into the lock and removed it. The light came on, and he opened the door. Mike followed him in. Rob pulled up his left pants leg, removing the two bundles of hundred dollar bills, ten thousand dollars in each bundle, threw them on the bed.

Ah," came a sigh from Mike, "planning on going shopping at Goodwill?"

Rob laughed. "No, just a little deposit. I think the words Jacobson used were 'earnest money'." Rob motioned for Mike to come over closer. He whispered, "Go down to the front desk and see if you can get us another room. I will explain later." Rob pointed to Mike and whispered, "Get it in your name." Rob pulled out three one hundred dollar bills from one of the bundles, and handed it to Mike. Mike folded the money, put it in his shirt pocket, and left the room.

Rob picked up the phone, took a piece of paper from his pocket, and dialed the number Jacobson had given him. The phone rang three times, then Jacobson answered. "All right, we'll do it, but there are some conditions. You need to meet with us first thing tomorrow. We'll explain everything."

"Sounds good," said Jacobson, "say eight-thirty in your room."

"See you then," replied Rob. He hung up the phone and looked at his watch. It was now seven-forty. They had twelve hours to get a plan together. They needed a simple plan, and one Jacobson and his men would not recognize, a way of guaranteeing payment and getting the airplane and their asses back home once they were through flying the cargo. Rob wanted a room that Jacobson didn't know about. It would give them time and a place to talk freely. He didn't feel comfortable in the rooms that Jacobson had gotten for them. More than likely they were listening to everything they said.

Damn, he'd made a big mistake. Eight-thirty was the time he had planned to call Anne and get that information. Well, Mike could call from the other room; that is, if they could get another room. He would stall Jacobson for a few minutes. No time to panic. He needed to be calm and think straight.

There was a soft knock on the door. Rob got out of his chair and walked over and looked through the peephole. There was Mike standing outside. Opening the door, Mike entered, shaking a card key but not saying anything. Rob nodded approval. "My old stomach is beginning to growl. It's letting me know it's feeding time. What you say let's go to the dining room and get something to eat?" Rob said while letting out a deep breath. They had a room. That was their first move. Their first act of rebellion against their entrapment. It felt good to do something, even as simple as getting a separate room on their own.

The men went down to the restaurant. While they were eating, Mike informed Rob that the room he had gotten was on the fourth floor. It was down at the far end of the hall from the elevator. They could use the staircase at the end of the hall to go from floor to floor and no one would notice. Rob felt sure Jacobson had someone around somewhere keeping tabs on them. It would be easy to take the elevator to the third floor then walk up to the fourth. Just in case Jacobson's person was watching from downstairs, the elevator would stop at the third floor.

"Did you have any trouble?" asked Rob.

"None at all," said Mike. "Walked up, smiled, said I needed a room for one night. Being Sunday, things were slow, so it was no problem."

The men finished their meals and then went over to the lounge and had a beer. They wanted everything to look normal. They went over to the elevator, punched the button for the third floor. Getting off there, Rob and Mike went to their room to check for messages. Opening the door, Rob stuck his head in. The light was off, so he closed the door, and made sure that it was locked. They then took the stairs to the fourth floor. Mike led the way to the room and opened it with the card key. Both men went in and sat down.

Rob pulled up his pants leg and took the money out. "We need a place to hide this," he began, "a place no one will look. Tomorrow, we will put part of it in a bank; then, we can wire the money back home to our bank in Virginia. Now we need a way to be sure we are going to get paid when we do the flying for these bastards," Rob continued.

"You're the business man. I'm just a pilot, or should I say, just the co-pilot, along for the ride. It's your shot," Mike said. "You make the call."

"Well," Rob paused, "I think this is what we need to do. If you don't agree with any of this, feel free to tell me," Rob continued. "We need a plan where we can be assured we get paid as we do the flying. We don't want to wait until the last flight. If we do, they'll feel it'll be better to get rid of us than to pay us. If we can make them put the total amount in a bank, then as we complete a delivery, they can transfer it to our bank account what is due us. We'll have Anne check with the bank after each transaction. If we get paid, we go again. We will also need access to support the flying, a mechanic, and spare parts to start. Maybe we won't need them, but you never know; so that is why I called Anne. She is checking on that now. We'll give her a call at 8:30 tomorrow morning. At least, you can call her from this room, then you come on down to the third floor for out meeting with Jacobson. Oh, one other thing, we will need some over-water survival gear, a life raft, a radio, and some fresh water. Most of this operation will be flying over open water, and that's not a pleasant thought considering we will be flying a forty-five year old airplane. We need to make a list of the basic supplies that we can get filled in Miami such as aircraft oil and hydraulic fluid. One of the main tires is questionable, so all of this must be addressed before we leave here. This is a complicated operation. I am not sure Jacobson has thought all of this through. We're not a mack truck; airplanes require maintenance, especially older ones. We need to make a list of maintenance needs and a list of essential necessities to operate such as food, water, first aid supplies, and a flare gun. I'm sure they haven't thought about this, and we need an escape plan. This whole operation could turn to crap in a hurry. We'll be the ones who are high profile. We'll be the ones flying an airplane that we already know in these parts is like advertising for trouble."

"You're right," Mike said, "but how do you plan for something like this, an escape?"

"I'm sure they know the exact range of the DC-3. Somehow we need to change that without them knowing. Let's think about it. I'll talk to the mechanic tomorrow. Maybe he'll have some ideas."

"Sounds real good," said Mike. "Now what are we going to do about sleeping tonight? I don't want to room with you again, and I am damn sure not going to sleep in that other room, the one where big nose Macedo started his permanent nap," Mike continued.

Rob said, "I'll go down and stay in the room on the third floor. You can come down and get your bag and stay up here, but don't be calling me on the phone. We don't want them to know about this room. In here, we can talk freely without someone listening, which I am sure they are doing on the third floor."

It was getting late as Mike and Rob went down the stairs to the third floor. Mike grabbed his bag and slipped into the hall door marked "stairs". Rob turned around and closed the door, then walked over, turned on the T.V., flipped to the news channel, and watched for a few minutes as he was preparing for bed. Basically, it was the same old politics plus some talk about the hostages and some squabbling between a Republican President and a Democratic Congress. Nothing had changed.

Rob called the desk and asked for a seven a.m. wake-up call, then turned out the lights and lay there thinking for a long time. A simple plan was beginning to emerge. Yes, a simple plan.

The phone rang. Rob sat up. It was his wake-up call. Putting the phone down, he sat on the side of the bed. He shook his head, walked to the bathroom, washed his face, and stood looking into the mirror. He needed all the confidence he could muster. That Jacobson was tough, but he had to be tougher. Rob knew Jacobson needed them, and he felt deep down in his gut Jacobson needed them almost desperately, but he couldn't be for sure.

Rob picked up the telephone and called room service. He needed coffee. He also needed to remind Mike to make that call at 8:30. Rob slipped on his jeans, shirt, and boots and ran up the stairs to the fourth floor to remind Mike.

He knocked on Mike's door. Mike opened it, and Rob slipped inside.

"I just wanted to remind you to call Anne at 8:30," he said.

"And a very good morning to you, too," Mike returned.

"Yeah, well, good morning, call Anne," Rob said as he backed out of Mike's door. "I've got to run. I need to get organized before Jacobson comes by. Tell Anne I will call her this afternoon." With that, Rob closed the door and headed downstairs.

Rob was shaving. As he looked in the mirror, he noticed that shaving cream was on his undershirt. Then he realized, "Hell," he said to himself, "I don't have any clean clothes. All this commotion, I don't have any clothes to put on."

This was supposed to be a two-day affair, and it was now four, going on five days. He had changed clothes only two times; that was in Orlando and here. Things had become so screwy, it hadn't dawned on him. He was putting on the same clothes each day. In fact, he had slept in them one night. He needed to add that to the list. Clothing, he scribbled. Before they jumped off into, God knows where, he needed to go to Miami. The things they needed would be hard to find in the Bahamas. Yes, Jacobson needed to take him back to Miami.

Just as Rob had finished shaving, there was a knock on the door-room service. Rob fumbled around in his jean's pocket looking for change as he approached the door. He opened the door to a young black man wearing a white jacket carrying a tray with a coffeepot, two cups, and a glass of ice water. Rob finally found a dollar bill U.S. He held it up and asked if it was okay. The young black man smiled, took the money, and exited.

Rob finished showering and then dressed back in his dirty clothes. "Man, this is the pits," he thought. It was now 8:15. He sat quietly, drinking his coffee and going over his list. Hopefully, he hadn't forgotten anything. There was the big question mark at the bottom of his list, not the list he had prepared for Jacobson, but the list that was a reminder to check on a way to extend the fuel in the DC-3 without being obvious. And it was just that-a big question mark. And Rob knew it.

17 PLAN TWO

There was a knock on the door. Rob got up and looked through the peephole; it was Jacobson and Juan Pablo. He opened the door.

"Good morning," said Jacobson with all the confidence a man in his position could have. And he appeared to be in a good position, or at least, it was evident he thought he was. "Where is our friend, Mr. Ricao?" were Jacobson's first words after he entered the room, looking around. "Oh, I apologize, how are you and Mr. Ricao doing? I expected Mr. Ricao would attend this meeting."

"He will," Rob replied, "and a good morning to you and Senor Ming. First, how is the DC-3? Have you checked on it?" Rob asked.

"Yes, Captain Mann made a call early this morning. He assured me everything was just fine. His exact words were 'I have a twenty-four hour around the clock guard on the airplane,'" Jacobson chuckled. "Now we need to discuss this matter. What do you expect in the way of conditions as you spoke of last evening?"

"Here is a list. These are the things that are absolutely necessary to make these multiple flights over water and to do them successfully. As you can see, it's materials to support the aircraft and supplies that the crew will need, down to flashlights and extra batteries," explained Rob. He paused then added, "There is also the matter of getting paid."

"Oh, that's no problem. I have the money. When we're through, I pay you in cash. No problem with cash, I assume," Jacobson said smugly as he sat in a chair staring at Rob. Juan stood looking out the window. He appeared to not hear a word they were saying.

"Well," Rob began, "since you say you have the money; then, there won't be a problem with depositing it in a bank, say in Miami. Then you can wire the money in payments to my bank account as we do the flying. To me that seems fairly simple and uncomplicated."

Jacobson sat quietly for a minute. It was apparent that he had not anticipated this and that he didn't like the idea, but he didn't say anything. He stood up suddenly and walked over to the window and looked out. "This is one beautiful view," he began. "That sun coming up in the east, the blue-green water. One of the most beautiful places on earth. Some of the locals don't appreciate the beauty. Some people rarely appreciate anything. But you, Mr. Marshall, are a businessman, and I appreciate that. I have a real respect for what you stand for. It is not what I had in mind, but I think I can arrange it. Yes, I think it can be done. As for your list, I'm not sure. Some of these things I don't quite understand, but I feel sure you know your needs better than I do. My suggestion is for you and Juan to go back to Miami. Take a day; get all this together. I'll stay here and keep Mr. Ricao company."

There was a knock on the door. Rob answered it. Mike's big 6'4" frame filled the door as he stepped through.

"Excellent timing," said Jacobson. "We were just talking about you." He turned back to Rob. "Juan and I will go make the arrangements for a flight back to Miami. I'll give you a call later on today. We'll try to get you there early enough to get something done this afternoon."

Jacobson and Juan exchanged handshakes with Rob and Mike and were out the door. Mike looked a little puzzled.

"What happened," he asked. "Did I miss something?"

"No," Rob replied. "I basically explained our needs and how I thought the payment should be handled. He balked a little at first but finally agreed." Under his breath in a low whisper Rob said, "I think the bastard is in a tight spot. Maybe he really needs us more than we need him. I feel a little better now. I think I saw past that poker face."

Mike nodded in agreement, "Let's go get breakfast, and damn, I need to get some clothes. These are beginning to smell. At least, I feel like they do."

"I know," Rob answered. "I have a feeling everyone may not know our name, but they sure know what we look like. They probably think we have our horses tied out back."

Both men laughed as they walked out the door. They had had a good night's sleep for the first time in three days, and things looked a little better. Now all they needed was a good meal and some clothes. Maybe a change in character was due. Definitely, the western look was out of place here on the islands.

Rob and Mike finished their breakfast and stopped by the gift shop looking for clothes. The clerk directed them to a clothing store around the corner and down a corridor past the casino.

After thirty minutes or so, the two men walked out. Mike was wearing a straw hat and sunglasses and carrying two large bags of clothes. Rob had also added to his wardrobe, a complete line of casual clothes including a swimsuit but no straw hat. "I guess this can be called a business expense," Rob said as they were entering the elevator.

"Yeah, we spent about eight hundred dollars out of Jacobson's money. I sure hope he doesn't mind," Mike said with a sarcastic laugh.

They were alone on the elevator. Rob took this time to talk. "Mike," he began, "I think we need our passports. I don't think Jacobson should know we have them. When we get back, go up to your room on the fourth floor and call Anne. Tell her my passport is in the small file cabinet beside my desk in the bottom drawer. Do you know where yours is?"

"Yes, it's at my apartment. It is in a briefcase in a closet in my bedroom," Mike replied.

"Okay," Rob said, "tell Anne to get them together and send them to Superior Air Parts to my friend Jim Wilson. Tell her to Federal Express them, and tell her to call Jim personally and tell him they're coming. I don't want Juan to know we are getting the passports."

The elevator stopped on the third floor. Both men got off with their bags in hand and headed for their room. Rob opened the door. They walked in and threw the bags on the bed. Mike turned without speaking, left the room, and walked up the stairs to the fourth floor. He opened the door and picked up the phone. He called the front desk. This was a real mess he thought. All calls had to go through the front desk. The operator finally answered. Mike gave the area code and number to the operator and waited what seemed to be an eternity. After several minutes the operator came back on. "Your number is ringing, sir," she spoke.

"Thank you," Mike answered. Anne's voice came over the phone. "How are you doing?" Mike began.

"I'm doing fine. The question is how are you doing, and what are you doing?" Anne continued.

"Maybe I better let Rob tell you all about this, and as for your other question, for now we are fine and we need a big favor. We need our passports." There was a long pause.

"Last Thursday when you left, you said you were going to be back Friday. Now it's Monday, and you want your passport. What's going on?" Anne asked.

"I know its doesn't sound so good, but we are okay. I had rather let Rob tell you all about this. I think he plans to call you tomorrow morning at the office, so send our passports to Jim Wilson at Superior Air Parts. Rob said to call Jim and tell him to keep the receipt of the passports confidential.

When Rob gets to Jim's place, he will have someone with him, a man named Juan Pablo Ming. He doesn't want him to know about the passports," Mike continued.

"What's all this secretive mess?" Anne asked. "And I don't have Rob's or your passports," Anne continued.

"I know," Mike said, "Rob's passport is in his office in the small file cabinet beside his desk in the bottom drawer. Mine is at home in my bedroom closet in an old brown briefcase with some aeronautical charts. You may have to dig around to find it," Mike continued.

"How am I going to get into your apartment, Mike?" Anne asked.

"Mrs. Merchant, the lady next door, has a key," Mike said.

"Okay," Anne answered. "I guess you want them as soon as possible," she continued.

"Yes," Mike answered, "send them Federal Express today, so Rob can pick them up tomorrow. Tell Jim that Rob will be there this afternoon or no later than tomorrow morning and to have Harris, that mechanic, there so that he can talk to him."

"I'll do my best," Anne said with a sigh. "I don't like this."

"I know," Mike replied, "but Rob will explain it all to you tomorrow, so hang by the phone. He will be calling you tomorrow before noon." Mike hung up the phone and went back down to Rob's room on the third floor. He knocked on the door. Rob opened it; Mike took a step back.

"Looks great," Mike laughed. "Well, that is, all but those white hairy legs. I think they would call you a snow bird," Rob chuckled. He was now a part of the local scene, and with his flowered shirt, shorts, and sneakers, he had the complete look of a tourist.

"Mike," Rob said, "if you will get out of those work clothes, I will have someone come up here and get all of these," pointing to a pile of soiled jeans, shirts and underclothes, "and have them laundered."

"Sounds good to me," Mike said, stripping off his shirt and jeans then throwing them in a pile on the floor. He slipped into a pullover shirt and shorts, putting on a pair of blue and white sneakers. "Feels good," he said with a big grin. "Boy, if Anne could see us now, she would think we both had lost it."

"When in Rome, do as the Romans do," Rob said smiling.

This was a new role for both men. They were usually very conservative and to them, a vacation was a three-day fishing trip to the coast or to the mountains. Neither would be considered sun worshippers.

Rob and Mike walked out the side of the hotel past the pool. Rob checked his watch. It was a little past eleven o'clock. Several people were out sun bathing. A few were in the pool, swimming. They went on past the pool, out the back gate, and onto the beach. Rob suddenly realized that it had been a long time since he had taken a leisurely stroll on a beach. But for now his thoughts were on his planned needs.

As they walked along the beach, they passed a group of young women, sunbathing. Mike tipped his hat, "A good morning to you, ladies," he said. An attractive blonde with big busts said for everyone to hear, "Now that's a big hunk!" Mike stopped, slowly turned around, and said, "Thank you." All the girls laughed. Rob shook his head without missing a stride. Mike walked a little faster and caught up with him.

"Now, when I get to Miami," Rob said, "I am going to Superior Air Parts and get all the aircraft supplies we listed. Then I will pick up the survival gear. While I am at Superior Air Parts, I will talk to Harris, the mechanic, and see what we need to do to extend our fuel range. There must be a way to add at least an hour or an hour and a half to the time we can stay airborne. I know they fly these old DC-3's long range. He'll know how they do it."

As they walked west along the beach, they heard the sound. Both men looked, first to their left and then at each other. There it was again, even louder.

"That sounds like an airplane," Mike said.

"I know," Rob added, "but on this small island? Let's go check it out. It must be an amphibian or something," Rob continued, as they trotted up from the beach into the parking lot of a hotel, around to the front, and down the drive to the street. They were approximately two blocks from their own hotel. As they were nearing it, the noise of the aircraft stopped. They were walking east in the direction of their hotel. There it was; a large amphibian parked on a blacktop ramp that sloped off into the lagoon. It had landed on the water and then extended its landing gear and taxied onto the ramp. The passengers were all disembarking as they approached.

Now this was interesting. Another way off this island. An air terminal at their back door. They stepped across the street from the small terminal and watched. In a few minutes, the aircraft was refueled, and they began to load with passengers. The men counted sixteen plus the crew. The ground crew closed the bottom part of the cabin door, then the engines started with a whine, and the airplane taxied out into the lagoon between the mainland and the island. The flight attendant closed the top door as the landing gear was retracted. They then eased down the lagoon and added power. Mike and Rob had gone across the street and onto the edge of the ramp to get a good look as the amphibious aircraft broke from the water and was airborne. It soon became a small speck off in the distance.

"Let's check this out," Rob said looking at Mike. "We need to know where this thing will take us if we need to leave in a hurry." Rob walked over and entered the small terminal office while Mike waited outside.

As Rob approached, a smiling clerk asked, "May I help you?"

"Yes, you can," Rob said as he returned the smile. "What's your schedule?"

"We have four flights a day. They are on this schedule," she said as she handed Rob a small one-page flyer with the Grumman amphibian at the top. The flights were from Nassau to Miami Harbor. There were two flights in the morning and two in the afternoon. Due to the sea landings, they were all daylight flights. He walked back outside and handed Mike the flyer. Mike looked at the schedule.

"We can use this if we have to," Mike said.

"Just what I was thinking," Rob added. "Now take this schedule and put it in your room. It has the phone number and times. We might need a reservation."

The men went back to their hotel. It was now twelve fifteen. They got off the elevator on the third floor, went to the room, and opened the door. As they entered, they saw that the message light was on. Rob went over and picked up the phone and dialed the desk. "Yes, do we have a message?" Mike stood waiting as Rob listened. Rob said thank you and hung up; and they stepped out into the hall.

"Juan wants us to meet him here at one thirty," Rob stated.

"I guess it's about time to go shopping," Mike said with a grin.

"Sounds like it," Rob answered. "While I'm gone, you need to stay in this room and wait by the phone and if I need you, I'll call. When I call you here and say we are going to another plan, then go to the room on the fourth floor, and I will call you there. Always remember they could be monitoring our call. They may know about the room on four, so we will say only what is absolutely necessary if and when I call."

"Let's go get something to eat before Juan gets here," Mike said heading for the elevator. Rob stepped inside the room and punched the remote to turn off the T.V. He followed Mike into the hall, pulled the door closed behind him, and walked to the elevator where Mike was waiting.

Rob and Mike had returned from eating lunch and were watching T.V news CNN when there was a knock on the door. Rob stood up, went to the door, and answered it. There stood Juan Pablo, punctual. That was the word to describe him. Organized and on time, yes, a detail person. No wonder Jacobson had so much confidence in him. He was the ideal employee. He did his job, never talked unless it was absolutely necessary, was always on time, and knew what he was doing. His never talking made Rob a little uneasy. Yes, you can never read a person who never says anything. You don't know what they are thinking, Rob thought to himself.

Juan spoke in his quiet way, "I have made all the arrangements. We will leave at four-thirty this afternoon and fly back to Miami. Lourdes is going to meet us and handle all the arrangements for lodging and transportation. I have us a reservation on a commuter that lands here on the island." Rob and Mike looked at each other.

Mike asked, "There is an airport here on this small island?"

"No," said Juan, "it doesn't use an airport. It is a seaplane. It lands in the lagoon and taxies up on land. It uses the water as a place for taking off and landing."

"Oh," said Mike nodding his head, "I thought I heard an airplane this afternoon but wasn't sure."

"Yes," continued Juan, "they are in walking distance of the hotel, only about two blocks."

"Sure sounds convenient," said Rob. "I guess I need to take that expense money with me," he continued.

Juan nodded yes and said, "If we take the flying boat, we can clear customs in Miami, and you won't need a visa. If we were to go to the Miami Terminal in Nassau Airport, you might have trouble since neither of you has a tourist visa."

"What about me?" Mike asked. "Don't I need a visa? What if the local cops stop me and ask me for my papers?"

"If you stay close by the hotel, nothing will happen. We will be back tomorrow around noon, and we will be getting out of here and heading south soon afterwards. I will call Captain Mann and have him make the arrangements for the necessary papers so you can leave when it's necessary," Juan continued.

"Well, I guess that answers that," Mike said. "That means keep my ass here and behave. I really didn't have anywhere to go anyway."

"I will return at three-thirty for you," Juan said looking at Rob. "We will be staying overnight in Miami." He turned and left, closing the door behind him.

"I guess he was telling me to pack a toothbrush," Rob said with a shrug of the shoulders, "and I suppose I will need to take enough money to pay for the supplies and things we are going to need on our venture," he said.

"Sounds that way," Mike added.

"I'll give you a call tonight when we get settled in. You'll need to call Anne when I leave and make sure she got everything together," Rob said looking at Mike.

"Can do," Mike replied. Mike started to say something, but Rob held up his finger placing it on his mouth then pointed to his ear, reminding him that they might be bugged. Mike stopped and nodded his head. This being secretive was not Mike's best trait. He had always been open and honest. This cloak and dagger bull wasn't his thing; he was about to say something he didn't need to say.

"Okay, I need my jeans if I'm going to Miami. I won't let Jim and his friend see me in the beach costume," Rob said as he picked up the phone and called to ask about his laundry. They had told him they could have it back by four; he needed it now. "Yes," he said, "this is Rob Marshall in room 318. You have some laundry for me."

There was a long pause, then the man came back on the line. "Yes, Mr.

Marshall, it's ready."

"Could you please have someone bring it up to me?"

"Yes sir," the man continued, "I will have it to you in ten minutes."

"Thank you," Rob said as he hung up the phone. "I'll get my jeans back. I won't feel uncomfortable going back to Miami. I'll be going dressed like a real person," he said with a smile.

18 Miami Heat

Rob and Juan walked down the street past two hotels and several small shops. As they neared the seaplane terminal, Rob could hear the plane taxiing up out of the lagoon onto the loading ramp. Neither man spoke on the walk over. As they came to the front of the terminal office, Juan said, "I made a reservation in your name and one in mine. It will be best if we each purchase our own tickets. They don't have assigned seats, so we can sit where we please. We're early, so there won't be a problem."

Rob didn't say anything, but he thought that they were real early. They had left the hotel at a quarter to four. It had only taken ten minutes to get to the terminal. They were thirty-five minutes early. As they entered the office, Juan approached the ticket clerk first. Rob stood back; this was the same young lady who he had talked with earlier. He waited until Juan had completed his purchase, then he approached the window. He stated his business without making eye contact. He definitely didn't want the clerk to say anything about his earlier inquiries. As he looked around, he saw several people lining up behind him. The young lady was now talking on the phone as she punched up his reservation on the computer. "That will be sixty-eight dollars one-way," she stated. Rob pulled out a hundred-dollar bill and slid it forward as the young clerk slid his ticket to him. Rob picked up his change and turned around looking for Juan. As he walked outside, Juan was sitting at a small picnic table. Rob walked over and held up his ticket so he could see it as he approached. Juan Pablo never spoke, only nodded. Rob sat down across from him. Over Juan's shoulder he could get a good view of the seaplane. It was an old Grumman that had been upgraded. Its piston engine had been replaced by modern turbine engines, and it had a pretty, dark blue paint job.

Both men sat quietly, not talking. Rob watched as the aircraft was serviced with fuel and the pilot did a quick walk around then went back into the terminal. In a short time he returned, carrying a small clipboard and handed it to the flight attendant. Shortly thereafter, the young clerk inside announced the four-thirty flight to Miami. Rob stood up, stretched a little, and looked at Juan. Juan Pablo stood up slowly, not making eye contact, and said only four words. "It's time to board." Rob thought at least he hadn't forgotten how to talk.

As they boarded, Rob and Juan were a little slow in getting to the plane. It was first come, first serve. Sit anywhere you want. Rob entered first to find that the only available seats were in the front or the very back. He walked to the front and sat on the right side, two seats back of the co-pilot. The pilot and co-pilot were busy running their check list. As he sat down, Rob watched a moment then remembered Juan. He then turned around, leaned over in his seat, and saw him sitting in the rear near the back door. It was apparent by Juan Pablo's actions, he was not comfortable with flying. As Rob turned back around and fastened his seat belt, he heard the starters engage and the engines whine into life.

Slowly they taxied down the ramp and into the lagoon. Rob could hear the landing gear retract. First one clicked and locked into place, then the other. The old Grumman slowly picked up speed as they cleared the end of the lagoon and went out into open water. After they became airborne, a pretty, blonde flight attendant in her early twenties held onto the hand grip with one hand and a microphone with the other and announced that the flight to Miami would take approximately forty-five minutes. She said that due to the shortness of the flight, only beer and soft drinks would be served. Rob looked at Juan. The fear of flying was etched on his face. At least that was one bit of information to store for later use.

The airplane landed and taxied onto the ramp in Miami Harbor. When the attendant opened the door, Juan was the first to exit. Rob waited patiently and was the last to get off. As he walked around the airplane, he noticed a roped off area with a walkway to the terminal and a door marked customs. Rob was a little apprehensive, but as he neared the entrance door, he saw Juan standing to one side of the line and waiting.

"Show them your driver's license, and tell them you are returning from a short vacation in Nassau," Juan said in a low whisper as he fell into line behind Rob. Rob gave a shallow nod without looking back.

The customs man was an older, gray-headed, fair-complexioned man in his fifties, a little on the heavy side. The name tag read Griffin, U.S. Customs. Rob walked up, presented his driver's license and a small blue form he had been given on the flight noting he had nothing to declare.

"Any luggage?" the man asked.

"Only this small bag," Rob said, setting the small gym bag on the counter. The customs man took both hands and mashed around on the bag, stamped the blue declarative, and handed Rob his bag with a "Have a nice day, Mr. Marshall."

Rob nodded and said thank you, then turned and exited through the side door. As he stepped outside, someone called his name, "Mr. Marshall". As he turned to his right, there stood Lourdes. Rob stopped and paused for a second. She looked even better than he remembered. Dressed in cream-colored walking shorts and a red and cream-colored top, she was holding her sunglasses in one hand and a small bag in the other. The effect was striking. Lourdes Gil Velasquez was a stunning woman with dark brown hair, deep brown eyes, and olive Latin complexion. Her full lips were accented with a contrasting shade of pink lipstick, framing a large sensual mouth. All of a sudden, Rob realized he was staring and not speaking. "Oh, hi," he said, fumbling for words. Damn it, he thought to himself, I sound like a bumbling high school kid.

Juan walked up, "Senorita Lourdes, how are you?" he asked with a slight bow.

"I'm fine," she replied. "Jacobson said for me to assist you two in anyway. He said we would be picking up some supplies, so I'm in a Chevy van. If this would not do, we are to give him a call."

"I think this will do fine," Rob said as they walked over to the white chevy van. Rob looked through the side window into the back. There were no seats, so there was more than enough room for what they needed. "Yes, this will be all we'll need," he added.

"I have rooms for both of you at the Airport Hilton. Jacobson made the arrangements. It seems he has some of his old friends who stay there on a regular basis and felt you would be comfortable there," Lourdes said as they pulled out of the parking lot into the street.

Rob made small talk. Lourdes asked about their flight and apologized for causing a mix-up in the directions she gave on delivering the DC-3. "Those things happen," Rob said, but deep down he knew people this organized didn't get screwed up on the delivery place of something as important as a two hundred thousand dollar DC-3. He knew he had to be composed and despite himself his eyes kept returning to Lourdes with growing appreciation.

Lourdes followed the signs to the airport. As she exited the freeway and went north two blocks, overhead was a bold sign "Miami International Airport." One block before the airport entrance, she turned right onto a street, then drove down one block and turned right again. Driving past several small hotels, she then turned left. As they made the last turn, there was the Hilton, a large, cream-colored building about five or six stories high, a big impressive front with tall pillows supporting a massive entrance. To his right as they passed was a black limo. The uniformed driver was standing by the front of the car talking to a bellhop. It was a nice place with valet parking he noted as a well-dressed woman stepped from her gold Mercedes convertible, and a young man wearing a red vest handed her a receipt and chirped the tires as he sped away. He didn't usually stay in places like this, but on their money, here he would stay.

Lourdes stopped the van directly in front of the hotel main entrance. Juan slid the side door open and Rob opened his front passenger door. As he was stepping out, she said, "I'll park the van. You two can go on in and register, and I'll be in shortly."

Juan walked in, and Rob followed carrying his bag. A man in a red uniform held the door open. As they entered, he looked around. He was surprised to see several men standing around in the lobby talking, dressed in cowboy boots and jeans. Well, he thought to himself, I don't feel so damn odd.

Juan went toward a large, marble covered counter with "registration" in bold gold lettering above. It was back and to their left. Rob caught up with him as he reached the desk. "Good afternoon," Juan said with a slight smile. "I am Juan Pablo Ming, and my friend is Mr. Rob Marshall. I think you have reservations for us."

"Okay," the middle-aged female clerk said with a big smile, "Let me check." She punched on the keyboard. "Yes sir," she said, "you are all pre-registered. Here are your packets. The bellman will help you with your bags."

"Thank you, but that will not be necessary," Juan said. "We can carry our own bags." The clerk slid Rob his packet. They waited approximately thirty seconds, and Lourdes appeared. Rob again could not help but stare. It occurred to him that the song "Spanish Eyes" might have been written for her.

"Okay," she said, "are you two taken care of?"

"Looks like they knew we were coming," Rob said. "They handed us a key and said go on up and make ourselves at home."

"Good," Lourdes said. "Why don't you two go put your bags in your rooms and come back down to the lounge and let me buy you a drink? It is a little past six, and I don't think there is much we can get accomplished today," she added.

"That sounds like a good idea to me," Rob said, "but where is the lounge?"

"Oh, go back to the front. Just before you get to the main entrance, turn right. You will see it just down the corridor," she added.

"Will do. See you in about ten minutes," Rob said, turning toward the elevator.

As he got to the elevator, he noticed several men dressed in boots and jeans waiting for the elevator with their bags in hand. As they stepped into the elevator, Rob looked at his key. He was in room 428. As he reached to punch four, he noticed that it was already punched. As he stepped back, the other three men began to talk in a very friendly manner. The man in the middle stuck out his hand and introduced himself. "I'm Jack Gibbs from Tucson, Arizona," he said looking at Rob.

"How are you doing? I'm Rob Marshall."

"I see you are one of us. Where is your permanent station?" he asked.

Rob was a little puzzled. "Oh, I'm from the East coast," he said.

"Good, glad to have you on board. This is my third time down here," Jack continued. "This is Thomas Bell. We call him T-Bell, and this is Ralph Winstead. We're all from Arizona. We'll be here for three months. You know the routine." Rob nodded.

The elevator stopped. They all got off and walked in different directions. After they turned the corner, Rob asked Juan what that was all about. Juan shrugged. "I'm not sure, but I think most of the people staying here on the fourth floor of the Hilton are government-like customs people who work and fly out of the Miami airport."

"Oh, I see," said Rob as they neared his room. Rob was in 428, and Juan Pablo was in 427 directly across the hall. Rob opened the door, walked in, and threw his bag on the bed. They had put him on the same floor with all the government agents. That way he had no idea who was watching. That Jacobson was a real smooth son of a bitch. Well, at least, he had given him a good-looking female to have a drink with, and that wasn't all bad.

Rob walked into the bathroom, turned on the light, and checked himself in the mirror. He decided that he looked decent enough. He walked out of the bathroom, picked up his key card, and put it in his pocket. Then he went out his door and across the hall and knocked on the door of room 427. Juan answered. "Ready?" Rob asked.

"No, I have some phone calls to make. You go on down without me. I will join you later," he answered.

"You sure?" Rob asked. Juan nodded. "Okay," Rob said, "I'll see you later." He headed back down the hall to the elevator. He waited a few minutes until the elevator car arrived. He left the elevator when it stopped on the first floor, then walked across the lobby and around the corner and down the corridor and stopped at two big, white double doors.

Rob opened the door to his right and stepped into a very large darkened room. The lounge was hotel plush, decorated in an island motif with flickering candles. He stood a moment looking around, letting his eyes adjust to the dim light. He heard a soft accented voice call his name. Rob turned around to follow the voice. There sat Lourdes Gil Velasquez. At the sight of her, he felt a moment of lightness, then his face darkened as a charge surged through his body. Until that moment Rob had not realized how long it had been since he had known that feeling. And now, despite the hotel air-conditioning, his flushed face misted lightly with a sudden burst of heat.

19 LOURDES, LOURDES

"May I join you?" Rob said with a smile, struggling to regain his composure.

"Yes, and I took the liberty of ordering you a beer," Lourdes said.

"Well, thank you," he said as he sat down. "This is a really great place. A man could get used to this lifestyle in a hurry," he continued, calmer now.

"I feel as if I owe you something," she said. "Juan told me what happened with your airplane. I can assure you I had no part in getting you into this trouble. I was only following his instructions. Jacobson never told me what happened to you, but I finally got Juan to tell me today. Jacobson said it was my mistake; I had misunderstood his instructions. I hope you understand."

"Yes, I am beginning to understand a few things. One is that Jacobson wants to have complete control, but that's enough business for now," Rob said, pushing back in his seat. "This beer is good, I'm in good company, and I think we need to make the best of it. Tell me about yourself," he said to her, gazing into her sparkling brown eyes accented by her smooth smiling face.

"I'm originally from Nicaragua. When Somoso was forced out in the late seventies, my father and I came to Miami. My father had close ties to Somosa. If we had stayed, I fear we would have paid with our lives," she continued.

"I'm sorry you had to leave," Rob said. "Are you still interested in the war effort?"

"Sure," she replied. "My family had large land holdings, or should I say, we were partners with the Somosa family in large land holdings. In Nicaragua," she continued, "the Somosa family owned a large interest in everything. You did business only with their approval. Like in the United States, you have the government as a partner. They take half of your income. We had Somosa. We paid a large part of our profit to the family, and in return, we operated freely; and no one bothered us because the Somosa family was very powerful. Some day we plan to return and have a free country where we can do business in a free way. No Somosas and no Sandinistas."

"Well, lots of luck," Rob said. "I'm not really a historian, but I have learned a few things by watching the news." He continued, "Your country is in a real struggle. You threw out a dictator, and now you have the communist. Doesn't sound like much of a change."

"Yes, I know," she said. "We need the help of the United States government, but they cut off all our funds. It is now very difficult to fight when you are without supplies. I think that is what Mr. Jacobson is doing. He is trying to get supplies to our people who are resisting the Sandinistas. That is why he needs your airplane."

Rob sat quietly, listening. It was all beginning to make more sense to him now. They were in the middle of a war and wanted them to fly supplies into a combat zone. That was not exactly on the top of his list of things he wanted to do. At least he had a better idea of what was going on, not that it made him feel comfortable. That Jacobson had sent her here to soften him up. The old S.O.B. couldn't come out and tell them all the details. He sent a good-looking messenger to do it.

"All right," Rob said, breaking out of his thoughts, "let's have another beer. Well, I'll have a beer. What are you drinking?"

"My drink is vodka with a twist of lime," Lourdes answered.

Rob, holding up two fingers, pointing first to Lourdes and then to himself, motioned for the waitress. "Where's Juan? He said he was going to join us," Rob said.

"I'll go call," she said sliding out of her seat and walking out the door.

Rob couldn't help it. He had found her very attractive from the first time they met in Orlando. What-four to five days back-it seemed like an eternity. The waitress brought the drinks. She was a cute thing, maybe, 21. She did a little flirting, trying to insure a good tip, Rob understood.

Lourdes returned in approximately five minutes. She slid into her seat, and as she did she asked, "Mr. Marshall, how would you like to go eat some very good Latin food?"

"That sounds good to me," answered Rob with a smile. "What about Juan?" he asked.

"He has some errands to run for Mr. Jacobson. Maybe he will join us later," she answered.

"Let's finish our drinks, and I'm all yours. Just lead the way, and I'll follow," Rob said with a laugh, picking up his bottle of beer and finishing it off. He pulled out a twenty-dollar bill and folded it, putting it under the empty bottle. "I'm ready when you are," he said.

They were out of the hotel parking lot and down the street and onto the freeway; they were going west. It was apparent Lourdes was quite accustomed to driving in the freeway traffic. Then, she turned south. "It seems you know where you're going," Rob said with a smile.

"Yes," she said as she returned his smile. "Most of my friends live in south Miami. The downtown area is not very safe. That includes the airport area, so be careful," she continued.

"Oh, I plan to," he answered.

"We'll be going to the southwest part of Miami-mostly residential and small shopping centers with a few good restaurants in them," she continued.

"I never miss an opportunity for good food," Rob said.

Lourdes exited the freeway and turned west on a boulevard and then onto a narrow side street and into the parking lot of a small strip shopping center. As they drove into the parking lot, Rob noticed it was mostly empty except on the east side. There was a concentration of cars in front of a business. She parked the van back about four rows from the front. "We have arrived," she said with a smile.

There was no sign or anything noting this was a restaurant. They walked up to the front of the building to a large, hand-carved wooden door. Lourdes knocked. A very heavy man pushed the door open from the inside. As Lourdes stepped inside, the man gave her a big hug. "Come in, come in," he said in broken English.

"Manny, this is a friend, Rob," Lourdes said. "Rob, this is Manuel Gitian or Manny."

"We are very glad to have you," Manny said as he escorted the couple around a divider and into the main dining room. Rob was impressed. To Rob's right, as they entered the dining room, was a big, red tapestry hanging from the wall. Also there were pictures of gauchos, working cattle on the other wall. The furniture was rustic, wooden chairs and tables. The chair seats were covered with cowhide. It was apparent these people liked their privacy. Manny was taking Rob and Lourdes to the back of the large dining room; and as they passed through the crowded room, she spoke to several different groups of customers. She knew most of these people. The restaurant was austere, no advertising, no sign, no frills. Rob felt a little uncomfortable as a tingle danced along his spine. He could feel everyone glance at them as they walked past, but they were too well mannered to stare.

As Manny was seating them, Rob noticed a particular group of distinguished, mostly older men who were sitting at a round table across the room. They seemed particularly interested in Rob and Lourdes. Rob didn't want to stare, but he could tell they were talking and the conversation definitely included the two of them. A waiter came and brought the menu. Manny introduced him as Faustino.

"You may call me Fred," the waiter said with a big, warm smile.

"Very nice to meet you," Rob returned with a smile and a nod.

"Faustino will be your waiter. If you need anything, anything at all, please feel free to ask," Manny said as he excused himself. Rob took the menu, which was mostly in Spanish, and looked it over.

"I see something I recognize," he said. "It's the cold beer," he said, smiling and looking at Fred, then back to Lourdes. "Yes, I'd like a beer. Would you like something to drink before dinner?" he asked her.

"Yes," she answered, "a vodka on the rocks with a twist of lime." Fred nodded his approval and exited.

"You will have to order for me," Rob said. "I'm not good at reading Spanish.

Lourdes smiled. "Do you like steak?" she asked.

"Sure," he replied.

"Okay," she answered, "then steak it will be."

As Rob and Lourdes sat and talked, Rob noticed that the several older, distinguished men at the round table across the room were still very interested in what they were doing. Rob was about to ask about the men when Fred returned with the drinks. As he was placing the drinks on the table, Lourdes asked to be excused. Rob admired her as she walked to the front of the restaurant. She disappeared around the divider. There was something about that woman that definitely had his attention. He sat alone, drinking his beer, trying to look comfortable, but there was something about this that made him uneasy. Yes, that was it. He felt like he was on display, the way people continued to catch a glance at him when they thought he wasn't looking. Rob sat quietly for a few minutes, collecting his thoughts and wondering how Mike was doing. His thoughts drifted to Anne and hoped she got those passports on FedEx. Well, he would know in the morning.

Rob heard some raised voices from across the room. He looked up in time to see the men at the round table all standing and greeting Lourdes. Some were shaking her hand. Some were giving her a gentle hug. His guess was right. He definitely was on display. This was not unexpected. It was apparent that the men sitting at the table were a part of the puzzle. As Rob watched, Juan suddenly appeared to join Lourdes at the table with the men. They all stood and talked for a few minutes and exchanged greetings. Rob didn't want to be rude and stare, but it was a very interesting group. Lourdes soon returned to Rob at their table.

"I hope you will forgive my rudeness," she said. "Those were old friends; I needed to speak to them. She continued, "I knew them when we lived in Nicaragua."

"I see Juan is with them," Rob said.

"Yes," she said, "he has known them most of his life. Those men were all important businessmen back home, and now they live here in the United States with very little to do. They sit around and plan and talk about how it was at one time. They dream of returning to Nicaragua and having things return to the old ways. When they should have been retiring, they were forced to leave their homes and lost most of their possessions. Some managed to get some of their assets out of the country, but many lost everything."

As she spoke, Fred came up carrying a tray with their dinner. He placed a covered plate before each of them. He removed the cover from Lourdes's first. Rob watched. She had ordered some type of seafood. Fred then lifted Rob's cover. "Is there anything else?" he asked. Lourdes glanced at Rob, then nodded no. He backed up a step, then turned, and was gone.

"Now, what do I have?" Rob asked rather puzzled. This did not favor a steak, and he knew it.

"That's a flank steak," Lourdes explained. "It's very good. The side order is rice with black beans. These are all Latin foods."

Rob tried his steak. "It's very good," he said with a smile.

As they were finishing their food, Juan came by. "How are you?" he said speaking to Rob.

"I'm fine, and the food is excellent," Rob replied.

"Good," Juan returned. "If you need anything, please feel free to let us know." He did a slight bow to Rob and Lourdes. He then turned and walked back to the round table and joined the older men.

Rob finished up the steak, folded his napkin, and placed it in the empty plate. Lourdes could see a puzzled look on Rob's face. She answered the question before Rob could ask it. "Juan is a partner in this restaurant."

"Well, that explains it," Rob said.

Fred appeared. "May I get you a dessert?" he asked as he removed the dishes from the table.

"No," answered Lourdes. "What about a coffee or an espresso?" she said looking at Rob.

"Sounds good," Rob replied. "Make mine a coffee," he continued.

"Yes, I will have a coffee, also," Lourdes said with a smile.

As they walked across the parking lot to the van, Rob checked his watch. It was ten thirty-five. "Lourdes, you did good. I really liked the food," Rob said.

"I am happy you did," she said smiling.

He followed her around to the driver's door, took the keys, and opened the door. She again smiled as he returned the keys to her. He closed the door and walked around the van, opened his door, and got in. The traffic was light as they drove back to the hotel.

As they entered the hotel parking lot, Rob spoke first. "Tomorrow's going to be a busy day. Let's have one more drink. It may be a long time before we get a chance to have another one."

Lourdes paused before answering. "Okay,' she said as she pulled into a parking spot.

As they entered the hotel lobby, Rob turned toward the lounge. Lourdes grabbed his right arm. "I have a suggestion," she said as they both stopped. "Let's go to your room and order room service. That lounge will be packed and very loud," she continued.

"Yes, let's do that," he said as he smiled at her. She held on to his arm as they walked toward the elevator. They got off on the fourth floor and went down the corridor to Rob's room. As they walked down the hall, she continued to hold Rob's hand. He pulled out the key card and opened the door and held it open as Lourdes stepped past him and into the room.

"You will have to excuse me," Rob said as he walked to the bathroom. "It's the beer."

"I'll call and get our drinks," she said as Rob closed the door. When he came out of the bathroom, she was standing across the room at the window looking out over the city. He walked up and put his arm around her waist. She turned and smiled, then placed both her arms around Rob's neck, pulled his face down, and kissed him. It was a short but passionate kiss. "I've wanted to do that since I met you," she said.

"I think we both have that feeling," Rob said. "I'm not sure what to call it, but it does feel good," he said with a smile still holding Lourdes around the waist.

"It's my turn in the bathroom," she said running a finger down the front of Rob's shirt as she backed away and then turned and walked to the bathroom, closing the door behind her.

There was a knock on the door. Rob went over to let in the room service waitress. She was carrying a tray with two beers on ice and a mixed drink. Rob tipped her and signed the check.

He picked up one of the beers, opened it, and stood looking out over the city. He admitted to himself it was exciting. Yes, he could see how people could get all caught up in something like this.

He heard the bathroom door open. In the reflection of the window, he could see her. She had changed and was wearing one of his shirts as a nightgown. Rob turned slowly as she came toward him.

"I made myself comfortable. I hope you don't mind," she said.

"Oh, no," said Rob with a big smile reaching out and grasping her hand. She smiled and kissed his cheek.

"I think I could use that drink," she said with a smile.

Rob pointed to the table. Lourdes walked over, picked up the glass, and added a few pieces of ice from the bucket containing the beer. She took a sip and turned and walked back over to him as he sat down in a chair. "You need to get comfortable," she said, kneeling down and pulling Rob's black, leather boots off. She then sat on the arm of the chair and began to unbutton Rob's shirt.

"What time do we need to be at your friend's place, the Superior Air Parts?" Lourdes asked. "I'll call and get a wake-up call," she said as she walked over to the bed, lying face down across it. Her shirt inched up, leaving little to the imagination. She picked up the phone and dialed the desk.

"We need to be out of here by eight-thirty, so let's get a seven-thirty wake-up call," Rob said. As she was lying on the bed giving instructions to the front desk, the shirt was now above her waist, revealing her lacy, sheer black and red bikini panties. She had a beautiful body, and he was excited. She knew what she was doing to him, and she knew that Rob knew. "Seven-thirty, thank you," she said as she hung up the phone. Rob watched silently as she rolled over. She was lying there in a half-sitting position on one elbow, and the shirt was loosely draped around her shoulders. She took her free hand and unbuttoned the two buttons holding the faded blue shirt, and it gracefully slid from her shoulders and down her back. Rob couldn't speak. He stood staring at her smooth tanned body and well-defined breast. His wife had walked away two years before and until now he had made it a point not to get involved with anyone. He knew this was going to complicate things, but all of those unsatisfied male urges were now dictating his thoughts and actions. To hell with logic he thought as he came to her and placed his muscular arms around her body and pulled her to him with a passionate kiss. He knew this wasn't right, but he was no longer in control.

20 Passports to the Unknown

The phone was ringing. Rob sat up and looked around. He was alone. He looked at his watch, seven-fifteen. "Damn, they're early with my wake-up call," he mumbled as he was answering it.

"How are you doing?" he heard Mike say in his most disgustingly fresh "on top of the world" attitude.

"Oh, hey, Mike," Rob responded.

"Well, I know I'm not the most charming person in the world, but you don't seem real happy to hear from me," he continued.

"Oh, it's not that," Rob answered. "I was asleep. I'm okay now. I had to get my head to working. You sound mighty chipper this early."

"Yeah," Mike said, "Juan called doing his duty checking on me this morning, so I got him to give me your phone number. I thought I better let you know I checked on our packages. It was confirmed that they will be arriving in the air mail today."

"Oh, that's good," Rob answered.

"Are you coming back over here today?" Mike asked. "It's not fun being on vacation by yourself," he said with a shallow laugh.

Rob knew Mike was in a strange place with lots of strange people, and that wasn't Mike's thing. "What did you do last night?" Rob asked.

"Oh, I had a few drinks, sat out by the pool in my vacation clothes, and talked to the bartender," Mike said with a big laugh. "I'm beginning to feel right at home."

Rob knew he was saying that so he wouldn't worry about him. Mike was that way. He didn't want to put any undue pressure on Rob. "Okay," said Rob, "I'll give you a call around two this afternoon and let you know our schedule. Thanks again for the information."

Rob could breathe a little easier. The passports had been Fedexed and would be at Jim's place by nine, so he and Juan needed to get there after nine. He didn't want Jim or his employees slipping up and announcing this delivery with Juan tagging along.

Now what had happened last night? When he went to sleep, Lourdes was snuggled up close. He sat up on the side of the bed, looking around. The room was empty except for him. He reached for the phone and called room service and ordered some coffee.

As he entered the bathroom and switched on the light, he was startled to see written on the mirror in bright red lipstick "good morning," with a curved arrow pointing to a folded piece of paper by the wash basin. Rob picked up the paper and opened it and read, "I had a great time last night. Had to go. Will call you around eight o'clock." No signature. No name. Rob thought these people keep everything in perspective. They don't take any chances. No name-no ties. Just good memories. This took a little getting use to. She was a professional. Maybe last night was a part of her job description. "God, I hate to think that way," Rob said out loud as he reached for some tissue and rolled it up and wiped off the mirror, then brushed his teeth and walked back into the room. There was a knock on the door. Rob eyed through the peephole in the door- only a black man with his coffee. He was beginning to be very cautious as he opened the door, letting in the young man in a red tie and blue jacket who smiled and placed the tray on the table. He signed the ticket, fumbling in his pocket, pulled out some wadded dollar bills, and gave the man two ones.

The waiter was out the door in no time. Before taking his shower, he poured a cup of coffee and took several gulps, went into the bathroom and dug through his bag, finding the clear plastic bottle. He took out two aspirins and washed them down with the last of the cup of coffee. His head was hurting a little, just a dull ache.

Rob was through with his shower, dressed, and had flipped on the t.v. It was the same news as yesterday - Congress and the President fighting over the Contra issue. Congress had cut off all aid and was questioning the President's use of private funds to keep the fight alive. As he sat staring at the news commentator, there was a knock on the door. He peeped out to see Juan. Rob opened the door.

Juan Pablo spoke, "Good morning", with his slight oriental bow.

"And a good morning to you," Rob answered. "I had an enjoyable time at the restaurant last night, and the food was good," Rob continued.

"Thank you," Juan said with a small smile. "Ms. Lourdes will be picking us up at eight-thirty," he continued.

"Good," Rob replied. "That gives us time to get some fresh coffee. Let's go downstairs to the restaurant. We'll keep our eyes open for Lourdes. If we aren't in the rooms, she'll know where to find us." Juan Pablo nodded his understanding.

Rob picked up the key. "Do we need to check out?" he asked.

Juan shook his head, "No."

Rob needed time. He didn't want Juan and Lourdes to get him to Superior Air Parts before the Federal Express got there. He looked at his watch. It was eight-fifteen. Jim's place was in north Miami at Opa Locka, which was about a thirty minute drive in morning traffic, so he needed about a ten to fifteen minute delay, and the coffee shop was a good place to drag your feet.

"I'll have breakfast," Rob said to the waitress. "How about you?" Rob said looking at Juan.

"No thank you; I'll have some hot tea," he said.

"Bring me some coffee while I decide," Rob said all the while thumbing through the menu.

The waitress returned with the tea and coffee. "I'll have a steak-medium rare, two eggs-overeasy, and some hashbrowns," Rob said, knowing the steak would take time to prepare. He checked his watch. It was now eight thirty-five. Eating breakfast would take at least another thirty minutes. That would work out about right he thought to himself. That will put us there around nine-thirty. Real good.

Rob was digging into his breakfast when he felt a tap on his shoulder. He turned to see Lourdes smiling. "Good morning," she said.

Rob quickly swallowed his food and smiled back. "The magic woman," he said with a locked gaze. "One minute she's here, and the next one she's gone."

"Mind if I join you?" she asked as she walked around to the other side of the table.

"Not at all," Rob said. "You have the wheels, and you have the keys, so it's obvious we need you."

As Lourdes was seated, Juan said, "Please excuse me. I will meet you in the lobby."

"Oh, you don't need to leave," Rob said.

"I have a phone call I need to make," he answered as he arose with a slight bow and walked out of the restaurant. He sensed some tension between Rob and Lourdes.

"Where did you go last night?" Rob asked.

"I do have other obligations," she answered. "Now is not the time to talk about it."

"If you say so," Rob answered slightly annoyed.

Lourdes kept looking at her watch. She was anxious to get started. They had not gotten anything accomplished the day before. It all had to be done today. As they were walking through the lobby, Juan joined them.

"Do you know how to get to Superior Air Parts?" Rob asked, looking at Lourdes as they drove north on the expressway.

"Yes, she answered. "I looked it up in the phone book and called for directions. It is on a side street by Opa Locka Airport, on the southside.

As they came around the corner and pulled up in front of Superior Air Parts, Rob breathed a nearly audible sigh of relief as he saw the Federal Express truck pull out of the alley beside the old gray block building, housing the air parts business.

Old and faded, it was obvious the building needed painting. The physical appearance of his business didn't mean a lot to Jim. Most of his business was done over the telephone. He knew most of his customers but very seldom saw them. It was that same way with Rob. They talked airplanes all the time but only saw each other once or twice a year; over the years they had become good friends. Rob led the way as the three of them walked into the parts sales office. It was a large room with a counter running across the front, and in the rear were several smaller cubical offices with large glass windows opening to the front sales office. Jim looked up and saw Rob as they entered through the front door. He came around his desk and out of his office to greet them. "Rob, how are you doing?" he said with a big smile.

"I'm all right," Rob replied as Jim stepped through a small, swinging door, leading through the counter into the customer area. They greeted with a hand shake. "Jim, I'd like you to meet some- ah-," Rob paused, "friends of mine."

"Good to meet you," Jim said.

"This is Juan Pablo and Lourdes. They were nice enough to give me a ride over here."

"Good, good," Jim said. "Can I get you something to drink - coffee or coke?"

"We're okay," Lourdes said with a smile.

"Well, make yourself comfortable. If you need anything, just call. Rob has a shopping list and he and I are going back to the warehouse and see how much of it we can fill," Jim continued.

"I won't be long," Rob said as he and Jim walked through the small door in the counter and out a side door into the warehouse.

"What is going on?" Jim asked as they went into the warehouse. "Anne called and said she was sending your passports. I just got them," Jim continued.

"It's a long story," Rob said. "I can't explain it now, but I do need your help with that list," Rob said. "We will be working over water on a few cargo flights."

Jim stopped walking and turned to Rob. "I've known you for a long time, my friend. Now, it's none of my damn business, but I've seen a lot of good

114

people get desperate and do some really stupid things, like flying into and out of South America. I am here to tell you, not all of them even lived to regret it. I know it's not my business, but...."

"I know," Rob said, "it's not that. We've agreed to do some flying for some people who are connected with that Contra thing in Nicaragua. I know I'm in over my head, but now I don't have a choice. I can't tell you everything. You'll just have to trust me and give me all the help you can," Rob said.

"Where's Mike?" Jim asked, still not satisfied.

"He's waiting for me in a hotel at Nassau in the Bahamas," answered Rob.

"Where's the old DC-3 you had for sale?" Jim asked.

"It's over there, too. We got our asses in a sling, and now we are going to have to work out of it the best way we can," Rob continued.

"Okay," Jim said. "I put your passports in a brown envelope in my office desk. When we get all this order filled and packed, remind me to give them to you. I think I have everything on your list, so let's go back over to the shipping office. David Harris, you remember him?" Rob nodded.

"He's waiting for us there. Oh, Anne said if you have time, you need to call her. She wants to talk to you. There are a few things back there that need your attention. When we get to shipping, you can make the call on the 800 line from the office."

They strolled along the aisles toward the rear of the large warehouse, filled with aircraft sheet metal, hardware, engine parts, and propeller parts. You name it; Jim either had it or could get it.

As they entered the shipping office, Jim called to Amy, a short, stocky girl with red hair and a big smile. "Amy, I need you to go up front. There are two people in the office lobby. Talk to them, show them pictures, whatever, but keep them occupied for the next thirty minutes. Okay, go," Jim said.

"Sure," Amy said as she stepped through the door and headed down the corridor to the front of the warehouse.

"She doesn't need to hear what we have to say, and your friends need to be comfortable. Amy's the one. She will talk them to sleep," Jim said with a smile. The side door opened and in stepped a tall man with black hair, graying at the temples. Rob recognized him. It was David Harris.

"How are you doing?" Rob said.

"Fine," David answered.

"I'll get right to the point," Rob said. "You know that old DC-3 you worked on for me?"

"Sure," said David.

"Well, I need some help. I need to increase the range about three hundred miles and don't want it to be obvious. How can I do it?" Rob asked.

"Legally you can't," David answered.

"Illegally, how can I?" Rob asked.

"Well, it's the bladder type fuel cell. The drug people use them on boats and in airplanes to increase their range, but with aviation fuel, it is very dangerous. A leak or fumes and you can be blown right out of the sky," David continued.

"Is there a place to put it under the floor?" Rob asked.

David thought a minute. "Yes, it can be put under the cabin flooring first section aft of the cockpit. Two one hundred fifty-gallon bladders, one on each side of the control cables, will fit. You need some plumbing and a transfer pump to pump the fuel into and out of the main tank," David continued.

"Okay," Rob said, "sounds like that's what I need - only thing is, David, I need it today. Can you get it for me?"

"I don't know," David said. He hesitated, looking at Jim.

"It's okay," Jim said. "He's not running drugs. It's for something else. You know me, I wouldn't be doing this or asking you to, if it was illegal," Jim said.

"It's ten now," Rob was thinking aloud. "I will need it by two-thirty to get it air freighted to Nassau this afternoon then on to the other island. Do you know anyone over there in Nassau?" Rob asked.

"Yes," Jim said, "I know a young man who has a one airplane charter service with an old Aztec, and he'll pick up in Nassau and deliver anywhere in the islands."

"I need these parts taken to Eleuthera and loaded on my airplane."

"When do you want us to deliver these parts?" Jim asked.

"Oh, if you can package them up now, we'll just take them with us," Rob answered. "Let me call Anne."

"Sure," said Jim, "David and I will be outside."

Rob picked up the phone and dialed his office number. Anne answered. "Hello," Rob said.

"What's going on?" Anne asked.

"Well, we've gone into the freight business," Rob answered.

"That's good," Anne said in a noncommittal fashion, "but Dan needs you to call him at the bank."

"Okay, you call him for me and tell him it's going to take a few more days to get this sale finalized. Don't tell him about us being in the Bahamas. Just tell him that I called you from Florida, and I'm in Miami at Jim's place now; and we are making some repairs to the airplane. That's all he needs to know," said Rob. "Oh, I need the bank's routing number so I can do some wire transfers," Rob continued.

"I have that in my computer," Anne said.

"Okay, go get it for me, and I do appreciate everything you're doing," Rob said. "Please call the kids and tell them we will need to postpone the fishing trip for a few days. They will understand," Rob said.

"Here's the number," Anne said, giving Rob a seven digit number, followed by a five-digit number, then the flying company's account number.

"This will get money from Miami to our bank?" Rob questioned.

"Yes," said Anne, "that's how you do it."

"Okay, I will be checking with you every few days. They are supposed to be paying us as we go and making wire transfers into our bank account after each flight," Rob said.

"Sounds good," Anne said.

"Just hold down the fort and keep your fingers crossed, and we will be home soon. We'll explain all of this then," he said.

Rob hung up the phone, opened the door, and stepped out into the warehouse. Jim and David were standing by a rack of aircraft sheet metal, and as Rob walked up, Jim spoke, "David and I have been talking about this flying over water. We would like to make a suggestion."

"Sure," said Rob with a puzzled look.

"Well," continued Jim, "David thinks you need a way to lighten your load in case of engine trouble. You know you will be over water, and you never know what will happen, maybe lose an engine. He thinks you need to replace the regular cargo door with a jump door," Jim continued.

"Yes, that sounds good," Rob said, "but the aircraft is in the Bahamas."

"I know," said Jim. "It doesn't take a lot of work, and you will be able to open the smaller jump door from inside during flight. In an emergency, that will give you a chance to jettison cargo."

"Sounds good," Rob said, "but where do I get one?"

"I just happen to have a special on them today," Jim grinned, placing his hand on a large, curved piece of sheet metal structure. "This is it. Now the colors may not match, but the door will definitely fit your airplane."

"There are only two hinge pins to remove, and then the door will come right off, and you can replace it with this one," David said.

"Okay," said Rob, "let me figure out a way to get it over to the airplane."

The three men walked to the front of the warehouse and into the sales office. Juan Pablo was standing, looking out the front window of the office as Amy and Lourdes were talking.

"Well, I think we are all set," Rob said. "Juan, take the van around to the back." Rob pointed to the side street. "You'll see a sign that says shipping," Rob continued.

"I'll ride with him," Amy said.

"While you are getting things loaded, I'll settle up with Jim," Rob said.

David only nodded to the group and did not speak as he walked through the sales office and out the front door, then got in his red and white Chevrolet pickup and drove away.

Rob went with Jim into his office and closed the door. "Add it all up, Jim," Rob began as he sat down in a small metal chair. "I'm going to pay for this now."

"Okay, but you don't need to do that. I'll bill you," Jim answered.

"No," Rob answered, "I want to keep this all slick. You never know what is going to happen." Rob pulled out a roll of hundred dollar bills. "How much is the damage?" he asked.

Jim turned to his calculator and began to add the following items: two three men life rafts, oil, hydraulic fluid, four flashlights, survival gear, and one jump door. "I'll give you a good price on that jump door if you want to bring it back when you're through," Jim said. "We'll work something out. Let's see; it all comes to fifty-three hundred twenty-two dollars," Jim continued.

"What about the fuel system, the bladder tanks, and the fittings?" Rob asked.

"I don't know," Jim answered.

"Here's eight thousand dollars. If it is more, put the rest on my tab and send a bill to the office. If it is less, run a credit," Rob said smiling.

"Can do," Jim said as Rob handed him the stack of bills. "I haven't seen this much cash in a long time," Jim said with a handshake. "If you need me for anything, here is my card. It has my home number written on the back. Call me day or night, and Rob, please be careful," Jim continued as he stood up. "Oh, I'm about to forget something," he said, sliding a large, brown envelope over to Rob. Rob opened it, removed the two passports, and placed them in his boot.

21 FINAL DESTINATION

Shimar stood in the pilothouse with the captain as he barked orders. The small freighter-"Star of Persia" in flaking white letters on her black, rust-streaked stern- was coming to a stop. The vibrations of the chain rattled through the hull as they dropped anchor. It was eleven-thirty Monday night, but they would have to wait until Tuesday morning for good light to enter the narrow channel leading to the dock. The shoaled-in river harbor shifted depth with each tide and with every heavy rain, making navigation perilous, so they waited until morning light and the arrival of a local pilot to get them safely into the main channel. The anchor chain had now stopped going out. They were at a full stop.

The Greek captain said, "We will be here until the pilot arrives in the morning," holding up both hands in a gesture of disgust.

They would not be unloading the ship tonight. It would be tomorrow. "Captain," Shimar said with a gesture of his right hand, "I think I will retire for the night."

Shimar walked out onto the deck of the ship, pulled out a cigarette, and lit it. Tomorrow was the day, the last day he would be cooped up on the small freighter. He would be going home, and the responsibility of this shipment would pass to someone else. They would be paid, and he could relax. Shimar finished his cigarette, opened the door leading to the stairs, and went down to the crew quarters, where he had a small room. He went into the room and looked around. This had been his home for the last ten days, and his personal things were all scattered about; they needed to be packed tonight. On a freighter, there was no maid service, but the packing could wait. He kicked off his shoes and lay down on the bed, and his thoughts drifted back home to his family in Israel. He wondered how they were all doing. In two days he would be home, and those were his last thoughts as he drifted off to sleep.

There was a loud banging on the metal door. Shimar sat up. The banging came again. He stood up, took the few steps to the door, and opened it. There was a small dark-skinned man. Speaking in broken English, he said that the captain would like for Shimar to join him for breakfast.

Shimar nodded okay. The crewman turned and walked away. Shimar closed the door and pulled on his shoes. He brushed his hair, turned and walked up the stairs to the captain's quarters.

He knocked, and the captain said, "Come in."

Shimar opened the door and walked in. Sitting at a small table was the captain, drinking coffee. "Well this is the day," the captain announced.

Shimar smiled. He knew that the captain was happy to be rid of him and his cargo. Shimar understood. No one likes to be riding around in a ship with a cargo hold full of explosives. The captain wasn't the only one who would be happy to be rid of this cargo.

"None of my crew will be allowed to leave the ship. Those are my orders. We don't need them spreading unnecessary information about this cargo to the locals," the captain explained. "You will be returning to the island on the boat that brings the channel pilot," the captain continued. "That will give you adequate time to make the necessary arrangements for storage or whatever," the captain said.

"Yes, that is an excellent idea," said Shimar.

"Now, may I order you some breakfast?" the captain asked.

"No," said Shimar. "I need to clean up and pack, but I thank you just the same. I will be prepared to leave when the pilot launch arrives. It has been a very pleasant trip, and I hope all the financial matters were satisfactory."

"Very much so," the captain said with a smile.

Shimar nervously showered and put on his last clean clothes he had saved for the flight home. He hurriedly crammed his belongings into his two bags and returned to the captain's quarters. The captain smiled. "It appears you are anxious to go," he said in broken English. Shimar smiled but did not answer. He was not accustomed to long rides on small freighters, and his demeanor made it obvious.

"Here. Have some coffee," the captain said. "The pilot will be here in about thirty minutes, so you have time."

Shimar graciously accepted the captain's hospitality. The captain's quarters were up high, just below the pilothouse, and there was a view of the island. Off in the distance were mountains with heavy green vegetation. This was the first time Shimar had been in this part of the world. It was quite different from the Middle East with its few trees and barren landscape. He turned and walked back and sat down at the small table with the captain.

"Are you sure I can't get you something to eat?" the captain asked.

"No." Shimar was too nervous to eat. Now was the most important part of the trip, the delivery and the finalizing of the sale. He was on his own. There was no one to back him up, a rather empty feeling. He sat quietly, not saying anything. Surely there were not going to be any last minute complications, but sometimes things don't go as planned he thought.

The captain's phone buzzed. The captain answered and spoke briefly and then hung up. "That was the bridge. The first mate has spoken to the harbormaster and the pilot is on his way. He should be here shortly," the captain said.

Shimar stood up. "Captain, I want to thank you on behalf of myself and my countrymen for what you have done."

"It was all part of my responsibility," the captain said, "and it has been very pleasant and, most of all, very quiet," he said with a big smile.

Shimar understood. No loud noises like explosions. He reached out and shook the captain's hand, turned, and walked out the door and down the long stairs to the deck.

He could see the launch coming about half a mile out from the small freighter. One of the crewmen came up and took one of his bags and smiled. He returned the smile. They could not communicate. The crewman was Greek and spoke neither Hebrew nor English.

There was a whine of the winch as the ladder was lowered along the side of the ship to allow the pilot to board and Shimar to leave. The launch pulled alongside and the pilot came aboard with two men. They were both well-dressed, but in casual clothes. One of the men spoke briefly with a crew member. The crew member nodded and pointed to Shimar. The men walked over to Shimar. The first was a medium built man in his late forties and with graying hair. He put out his hand. "Mr. Shimar?" he asked.

"Yes," Shimar answered.

"I'm Jacobson. I flew down last night. I felt it would be safer if we met on the ship and did our inspection here. Then there would be no need to reopen the containers at the dock."

"What about customs?" Shimar asked.

"Oh, that little problem has been addressed. Our trucks are waiting. We will unload the cargo and move it to a warehouse for safekeeping. I've spoken with the captain of the ship. He is going to delay for a short period and allow us to check the cargo. This is just a formality," said Jacobson.

Shimar nodded as they walked along the deck to a staircase leading into the cargo hold. All the containers were locked. Shimar had the keys. He placed them in Jacobson's hands and pointed to the five large gray containers. Shimar stood back as Jacobson methodically, one by one, did his inspection and put the locks back on the container doors. He pulled a small list from his pocket, looked it over, then put it back. "We are okay," he said with a smile. "Let's go make a phone call."

The three men climbed back up the stairs and walked across the deck to the boarding ramp. Jacobson and Shimar climbed down and boarded the launch, leaving Jacobson's man onboard with the cargo.

The ride back to shore took approximately fifteen minutes. There was a car waiting. The driver sat quietly as Jacobson and Shimar got into the back. They drove without talking to a hotel then went up to the third floor, and Jacobson placed a call with the operator, then he waited approximately ten minutes. The phone rang. It was the operator who said that the call was completed. Jacobson's words were, "All the cargo is as ordered. We can take delivery. Call and finalize the contract. Call me back when it is finished," he said as he hung up the phone. "Well, they're doing the paperwork. They'll call when it is complete."

Shimar knew what he meant. The funds were being transferred, and as soon as the transaction was complete, Vlasenko would call with the pre-arranged code. If he didn't hear those words, he was ordering the captain to return with the cargo.

They sat waiting for the phone call. Fifteen minutes passed; no one talked. The telephone finally rang. Jacobson answered. "Yes sir, I understand," he said. He hung up the phone. "Mr. Vlasenko will be calling shortly. Everything went as planned. The transaction is complete," Jacobson continued.

Shimar didn't speak. Another ten minutes passed. Shimar was a little nervous. Then the phone rang. Again Jacobson answered it. "Just a minute," he said as he handed the phone to Shimar.

"Shimar," Mr. Vlasenko said, "how are you? It's good to hear your voice. It's completed. Oh, I sent the yellow roses to your wife on her birthday. She was so happy you remembered."

Shimar breathed a sigh of relief. That was the code - yellow roses. He smiled and handed the phone back to Jacobson. "I'll need to talk to the captain," he said to Jacobson.

"No problem," Jacobson answered. "We will go down to the harbor and use the harbor master's radio," he continued.

They arrived at the small, neat but worn office shared by the harbor master and customs. As they entered, it was apparent everyone knew who Jacobson was. He smiled and shook hands. He spoke briefly with an operator then nodded. Jacobson motioned for Shimar. Shimar walked over to the radio operator. "We have the captain on the radio," Jacobson said, handing the mic to Shimar.

Shimar spoke a few words in Hebrew to the captain. The captain then answered. Shimar then handed the mic back to Jacobson. "I think that completes our transaction," Shimar said smiling. "Now I need to clear customs and get a ride to the airport. I'm ready to go home," he said smiling.

"I'll have one of my men take you," Jacobson said putting his hand out. The men shook hands. Shimar picked up his bags and walked out the door.

22 IT WON'T BE LONG NOW

The early afternoon breeze gently swayed the partially drawn curtain as the restless figure of the gentle giant of a man watched the foaming surf break on the white sandy beach. A beach bubbling with activity as some played in the water and others restfully soaked up the summer sun. Yesterday at this time, several dolphins had made their presence known as they romped in the rolling surf. Mike strained with his hand shading his eyes, they weren't there. Only thing out there was a blue speedboat pulling a white parasail with a young man in bright orange bathing trunks and a faded t-shirt. Mike stood and watched as it floated by and disappeared from view. He paced across the room to the phone. Rob was supposed to call no later than two. He stood looking at the phone as if that would make it ring. Then he turned back to the open window. Now he knew how the caged animals at the zoo felt. He could look out but couldn't go anywhere. As he leaned forward on the window ledge, the phone rang.

"How are you doing, Mike?" Rob began.

"I'm all right. This view from the room is like looking at the same picture and is getting a little old," said Mike.

"Well, don't worry. You won't have time for it to get too old. We'll be leaving there in the morning and going South. I don't know where, but we'll find out tonight. I'll explain our plans when I get back. I've gotten together all the gear we'll need, and we'll be leaving here as soon as Jim gets some life rafts packed and ready. Those are some of the things we definitely need. Hopefully, he'll have it all ready in the next two hours, then we'll fly it all

125

over there on one of the commercial airline flights," explained Rob.

"Sounds good," Mike said, " so you and Juan will be back later this afternoon. Have you heard from old man Jacobson?" Mike asked.

"Yes and no," Rob replied. "He's disappeared. Maybe he is out making someone else miserable."

They both laughed. It was strange that Jacobson was gone at this critical time. Today they were supposed to leave for the islands. He was usually around, letting everyone know who was in charge.

"I'll call you back around three-thirty. We should be leaving then," Rob said.

"Okay," Mike said and hung up the phone. He left the room on the third floor and went up to the room on the fourth floor. He picked up the phone and called Anne at the office.

"Hey, girl," Mike said, "just thought I'd check in with you. All this sunshine and beautiful women are wearing me down."

"Mike Ricau, you better behave yourself. You know that's not a part of the United States," Anne said. "You are still in the Bahamas?" she asked. "You move around so much I can't keep up with you."

"Yeah," Mike said, "we're real world travelers." They both laughed. Mike got serious, "We're okay, but the near future is a little cloudy."

"I know," said Anne. "Rob called this morning. He didn't sound good. He didn't want to talk to Dan down at the bank, and that's not like Rob."

"Yeah," said Mike. "He's under the gun. Well, we both are. We are playing a game, and it looks like they have a stacked deck," Mike added. "Did Rob talk about the money?" Mike asked.

"Well, not really. He just got a routing number to do wire transfers to our bank," Anne answered.

"Well, we don't exactly trust this bunch, so we decided we'll get paid every time we do work. We should be transferring money about every few days if things go the way we planned," Mike said.

"Okay," said Anne with a slow southern drawl. "I guess it's good that things are slow around here. I've asked Jeff to come in if we need him. He said he could fly for the next week, and then he will have to go back to his other job."

"That's good," Mike said. "Did you talk to Rob about this?"

"No," said Anne, "he wouldn't let me. He seemed in a hurry and had other things on his mind," she added.

"Yes, he is carrying a load, and it's tough," said Mike.

"He owes the bank over one hundred thousand dollars on the old DC-3. If he lost the plane, he would be shut down. He's worked fifteen years building that business, and it could be gone over night. I'd say he's got a right to be a little uptight," Mike added.

"Who are these people?" Anne asked.

"You know about as much as we do," Mike said. "They are real secretive."

"Oh God," said Anne, "don't get involved with those people who are running drugs."

"No, this doesn't have anything to do with drugs. At least, that's what they are telling us," Mike answered. "Supposedly, we will be doing something that will help our government, but you know how that goes. Never know who's just shooting the bull and who's telling the truth," Mike added.

"Yes," said Anne. "I'll say a prayer for you when I go to church."

"I think we'll need it," Mike said.

"Please be careful," Anne said, "and tell Rob to call me either here at the office or at home. Tell him I talked to Dan at the bank. Everything is okay for now."

"All right," said Mike. "I need to go. I'll tell Rob to call," he added, "and you be careful. Oh, it might be a good idea to call Jeff and have him hang around the office until we get back. Tell him I owe him one. Yeah, tell him I'll take him deep sea fishing when I get back, my treat. That'll get his attention."

"I'll call him now," Anne answered.

"I'll talk to you tomorrow," Mike said, hanging up the phone.

Mike looked around the room. It was real neat and clean. It seemed evident no one was staying in this room. He walked over and pulled the cover back on the bed. He then walked into the bathroom and pulled off his clothes and took a shower. He threw a few wet towels around. "Now," he said out loud, "they won't get suspicious. They'll know someone is staying here."

Mike dressed and headed down to the room on the third floor. He unlocked the door and walked in. He checked the message light on the phone. it was out. At least no one had tried to call. He sat down on the side of the bed. This damn waiting was getting the best of him. He didn't have a lot of patience, especially sitting and doing nothing. He had to get out; no one to talk to and being in this room was too much. He picked up the phone and called the desk.

"This is Mike Ricau," he said. "I'm expecting an important phone call. Will it be a problem to have you forward the call to the restaurant or lounge?"

"Uh, no," the operator answered.

"Then I will be in the restaurant, and then I'm going to the lounge," he said with a deep sigh. "What a day!" he said as he hung up the telephone.

Mike walked into the dining room. Things were quiet in the middle of the afternoon. A few people were scattered about, but mostly, the dining room was empty. There was no one at the door to seat him, so he went on in and sat at a table by the wall to his left. He noticed two black men in white uniforms sitting across the dining room. They both looked him over as he entered the room. Mike didn't want to stare, but he was almost sure they were not police, maybe customs. He was certain of one thing; he didn't need to talk to them. He didn't have a passport or a visa and for damn sure, there wasn't anyone here to get his ass out of jail if they arrested him.

Those officials made him uncomfortable. He needed to be calm and relax, be a typical tourist and enjoy himself.

"How are we doing?" Mike was a little startled by the question. "I didn't mean to scare you," the older waitress said as she walked up to Mike's side.

"Oh, that's all right," Mike said with a big smile. "I'm just sitting here daydreaming."

"Well, what can I get for you?" she asked.

"You can bring me a cup of coffee and a menu for now," said Mike.

"I can do that," she said with a smile, dropping a menu on the table before him, and turning, disappeared to the back of the restaurant through a set of double doors.

Mike sat looking at the menu. Half the dishes on the menu he didn't understand, and the other half, he had tried. The waitress returned with the coffee. Mike studied the menu. He finally decided on a small steak and salad. As the waitress walked away with Mike's food order, the two men in their white uniforms passed her and said a few words. All three laughed, and the two men exited the dining room without looking back. Mike now breathed a sigh of relief.

A few minutes later, the waitress returned with Mike's salad. Mike smiled. "Your policemen have a very different uniform," he said waiting for a response from the waitress.

"Oh, they were not policemen," she answered. "They are from customs." Mike was right.

"They work the incoming passengers from the flying boats that come over here from Miami," she added. "They come over here and have a spot of tea in the afternoon."

"Very interesting," Mike said smiling.

"Yes," she added, "we were a part of the British Crown until a few years age, and now we are self-governed; but we still have a few of the old traditions, like our speech and drinking tea," she said smiling.

"Well, I'm not much on tea, but I do like my coffee," Mike said.

Mike finished his meal and stepped across the lobby to the lounge. Checking his watch, it was twenty minutes till four o'clock; he should be hearing something from Rob. I'll go into the lounge and have a beer, no more than two. Maybe, just maybe, Rob would call soon.

Mike sat down at the far end of the bar with his back to the wall. He didn't need any more Bahamian officials checking him out. As he was sitting down, Sam, the small, thin, light-skinned, black man, came up with a big smile.

"How are we doing, Mike," he said. He was now on a first name basis with the hotel bartender.

"I'm doing fine," said Mike with an extended hand. They shook; Sam turned and took a few steps to the cooler and returned with Mike's beer. Mike sat, sipping the beer, trying to relax, although all this cloak and dagger B.S. was getting to him.

Mike and Sam talked as Mike finished the second beer. Still, no phone call. He was getting a little nervous. Maybe they had forgotten to forward the call into the lounge. Yes, it would be best to get back up to the room on the third floor. It was now four-thirty. Mike paid his tab and walked away with a "see you later, Sam." He stopped by the restroom on the way out of the lounge. Then as he passed the front desk, he heard someone calling, "Sir, Sir." He looked up at the desk, and a young woman was calling him. He walked over to the desk.

"Are you Mr. Ricau?" she asked.

"Yes," Mike replied rather cautiously.

"Then I have a long distance phone call for you," she added. "I called the lounge. They said that you had just been there. Sam identified you," she said with a smile. "You can take the call on the house phone, hanging on the wall to the left of the front desk. Wait for it to ring," the girl said with a smile.

Mike walked over and waited. The phone rang. "Hello," Mike said.

"Mike," Rob said, "I had a little trouble finding you. We'll be back at the airport around seven. We'll see you around seven-thirty. I'll explain everything then," Rob added.

"Man, it's good to hear from you," Mike said when Rob stopped talking. "I've had all of this place I can stand," he continued.

"It won't be long now," Rob replied. "I'll tell you everything tonight."

"Oh," said Mike, "if I'm not in the room, I'll be down there, keeping the bartender busy."

"Well, don't drink too much. We have to work tomorrow," Rob said.

"Okay, see you when you get here." Mike hung up the phone and headed back to the lounge. Damn this sitting in a room with no one to talk to.

23 Back to Paradise

Lourdes pulled the gear selector into drive and slowly eased away from the loading dock of Superior Air Parts and into the street. They were one block from Eighth Avenue, which would take them to Opa Locka Airport.

"I'm sorry we had to wait on the last life raft, but with that we have all the supplies we need," said Rob. "Now, how do we get them over to the airplane?" he asked. "We're running out of time; it's already four o'clock."

"We've taken care of the transportation," Lourdes said. "All we need to do is take the supplies to George's hanger at Opa Locka. They will fly the supplies over to your airplane early tomorrow morning."

Rob was a little uneasy. That second life raft wasn't really a life raft. All the survival gear and everything other than the liner of the raft were removed. In its place, David had placed the two fuel bladders and the necessary rigging to make them work with the fuel system of the DC-3. This could be a bad situation. Maybe this was a bad idea he thought. If George or some of his crew opened up everything and saw the fuel cells, then what? I can't change it now, he thought. Maybe they won't look. For damn sure, he didn't want anyone probing in the oil or hydraulic fluid and getting it contaminated. Yes, that was it. "Can we lock the supplies up?" asked Rob.

"I don't know," answered Lourdes.

"Well, we need to," said Rob. "The oil and hydraulic fluid can easily be contaminated. That would foul up the systems on the airplane," he explained.

"We're supposed to drop it off at the airport now. We were to leave it in the back of George's hangar, and I'm sure there are several people who have access to that hangar," Lourdes stated.

"I'm not real comfortable with that," said Rob. "It will be really difficult to stop and do repairs to that old DC-3 out over the water." They both chuckled.

"I think you are right," said Lourdes. "I'll just drop you off at Miami International and keep the supplies in the van until tomorrow morning. Then I can deliver them to George, and he can bring them to you at the island tomorrow morning."

"Yeah," said Rob, "I will feel a lot better if you have all this locked up in the van rather than it sitting out in the open in a hanger at Opa Locka, with a lot of people going and coming, and you never can be too careful," Rob added.

Lourdes drove by George's office and talked to his mechanic, explaining the situation. She returned to the van. "It's all right," she said. "The mechanic said we were doing the right thing because he would be leaving around five-thirty this afternoon; and after that, he couldn't be responsible. I do have to be here by six-thirty in the morning, so that he'll have time to load the supplies on the airplane. He wanted to know how much all this weighs," Lourdes said.

"Let's see," said Rob, pulling out his list. "I can give a good educated guess." He went down the list and put a weight beside each item. "Oh, Juan," Rob said, turning in his seat to face Juan Pablo who was sitting in the back on the supplies, "look on the life rafts. The weight should be written on there somewhere."

Juan rolled one of the life rafts around until he could see the data tag. "Here it is," he said, "eighty-seven pounds."

"Okay," said Rob, going down the list and adding the numbers. "Well, it is about four hundred seventy-six pounds. Let's just say five hundred, and that will be a safe guess," Rob said.

They were now back on I-95, heading south. They then turned east on the expressway and drove off at LeJeune, then turned right into the drive leading to the Hilton. They checked out, loaded their bags into the van, and drove back onto LeJeune and over to the airport.

Juan opened the sliding door and picked up both his and Rob's bags. Rob sat a minute, staring over the front of the van. Juan Pablo walked on toward the entrance. As he approached, he stopped and waited for Rob. Rob was thinking he really wanted to talk to Lourdes, but what could he say? It had been that way all day. They had only spoken when it was necessary. He knew that anything he said would make him feel like a fool. Sometimes it was best to leave things unsaid, and this was one of those times.

Lourdes reached over and placed her hand on top of his. She squeezed, placing a small, folded object in his palm and said, "I'll light a candle and say a prayer for you."

Rob opened the door and stepped out without looking at her. It wasn't the right time. He had other things to do and needed to focus on everything else. He pushed the door closed with one hand on the window opening. He looked up with a smile and said, "Thanks," quickly turning and went towards Juan. The two men walked together into the airport main lobby.

"I hope you have the tickets," he said to Juan Pablo with a smile. Juan held up two tickets and smiled back. As they hurried toward the boarding gates, Rob stopped. "Juan Pablo," he said, "I need to take a restroom break. I'll be back in a minute."

As he rounded the corner in the restroom, he opened his left hand; there was a small piece of folded paper. Lourdes had placed it in his palm while squeezing it in the van. Rob unfolded the paper. There was a phone number followed by the word, home. Rob's heart skipped a beat. So, maybe last night wasn't part of her job. Rob folded the paper and placed it in his wallet. He waited a minute and exited the restroom to see Juan Pablo waiting just outside. They scurried down the corridor and through the gate, presenting their tickets and boarding the plane.

The pilot bumped a little hard on the landing as some pilots do, Rob thought. That's sloppy. If he would only concentrate, they would have landed smoothly. "I've got to stop grading everyone," thought Rob. As they exited the airplane and were clearing customs, Rob saw the smiling Captain Mann standing over by the exit. Rob presented his driver's license and was issued a visa, good for ten days or until you leave, whichever came first, the custom's officer had explained.

Mann was there to pick up Juan and Rob and take them back to the hotel where Juan Pablo had left his car. They walked out of the small terminal and across the street to Captain Mann's car. Rob was a little surprised to see a government official driving a black Mercedes, even though it wasn't new. It was very nice and for the Bahamas, very expensive. It was evident the Captain had an outside income, and Rob was sure he knew who the employer was. The car was very clean and well-maintained. Rob guessed it was maybe three or four years old and looked new. The Captain was unmistakably very proud.

He opened the trunk and gently placed their bags on the floor, then went around to the side and unlocked the door for Juan. It was obvious who was helping whom. Rob sat on the right front. It took a little getting use to, sitting on the side meeting all the traffic.

They crossed over the bridge and drove into the hotel parking lot. The Captain parked in the back away from all the other cars. He was very careful and did not want his Mercedes scratched or damaged.

Captain Mann walked with the two men to the front entrance of the hotel as Rob went on in. Juan Pablo and Captain Mann stood outside and talked briefly. While waiting for Juan, Rob strolled around the corner and stopped at the entrance to the lounge and glared into the dim-lit room full of shadows. There he was at the far end of the bar talking to a very cute girl and the bartender. Yes, Mike was a little too relaxed Rob thought. He stepped back from the entrance and went around the corner and waited on Juan.

Juan Pablo finished his conversation with Captain Mann then rushed to join Rob.

"My old partner is in the bar and seems to be having a good time," said Rob with a smile to Juan. "I think I'll take my bag up to the room and come back and have a beer. You are welcome to join us," Rob said looking him in the eye.

Juan paused a minute and then looking away said, "No, thank you. I think I'll go home. I'll see you both in the morning before eight o'clock." With a slight bow he turned and walked out the front door of the hotel.

Rob stood for a minute and thought maybe he had better say something to Mike, then take his bag up to the room. He rounded the corner and stepped to the front of the ornate lounge covered with stained glass and brass and casually strolled up behind Mike, placing one hand on his shoulder. "You think I can get one of those?" he said, pointing to Mike's beer.

"You definitely can," said Mike, reaching out his big hand to Rob with a warm smile.

"Okay, you hang onto that beer. I'll take my bag up to the room and be right back," said Rob.

"Can do," said Mike a little too loudly.

Rob knew Mike only spoke this way when he had too much to drink, so he hurried out of the lounge and across the lobby to the elevators. As the elevator stopped on the third floor, he fumbled in his wallet for the door card, swung the door open, and threw his bag on the bed and looked around at the clock; it was eight o'clock. He had gone all day on breakfast and a little snack at lunch, now it was time for some real food.

He hurried back down to the lounge. Mike needed to slow down on the drinking. Maybe food would do the trick. He went in and sat down at the bar with Mike.

"This is Christy," said Mike, looking at the girl sitting on his left as he leaned back. "And Christy, this is a very good friend, Rob," Mike said with a big glowing smile. "And Rob, here's your beer," he said while sliding a long neck toward Rob. "I had them keep it on ice until you returned," he said with a wink and a smile.

Rob took a long drink from the beer, put it down, and wiped his mouth. He let out a long breath and said, "I needed that."

As he finished the beer, Rob stood up and stretched. He'd had a long, rough day. "I am going to get something to eat. You want to join me?" he asked, looking at Mike.

"Sure," said Mike. "That's all I do, drink beer and eat food. Christy, do you want to go with us?" Mike asked as he slid off of the barstool and stood up.

"No thank you," she said. "If you're coming back, I'll be here."

"Sure thing," said Mike.

The two men went across the lobby to the dining room. As they walked, they were talking. "I need to get out of here," said Mike. "I'm getting on a first name basis with everyone. All I do is eat, drink, and sleep."

Rob laughed. He knew Mike was feeling no pain, and the morning would be coming early.

24 THE MAN'S BACK

Jacobson looked to the east. The sun was beginning to show through the early morning haze. Red and yellow rays played against the backdrop of the soft blue sky. He walked up to the door of the light blue and white Piper Navajo twin engine airplane. Peering inside, George and the mechanic were stacking brown paper boxes under the seats. Some larger ones were stacked in the back near the door.

"What have we got here?" Jacobson asked.

"Oh, good morning Mr. Jacobson," George said.

"What's all this?" Jacobson asked again.

"These are the supplies for your air crew on the DC-3," he said.

"I thought all of this was shipped air express yesterday," Jacobson continued.

"I think the decision was made to take all of this with us this morning," George said.

"Who made that decision?" Jacobson asked.

"I'm not sure," said George. "Lourdes called and talked to Manny, my brother. I think they decided it was best if we took it with us this morning," George continued.

"Great!" exclaimed Jacobson. "Where are all the people going to sit? You know we have to pick up four passengers in Nassau."

"Yes sir, I've taken care of that. I have chartered another airplane in Nassau to take all the others over to Eleuthera. That way we won't have to stop in Nassau and have customs people poking around and asking for a manifest describing all of this," said George, putting both hands out in front and pointing to the boxes and two large bags containing the life rafts.

"You're right," Jacobson said, turning around. "I think I need another cup of coffee. Is there any made?" he asked.

"Yes sir," George said, stumbling over the boxes in the isle, trying to get to the door. "Mr. Jacobson, I'll get it," he said, stepping down from the airplane and going hastily over to the office. He returned in a few minutes, carrying two plastic cups of coffee.

He handed one cup to Jacobson and took a sip from the other one. They were both tired. They were past eleven o'clock last night getting back from Haiti, and now they were going back to the Bahamas. Then they were going on to Port-Au-Prince. The two men stood in the fresh morning air, drinking the coffee and making small talk. Jacobson was concerned about the weather on the flight back last night.

"There were just a few scattered thunderstorms," George said. "Aw, nothing for you to worry about, Mr. Jacobson."

Now Jake wasn't the most comfortable person when it came to flying in a small airplane, and bad weather made him very nervous. He knew he had to go to the Bahamas, but he was tired; and he didn't relish the thought of flying again.

They stepped back out of the way as the mechanic brought the last box and slid it in the door. He first stepped up on the bottom step, looked into the airplane, paused, and turned around. "George, where do you want this one?" he asked.

"Oh hell, I don't know," George said, putting his empty hand up. "Put it in a seat and put a seatbelt around it."

The mechanic stood and looked at George, then cautiously turned and stepped up into the plane. He picked up the box and put it in the right rear seat, turned and walked back to the door, stepped down, and said, "It's all loaded. I've checked the oil, fuel, and the sumps are drained, and you're ready to go." The mechanic turned and walked away.

George said, "Thank you." The mechanic waved his right hand in recognition as he moved toward the hangar.

"It's a two hour flight. We need to be loaded and ready to go by seven-thirty. That will put us out of here by seven forty-five. Then we will arrive there before ten o'clock," said George.

Jacobson nodded and walked toward the office. He had started the morning with a cup of coffee. Now he was finishing his third cup. He had to hit the restroom before he boarded for a two- hour flight.

George taxied the little airplane out onto the runway, and after receiving clearance from the tower, eased the throttle forward, glancing down from time to time, scanning the engine gauges. Everything appeared normal. They broke ground. The gear was up, and they began a gradual climb out to the east. George made a few course changes, and then was cleared by air traffic control; they were on their way to Eleuthera.

It was a beautiful morning, but the sun was shining directly in George's face. He pulled the shaded visor down. Yes, that helped somewhat. As they reached their altitude, George trimmed the airplane, pulled the throttle back to cruise, and set the autopilot. He turned on the radar. Everything was clear for the next one hundred fifty miles. It looked like a nice, clear, smooth morning flight. George scanned the gauges. Everything appeared to be okay. George was cautious after many years of flying. What seemed to be great one minute, could turn to crap the next. Flying is what they say it is-hours and hours of boredom punctuated by moments of stark terror. "You should always be prepared for the unexpected," he said in a whisper to himself.

25 RETURN TO THE TRAP

Rob rolled over and looked at his watch. It was six o'clock in the morning. He answered the ringing phone. "It is now six o'clock," the recording said. Rob sat up on the side of the bed. This was the day they were going south to what? He didn't have a clue, only the word of a man he didn't trust. There was a gut-wrenching sickness. Hopefully, it would go away. To make plans was one thing. To carry them out was another. It took a special person, and Rob wasn't sure he had what it took. One thing was sure; he would have the answer to that question in the near future.

He picked up the phone and dialed Mike's room on the fourth floor. The phone rang several times before he heard Mike answer. There was a half grunt, then a weak "Hello".

"You need to get up." Rob said.

"Oh, okay," Mike said.

"Juan Pablo will be here by seven-thirty. We will be checking out," said Rob.

"I'm ready," said Mike. "I've had all of this vacation I can handle."

"Before you leave the room, call Anne and tell her we will be calling her in a few days. Don't go into detail," Rob added.

"Sure," said Mike. "I'll do it after I shower and find some aspirin. I've got a little man pounding in my head. I really want him to stop," he said with a slight sigh.

"Okay," said Rob. "Meet me here in the room when you've finished. We'll go get a hot breakfast; maybe the last one for sometime," Rob added with a nervous laugh. He felt somewhat like an inmate on death row. Maybe his last meal. Rob showered and packed his small, blue bag then set it on the floor by the door and sat and waited patiently for Mike.

Rob's thoughts drifted back home to his children, Annie, who was nine, and Robert, who was six. He had planned to take them fishing this week. They were always looking forward to the fishing trips out on the lake in the cool, early morning. Usually, there wasn't much fishing, or at least, they didn't catch anything. Little Rob was too busy playing in the water, and Annie, the serious one, always got upset and tried to make him behave. They were making memories with those trips and that's what life was all about. As soon as he returned home, he would make it up to them. Yes, he'd do that. He would bring them something special that would make them forget the disappointment of delaying the fishing trip.

There was a knock on the door. Rob opened the door without looking. He knew it was Mike.

They were finishing up with breakfast as Juan came over to their table. Juan spoke first. "A good morning," he said with his usual oriental bow.

Juan pulled the chair out gently and sat down quietly. "Would you like a cup of tea?" Rob asked.

"No, thank you," Juan replied. "I see you are nearly finished. I will excuse myself and go complete the arrangements for your stay. I will meet you in the lobby," he said as he stood up and quietly placed his chair correctly at the side of the table.

As Juan walked away, Mike looked up and spoke, "I'll bet there's not a thing that he hasn't got control over, or that is out of place in his world. This guy bothers me. Everything is so organized, so arranged," Mike continued with a slight shake of his head.

The men finished breakfast, picked up their bags, and went out into the lobby. Juan Pablo was standing and talking to Captain Mann. "It looks like we get to ride in a Mercedes," Rob said in a low voice as they approached the other two men.

"All of the arrangements are concluded," Juan Pablo said. "We can now go. Captain Mann was courteous enough to give us a ride to the airport."

"Good," Rob said as he grasped the captain's hand and they shook.

"Captain Mann will be accompanying us to the island to see that there are no problems with the airplane," Juan said.

"Good, nothing like being personally escorted by our own problem solver," Mike said sarcastically.

The four men made little conversation as they rode to the airport. Each man was deep in thought about the task ahead.

"What are we going to do about me?" Mike cleared his throat. "Remember, I don't have a visa."

"I'll take care of that," Captain Mann said with a smile.

"I thought maybe ya'll had forgotten," Mike said as he leaned back in the large, leather seat of the Mercedes.

"No, that is not a problem," Juan Pablo said.

Captain Mann drove the Mercedes around to the executive side of the airport. He parked in a space behind a large, white block building. The four men got out and went to the rear of the car. Captain Mann lifted the trunk lid and set their bags on the ground. The men picked up the bags and fell into step behind Captain Mann as he entered the building through a rear door.

The four moved along a shadowy, dim-lit corridor with several offices opening onto it. Near the end was a door to an office with a small, black shingle hanging out into the corridor with white lettering, customs. Mike looked at Rob; Rob held his hand out with the palm down and made a downward motion several times without saying anything. Mike understood. Calm down. Mann stepped into the office and closed the door behind him. Juan, Rob, and Mike were left standing outside in the corridor.

Through the glass window in the door, Rob could see two younger men sitting at their desks. Captain Mann was leaning over and talking to one of them. Rob knew they were being discussed as the young men looked around Mann and stared momentarily at him. One young man stood up and shook Captain Mann's hand and smiled. Captain Mann opened the door and came out of the offices and motioned for the three men to follow him. They went along the corridor to the end then turned left into a small waiting area where there were a few chairs and an old, worn couch. Seated on one end of the couch was a clean, neatly dressed, black man. "Gentlemen," announced Mann, "this is our pilot, Tony. He will take us to Eleuthera this morning."

"Good morning," Tony said with a smile as he rose to his feet. "At you service." Rob and Mike nodded. Juan shook his hand. "May I help you with your bags?" Tony asked.

"We don't have much," said Rob. "We'll carry it."

"That's great," Tony said with a slight British Bahamian accent.

Tony led them out to an old, faded brown and white Piper Aztec. One by one they climbed on board and stowed their bags under the seats. In no time, Tony was starting the engines and talking on the radio to the tower. There wasn't a lot of air traffic this early in Nassau, so Rob and Mike could hear what was being said between the tower and Tony as the conversation was carried over the speaker. Then Tony put on a headset, and the speaker was turned off. It was a beautiful day, a little gray with a big, orange sun shining through the morning haze as they departed on a runway to the northwest. After take-off, Tony slowly turned right to an easterly heading. The conversation was sparse. Occasionally, Tony talked on the radio, but the noise of the aircraft engines made it impossible to understand what he said.

Rob, ever the pilot, was curious at first but finally gave up and spent his time looking out the window at the blue-green water and all the islands nestled in the setting of the landscape. The islands were a beautiful place for a vacation if a person had time to relax and forget about everything else, but that wasn't their situation. A small feeling of anger swelled up inside as his fears were changing. He would like to see all the sob's get what was coming to them and the sooner, the better. Yes, he felt it all eventually came full circle, and it usually did if you had time to wait.

Mike was sitting in the right front seat. Rob was all the way in back. Juan and Captain Mann were sitting in the seats in between. Rob saw Mike, pointing, then he turned in his seat and faced the other three men sitting in the back, and with a big smile said, "looks like the old DC-3 is still parked where we left it." He pointed over the nose of the aircraft. Rob leaned over into the aisle of the small airplane, sitting on the front of his seat and glanced over the nose of the plane.

He could only see the small island at first, then he spotted it. There it was! He breathed a sigh of relief.

Captain Mann turned toward Rob and smiled. "I have taken care of everything. There are no problems," he said in his strong Bahamian accent.

Rob smiled back and nodded an okay. Tony entered a downwind approach to the airport, then turned base leg, and then final. He made a smooth landing, taxied the small Aztec up beside the large DC-3, and shut the engines down. Mike opened the door and crawled out first as Tony held the right front seat forward as Captain Mann stepped out onto the wing then to the ground, followed by Juan Pablo and then Rob. Mike stretched as Captain Mann and Juan walked past him and over to the two uniformed men standing out front of the small, faded white wood-frame customs office building.

"I don't have good memories of this damn place," said Mike. "I know we need to come over here to get the old airplane, but I don't like it," Mike said as he reached up on the wing of the Aztec and picked up the small bags, handing Rob his.

The two men started a slow walk over toward the DC-3. Rob paused then tossed his bag to Mike and said, "I think I'll go see what's going on with Juan Pablo and Mann. You go on and start a pre-flight inspection on the old bird."

Rob walked up the slight incline to the small faded wooden building. The door was open, so he stepped in rather reluctantly. Captain Mann and the two local officials were talking very softly. Juan Pablo was sitting across the room on a small wooden bench. This all looked much too familiar to Rob. There was the small customs office in the corner. Juan motioned for Rob to join him. Rob walked over and sat down. "Where do we go from here?" He said looking at him.

Juan sat for a minute, then answered. "Mr. Jacobson will be arriving very soon. He will explain all the details."

"Okay," said Rob as he stood up. We'll be down at the airplane getting it ready to fly. Oh, we only have about two hours of fuel, so we will need some; and it doesn't look like there is any here."

Juan nodded. It was apparent he didn't want to disturb the conversation between Mann and the local officials. There seemed to be some type of negotiations going on between the three.

Rob quietly walked back to the airplane. Mike had opened up the large cargo door and the small cockpit windows.

"It's beginning to get a little warm inside," Mike said. "I've checked the oil. We'll need about five gallons between the two engines and a little hydraulic fluid, not much, maybe two quarts. I drained the fuel tank sumps and checked for water. They were all okay."

"Good," said Rob.

"Also I switched on the batteries. They seem all right, but we won't know until we get ready to start the engines. I've done a visual check on the inside. I didn't do any operations check or anything. I didn't want to drain the batteries; we'll need them to start the engine," Mike continued.

"That's good," Rob said, "We'll wait until we've started the engines. Then we'll check out the electrical system." As they stood talking, Rob had his back to the west.

"Oh lovely," said Mike, "I think our host is arriving."

Rob turned as he heard the faint sound of the blue and white Navajo making its approach to land. "They're here," Rob said. "Now we should get some answers to all our questions, and I do hope they remembered our supplies."

Rob bent down and looked under the DC-3 toward the customs office to be sure no one was around. "Mike, we will have two life rafts. One is kind of special," Rob said.

"How special?" Mike asked.

"It has two fuel bladders and all the necessary hardware to hook them up," Rob answered.

"Hmmm, sounds real special, one to save our asses if we go down in the water and one to save us if we keep flying," said Mike.

26 Flying South

The remote silence of the distant island was for the second time that morning disturbed by the sound of a small airplane as it approached and landed. The pilot maneuvered the blue and white twin engine airplane alongside the Aztec and DC-3. The rear door sprang open and Jacobson took the small steps in one stride and stopped on the asphalt surface, stretched his tired shoulders, rolling them from side to side. Juan, with his deliberate stride, passed Mike and Rob without looking or speaking as they stood beneath the right wing of the DC-3, and he rushed to greet Jacobson. They met at the nose of the Navajo with a hand shake and few words. The meeting was finished. Both men turned and approached Rob and Mike as they now stood near the cargo door of the DC-3. "How are you men doing?" he asked with a big smile and thrust his strong hand out to Rob.

We're okay," Rob said as he shook Jacobson's hand.

Jacobson turned to Mike, "How are we doing this morning?" he asked, patting Mike on the arm with the other hand as they shook. "I have all the necessary flight charts you'll need, and I've brought over your supplies. I think it's time to go to work."

Rob and Mike stood without saying a word letting Jacobson do the talking.

"I need to go over to the office for a minute and talk to Mann. When I'm finished, we'll sit down and I'll explain all the details," Jacobson said. "The supplies are under the seats in the Navajo. Juan Pablo, help them unload," Jacobson said as he walked off.

As Jacobson strode off to the office, Mike said, "Nothing like being hired

147

help." Juan smiled as they walked over to the Navajo to begin unloading the supplies.

George removed the cargo tie down and handed the supplies to Juan, Mike, and Rob as they carried them over to the DC-3. "What about customs?" Mike asked.

"I think customs is doing their inspection in the office now," Rob said with a grin.

"I think I understand," Mike said as he lifted one of the life rafts on his shoulder and started over to the cargo door of the DC-3. Rob followed with the other life raft. David Harris did an excellent job of packing the special life raft. Rob couldn't tell the difference from the regular raft. David had stamped yesterday's date on the special raft as an inspection date. That was the only visible difference.

The three men opened the boxes and unpacked the supplies, storing them in the DC-3. Mike took a small stepladder from the rear compartment of the DC-3 and climbed up on the wing with a five-gallon container of engine oil. He serviced the left engine first and then the right. Rob was busy sorting and storing the food, water, and survival gear. A few minutes passed, and Jacobson returned with Mann.

"Gentlemen," Jacobson began, "I understand you need fuel." He said this as he and Mann climbed the small crew step into the DC-3.

"Yes, we do," Rob said without looking up from assembling a small electric lantern with a battery.

"Mann has called. There is another airport about thirty minutes flying time to the south. That's on our way," he continued. "They have all the fuel you'll need."

Rob sat without saying a word.

"Captain Mann will be leaving in a few minutes with Tony, returning to Nassau. If there is anything we need him to do, now is the time," Jacobson said, as he was standing in the middle of the cargo compartment of the DC-3, wiping his face with a small white handkerchief.

"Fuel is the only thing I can think of now," said Rob.

Mike finished servicing the engines and was standing in the door of the DC-3 with perspiration all over his face. "If you are taking orders, a cold beer would feel real good about now," he said.

Jacobson turned slowly and stared at Mike without saying anything. Mike stared back. "Well, maybe a big glass of ice water," he said.

Rob looked up at Mike, grinned, and shook his head. Rob was sitting on one of the other five-gallon oil cans. He slowly stood up.

Jacobson turned, and he and Captain Mann walked back to the cargo door of the airplane. "Mann, I guess you and Tony can go on back to Nassau. If I have any problems, I have your numbers," Jacobson said as they carefully climbed down from the airplane.

Jacobson and Mann spoke softly as they walked over to the brown and white Aztec where Tony was sitting on the wing with the door open, waiting for further instructions. Jacobson talked with Tony, then to Captain Mann. Tony bent over and crawled through the door and into the left seat. Captain Mann got into the right seat and held the door open with his hand. The small airplane had gotten hot, sitting in the sun. Tony started the engines, talked briefly on the radio, then taxied onto the runway. Mann closed the door as the small plane began its take-off roll.

Jacobson had stood watching as they departed. Now they had to have a very serious talk. It was time to give the other men all the details of their mission.

Jacobson turned back to the DC-3. He stood in the door watching as Juan walked up and handed him a small brown briefcase. Jacobson set the briefcase in the floor of the airplane by the door. He opened it and motioned for Rob and Mike to come over. Both men came over and squatted down in the door opening as Jacobson unfolded a large flying chart of the Caribbean. He then laid out two others charts to the side.

"This is the one you will need for now," Jacobson said. "I've had George help me lay out all the routes to Port-A-Prince, Haiti. That is where you will be going today. It's about two and one-half hours from here. With a fuel stop you need to add an extra hour. It's now eleven o'clock. You should be there no later than five o'clock if you leave in the next hour. Now," he said, pointing to the two other charts, lying to one side, "these will cover the area from Haiti to you destination. Hang on to them," he added. "George and I should be in Haiti by the time you arrive. If not, here is a name and phone number. It's a Colonel Chenier. He is the one in charge of the airport. Don't talk to anyone else. I must emphasize this. No one must know what we are doing, no one," Jacobson said, staring at Mike first, then at Rob.

Both men nodded that they understood.

"Now, how's your money holding out?" Jacobson asked, looking at Rob. "One thing to remember, in this part of the world, the greenback talks loud and clear. Always remember that."

"I have about twenty thousand dollars with me," Rob said.

"Good," Jacobson said. "Now are there any questions?" Jacobson asked in a stern voice. He paused. "Juan Pablo will be riding with you. He will know how to get me if there are any problems."

"I'd feel a lot better," Rob said with a pause, "if you would stick around until we make sure this thing is going to start. It has sat here for over four days, and we don't have a power cart. We'll have to rely on the battery to get us going."

"No problem," Jacobson said as he picked up his briefcase and walked away. Juan followed him over to the Navajo. They stood outside and talked briefly.

Juan returned. Mike and Rob were out front pulling the propeller blades through to make sure there wasn't a liquid lock on the old radial engines. Juan stood, patiently waiting, a few feet outside the cargo door. Both men finished and walked back toward him.

"Let's see what this thing will do," said Rob as they climbed up the steps into the cargo cabin.

Juan followed Mike up the steps. Mike got down on one knee and pulled the crew step into the cabin. He reached around and pulled the open half of the cargo door closed. He shook the handle to be sure that it was safely locked.

"Okay," said Mike, looking at Juan as the two men walked up the inclined cabin floor, "let's go see if we can help Rob make this thing fly."

Rob was going through the checklist. As Mike sat down, Rob turned on the boost pump.

"We've got fuel pressure," Rob said. "Now let's see if it will start."

Rob pressed the starter button, counted six blades, started priming, and then turned on the magneto switch. The left engine sputtered and puffed out some smoke then began to pick up speed. Rob pushed the mixture forward. The engine was running. He adjusted the throttle while checking the oil pressure. Everything looked good. Rob turned on the generator switch. He then repeated the process on the right engine. It started. Everything was going smoothly. Rob looked over at Mike. They stared at each other for a brief period. Rob picked up his headset and turned on the radio. He carefully finished the pre-taxi checklist. Mike put on his headset. Rob pushed the button for the intercom.

"That's that," he said. Mike nodded his head in approval as he picked up the chart Jacobson had given them then carefully unfolded it, showing their planned flight route. Running his fingers south along the chart, he picked out the airport Jacobson and Mann had said was cleared for them to stop and get fuel.

"I hope those sons of bitches know we are coming this time," Mike said over the noise of the engine of the Piper Navajo as George and Jacobson departed to the south.

"Me too," said Rob as he reached down and unlocked the tail wheel and released the brakes and began to taxi the old lumbering DC-3 out to the runway. "See anything?" Rob asked Mike as they were starting out onto the runway.

"No traffic," Mike answered. "Everything looks clear."

Rob taxied out and swung around on the end of the runway. He lined up the DC-3 and locked the tail wheel. He then set the brakes and began a run-up. Everything checked out okay. "Let's go," said Rob, looking over his shoulder at Juan, who was sitting in a small fabric jump seat behind the cockpit.

Rob pushed the throttles forward, and the old DC-3 shook. He released the brakes, and then he advanced the throttles slowly, watching the manifold pressure and the engine tachometer. The airplane began to gain speed, then lifted off the runway.

"Gear up," said Rob. There was a pause.

"Gear up and locked," Mike said.

Rob adjusted the throttles and began a slow climb.

"We're off," said Mike, speaking over the intercom to Rob. "This is the beginning of the beginning. Where it will end," he paused, "we will know soon enough.

27 One of Them

The flight was going smoothly. All the systems on the old airplane were performing as well as could be expected for a forty-five year old airplane. Rob looked closely at the chart, checking for landmarks. Most of the flight was over the water along the coastline of the island. The island had the shape of a crescent moon, and they were flying along a southeastern heading. That would put them over the airport in the next fifteen minutes if his calculations were correct.

As Rob was again checking the landmark on the chart, Mike came on the intercom. "There it is," he said.

Rob looked out over the nose of the airplane. There, a little off to the left was an airport with two small buildings and one larger one. Rob spoke on the radio, using the unicom frequency. He was given an airport advisory; the winds were from the south, so they would land from the north to the south. All the buildings were on the southwest side of the airport. Rob slowed the old DC-3. "Get the gear," he said to Mike as he turned the aircraft on a base leg.

"Gear down and locked," Mike answered.

Rob slowed the airplane down on the final approach then made a smooth landing. They taxied down to the south end of the runway. Rob reached and unlocked the tail wheel and then made a right turn into the parking ramp. They looked around for a fuel truck. A black man in blue work clothes came running out to meet the airplane.

Rob spoke," Mike, have Juan go and tell them we need fuel."

Mike nodded and took off his seatbelt and headset. He stepped over the console, motioning for Juan to follow. They descended down the inclined cargo cabin floor. Mike opened the door, pushing with his shoulder into the large cargo door, holding it open as the blast from the propeller tried to close it. Juan jumped down, disappeared, then returned shortly. "The only fuel they have is a pump over by the hangar," he said, pointing under the aircraft toward the large faded orange building.

"Okay," Mike said, "tell them we will taxi over there and get as close as we can."

Juan stepped back, and Mike released the door, which closed with a bang. He struggled back up the cabin to the cockpit, leaned over and explained to Rob. They both looked over toward the faded orange building. There it was- an old, faded blue gas pump with a hose reel attached to the side- one like you would see at some rural store back home.

Rob released the brakes and made a slight turn to his right. Cautiously he taxied the airplane up to the front of the pump, then made a turn to his left and swung the right wing out over the pump. "How's that for service?' he said, smiling at Mike, who was still standing in the cockpit door.

Rob shut the engines down, turned off all the switches, set the brakes. They scurried down to the back of the cabin. Mike swung open the door as Rob placed the crew steps in place. The two men stepped down on the pot-holed ramp. The black man came up and smiled. "What can I do for you?" he asked.

"We need fuel for starters," Rob said.

"I can take care of that," he answered.

"We don't have any Bahamian money. All I have is U.S. greenbacks. Will they take that?" Rob asked.

"I don't think that will be a problem, but the airport manager is inside. Talk to him," he said.

Rob and Mike sauntered cautiously toward the office area of the building. This was the terminal where all traffic either inbound or departing had to clear. They weren't sure of the procedure.

"I'm not real sure what we need to do here," Rob said. "I thought Jacobson and George were going to stop here and wait on us."

"You're saying Jacobson misled you," Mike said sarcastically. "I can't believe that. We don't know the procedure, but I am damn sure someone will explain it to us," Mike said shaking his head in disgust.

As they entered the terminal, Juan was talking to a well-groomed man. "This is Eiland Smith," he said. He is the airport manager and has agreed to help us with the fuel. This is Rob and Mike," Juan said, introducing the men.

"We only have U.S. money," Rob said. "Will that be a problem?"

Mr. Smith shook his head slightly. "Come into my office," he said.

The four men went with Smith into a corner office. "When the refueling is complete, don't pay the cashier. Come to me and I will handle everything," said Smith.

"Sounds good," said Rob.

"What about customs?" asked Mike. He knew he didn't have a visa, and it made him very nervous.

"The custom agents are in and out. They usually only appear at scheduled airline landings. Today they have a supervisor with them, and they've gone over to one of the men's homes to eat lunch. You should be refueled and out of here before they return." He paused. "Speaking of lunch, we have a small lunch counter where you can order something to eat," Smith said as he stood up from behind his desk. "If I can be of further assistance, let me know."

"Thank you," Rob said as they all shook hands and left the office.

They all filed out to the counter where the menu was printed on a billboard overhead.

"I think I'll play it safe," said Mike. "Give me two hamburgers and a large coke."

"I'll have the same," said Rob.

Juan ordered a conch chowder plate and tea. The three men sat on a picnic table outside and were finishing eating when the fuel attendant walked up and said, "I have the airplane serviced with fuel."

Rob crossed his legs under the table and took out several hundred-dollar bills from his boot.

"How much fuel have we burned?" asked Rob, looking at Mike who was finishing his last bite of hamburger.

Mike finished chewing and thought three and one-half hour's maximum flying time and four hundred fifty to five hundred gallons. Rob walked into Smith's office. "How much do we owe you?" asked Rob.

"The fuel is twelve hundred dollars U.S.," Smith said. "Mr. Mann said this was a special favor and that you will show your appreciation."

"Sounds reasonable," said Rob. He counted out twelve hundred dollars. Then he counted five hundred to one side. "How's that?" he asked. Before the words were out of his mouth, he had the answer. Smith quickly picked up the five hundred dollars and pushed it in his pocket with a smile.

Rob turned, then walked out of the office and across the terminal building. Mike and Juan were standing outside the main entrance.

"I think we have a problem," said Mike.

"What's that?" asked Rob.

Mike pointed to the DC-3. There were three men in white uniform walking around, looking. One walked over to the door of the airplane and stood looking inside.

"Let's go see what is going on," said Rob. Rob, Mike, and Juan walked reluctantly over to the airplane. The man standing in the door was apparently the senior member of the trio.

"Who's flying this airplane?" he asked in a slurred British influenced Bahamian accent.

"I am," answered Rob.

"May I see your papers?" he asked.

"What papers?" asked Rob. "You will have to be more specific."

"For starters, your entrance visa," he said.

Rob opened up his wallet and handed a folded piece of paper to the man. He looked briefly at it and said, "Your flight plans?"

"We're only passing through on our way to Haiti," Rob said.

"Yes, yes, I know. I've heard this before. I want to look inside," he said.

"Sure," said Rob. "We don't have anything to hide."

The senior member climbed up the crew steps and walked around in the cabin. It was apparent there wasn't anything in the airplane. Rob began to sense the problem. This was another shakedown. He remembered Jacobson's words, "greenbacks." They'll speak loud and clear.

"Would you like to see the cockpit?" Rob asked.

The two men walked up to the front of the airplane. Rob had four hundred-dollar bills in one of his pockets. He pulled them out and stuffed them in the official's shirt pocket.

"Now is there a problem?" he asked.

"No, no," the official said. "Everything is in order as far as I can tell," he said, walking back down the slanted floor of the cabin.

"Good," said Rob. "Are we free to go?"

"Oh, I don't make that decision," said the senior official. "Those two men are in charge over here," he said, pointing to the two men standing on the ground.

"Come on, Mike, Juan," Rob said. "Let's go."

One of the younger men said, "Not so fast. We need to talk about this,"

"Mike, go start the engine," Rob said.

"If you start this airplane engine," the customs man said, "without our clearing it, you will be under arrest."

"Here," Rob said, handing the last three hundred dollars he had in his other pocket to the man doing the talking.

It embarrassed the official to be seen by the others taking a bribe. "You are under arrest," he said, "for bribing an official."

"Do you have a gun?" Rob asked. The official backed up. Rob pulled the door closed and locked it. "Let's go," he said as he entered the cockpit. Mike was starting the second engine. "These people are sons of bitches," said Rob. "They all want a piece of you."

"What are we going to do?" asked Mike over the roar of the engines.

"We are getting out of here if they don't stop us," Rob said.

Rob climbed into the pilot's seat. The officials from customs were all now standing in front of the terminal building, watching. Rob strapped his seat belt on and released the brakes. He eased the throttles forward and began to taxi. It was evident the government officials were making no attempt to stop the DC-3. Rob and Mike scanned the skies around the airport. There was no traffic. Rob taxied onto the runway, locked the tail wheel, and departed to the north. When they broke ground, Rob breathed a sigh of relief. "Well, I am in it now," he thought. "I've bribed my first public official. I now have become one of them."

28 Gateway to Hell

Mike folded out the aeronautical chart. "The next step-the gateway to hell," he said. "I've heard it called that," Mike said, talking to Rob over the intercom. "All the South American drug runners coming into the U.S. pass between Haiti and Cuba. That is, the ones who don't have permission from Castro to fly over Cuba. It seems the leadership of Cuba is sometimes involved in the import and export business," he added. "The more I think about it," Mike continued, "we are dealing with the sorry end of humanity."

Rob looked at Mike, "I gave you a choice," he said.

"I know," said Mike, "It's this feeling I'm getting. Everywhere we go there's a problem. These people seem to thrive on conflict and confrontation. Yeah, I guess if you grow up living in it, you always smell like it."

Rob shook his head. Mike definitely wasn't happy. He'd give him a little time to cool down. "Get us a heading," he said to Mike, pointing to the chart.

Mike unfolded the chart on his knee until he found Port-au-Prince. He picked up a small plastic compass and placed it on the chart and made a mark. "Turn to a compass heading of 164 degrees. That puts us close enough," Mike said. "There are some land masses along the way we can use as landmarks to make the necessary course adjustments if we need to," Mike added.

Rob turned the DC-3 again to the southeasterly heading. Mike folded the chart and placed it on the console in front of the throttle quadrant.

They had climbed to sixty-five hundred feet and leveled off. The visibility was excellent; they could see for miles. Off to the southwest were a few scattered clouds. Everything was looking good as Rob trimmed up the airplane, set the autopilot, and relaxed. There was another hour and a half of sitting, scanning gauges, monitoring fuel systems, and boredom. They passed several small islands and then one larger island off to the west.

Rob made a slight course correction a few degrees to the east. Mike pointed off to the right on the horizon. There was the top of some low mountains in the haze. Rob checked his watch. They were now an hour and forty-five minutes into the flight. "That must be Haiti," he said. The landmass was getting larger as time passed. Then there was Cuba off to the west. They were getting close. Rob reached for the chart and looked up the radio frequency for Port-au-Prince.

He set the frequency on the radio and listened as a commercial airliner departed Port-au-Prince. Rob waited until he had the airport in sight, then he called the tower and received landing instructions.

Everything went smoothly. They landed and were given instructions. As they were taxiing across the airport to the far side away from the terminal, they saw a gray, streaked DC-3 and a shiny Loadstar 500. "Now that Loadstar 500 is what we need," said Mike. "That thing's fast."

"I'll take the DC-3," Rob answered. "It's more reliable."

Mike laughed. As they taxied past the two airplanes, Rob noticed an old brown pickup truck parked on the grass. A man in faded blue work clothes walked out onto the ramp. As they approached, he signaled them to park alongside the other DC-3. Rob taxied the plane into the spot, turning and lining the nose up with the other planes, pulled the mixtures and shut the engines down, then shut off all the other necessary switches and the fuel selectors. He then did a quick glance of the checklist to make sure he had not forgotten anything. Last, he set the brakes.

"Let's put some control locks on," said Rob, looking at Mike. "I'm not sure what the weather is like around here," he continued. Rob remembered another trip a few years ago when he almost lost a plane to the winds of an unexpected tropical storm.

"I'll get them out," said Mike as he climbed from the right seat and scurried down the cargo cabin. He went past the cargo door and to a small door in the aft of the cabin and pulled out the control locks. Juan had already opened the cargo door. The man in the blue work clothes was talking to him as Mike stepped down.

"Sir, could I please help you with that?" he said with a strong French influenced accent.

"Sure," said Mike as he walked around to the rear of the airplane. The man followed. Mike carefully slid the locks on the controls' surfaces as the man held them in place.

"I have been instructed to give you a ride over to the terminal," he said. "We have parked you over here away from the busy terminal for your privacy," he continued.

Mike walked back to the side of the airplane. He stood on the ground as Rob handed down their bags and then stepped down. Rob took the crew steps and slid them inside, closed the cargo door, and locked it.

"What about security?" said Rob, looking at the man as they were approaching the truck.

"Oh, no problem," he said. "We have a military force on the airport at all times. They will protect your airplane. No problem," he repeated with a big smile as he loaded all the bags into the back of the truck.

Juan said, "I'll ride back here."

Rob crawled in the middle. "I've got shot-gun," said Mike with a smile. Rob sat a little sideways as the manual shift lever from the old Ford came up through the floor beside his legs.

The man started up the truck and, shimmying and shaking, they were off. Rob looked at Mike. He knew what Rob was thinking. Back home this thing would be considered a piece of junk. It would have gone to the crusher years earlier. One thing was for sure, maybe it rattled and squeaked, but it beat walking, he thought.

The man drove around the end of the runway across in front of the terminal building and over to the hangar. There were several smaller twin engine airplanes parked on the ramp. Rob and Mike both looked for the blue and white Piper Navajo. It wasn't there. They looked at each other and rolled their eyes.

"He said he would be here," Mike said. They pulled up and parked beside the large hangar.

The driver got out and said, "Follow me." He walked over and opened a side door, then held it while Mike and Rob retrieved their bags from the rear of the pickup truck. Juan stepped down and waited as Rob and Mike followed, then walked along behind them.

As they stepped into the dark hangar, it took a moment for their eyes to adjust. In the back there was a light coming from what appeared to be a small office of some type. They followed the man as he walked around the equipment and down a small aisle toward the office. The man knocked on a metal door and waited. There was a muffled voice, "Come in." The man in blue opened the door, then stood to one side and motioned for them to go in. Rob stepped in cautiously, looking around.

Sitting behind a brown, painted wooden desk was a very neat, light-skinned black man in a starched tan military uniform. As he stood up and extended his hand, he introduced himself, "I am Colonel Chenier."

Rob stepped forward. "Rob," he said as they shook.

"And this is Mike and Juan Pablo," as both men leaned forward and shook his hand.

"Yes, it is very nice to meet you. Please be seated," said Colonel Chenier.

"Your friend, Mr. Jacobson, arrived earlier. He asked me to make you comfortable and tell you he will be returning soon."

"Good," said Rob. He didn't like Jacobson at all, but one thing was for sure, he seemed to exert much more influence over these people than they did. Yes, to some extent, Rob's comfort zone expanded with Jacobson around.

"Colonel, what about a restroom?" Mike asked with a smile.

"Behind me," the Colonel said, pointing with his left hand to a door in the rear of the room. "Down the corridor, second door to the left."

"Thanks," Mike said as he stood up and stepped briskly across the room.

"How was your flight?" the Colonel asked.

"Excellent," Rob answered. "No problem."

"Good, we parked you across the airport for you own privacy. No one coming or going from the airport will have access to your airplane except through this office. We can provide transportation for you over there, and the tower has full view of the airplane at all times. That is to your advantage."

And to yours thought Rob. I can't get to my own airplane without your permission. All a part of Jacobson's plan. One by one the three men took turns using the restroom as they waited for Jacobson to return.

"I see you made it without any problems," Jacobson said, reaching out and shaking hands with both Rob and Mike as he entered the office.

"I wouldn't say without any problems, but I'd say we didn't have any we couldn't handle," Rob answered.

Jacobson looked a little puzzled, but he knew this was not the time or place to discuss the matter. As Jacobson entered the office, he had two strange men tagging behind him. Even though they did not speak, it was obvious they were American by their dress and mannerisms. "Let's go. We've got you a place to stay, and I'm sure all of you could use a break."

Without speaking, Rob, Mike, and Juan picked up their bags. They thanked the Colonel for his courtesy as they were leaving and followed Jacobson down the corridor past the restroom and out a back door into a sandy parking lot. There sat a 1968 rusted blue Dodge van. An old black man was sitting patiently, waiting at the wheel with the sliding side door open.

As they stepped from the hangar, one of Jacobson's men held the door open. Jacobson, as usual, led the procession, setting the mood with his normal "take charge" behavior. He walked up to the side of the van and stated, "This is our transportation to the hotel."

Boarding first, Mike and Juan squeezed into the back. Rob sat on the middle seat behind the driver. Jacobson's two men slid in beside him, and Jacobson sat up front with the driver.

On the drive away from the airport, the road gradually climbed up the terrain and became rough and bumpy with continuous areas of potholes. Most of the local people were walking. A few rode on bicycles, but there were virtually no cars, only one older large truck and a few small pickups. It was a poor country and signs of poverty marked all aspects of life.

Along the drive, there was an occasional big house with large stone or cement fences protected by armed guards (the haves versus the have nots). Jacobson had chosen a great place to work, where a little money went a long way.

At a snail's pace they wound around and up the terrain to where the city sat on the side of a large hill or small mountain, depending on one's perspective. It was larger than Rob had expected. As they entered the heart of the city, the houses of cardboard and driftwood dwindled, giving way to a better section. It was cleaner and had the appearance of an older business district. There was a hotel tucked in between several other buildings. The van pulled up to the front, and the men all unloaded. As they entered through the front door, Jacobson walked on ahead and returned with the keys. These are real keys Rob thought, unlike the cards they had in the Bahamas. The hotel staff was very anxious to help them carry their bags and asked the group to follow them as they proceeded around to the elevators where only one, it appeared, was working. The other three elevators had small chains hanging across the front doors. This would limit access to their rooms on the second floor. One of the staff, a man in a little white vest, spoke, "Kind sirs, would some of you consider waiting until the elevator has returned? I feel all of us on the elevator at the same time could possibly cause an overload."

"No problem" said Mike as he backed up.

"I'll wait, too," said Juan Pablo.

One of Jacobson's men stepped back with Mike and Juan.

"All right," Jacobson ordered, "Let's go." He stepped in and stood to one side, giving the three hotel staff members room. The old elevator rumbled and shook as it strained and made its way up to the second floor. Apparently the elevator was used only on special occasions. The staff normally used the stairs. The elevator stopped with a shudder, and Rob felt relief. Next time he would take the stairs. That was his first and last ride on the out-dated contraption.

The three men followed the hotel staff members down the hall to the first stop. "Mr. Jacobson, this is your room," he said as he opened the door.

"We have three other rooms. They all have accommodations for two persons," the second attendant said.

"Anywhere's good. That big guy downstairs will be sharing with me," Rob said as they entered the room to his right.

"Yes sir," the man said, putting Rob's bags on the floor and walking out the door, pulling it closed behind him as he left. Rob looked around. It was

163

like going back in time. It was old, very old, but it was clean. That was the most important thing, Rob thought. Jacobson had made the arrangements; they were out of the area of the city that usually accommodated international travelers. Jacobson was taking no chances. He wanted no one to observe this odd gathering. So here they were in an old hotel off the beaten path.

Rob turned around as the door opened and in stepped Mike. "No phone, no TV," he said as he walked around the room. "But we do have indoor plumbing," he said as he opened the door to the bathroom. If we bundled up all this crap and took it back to the states, we'd be one hell of an antique dealer."

Rob was sitting on the side of the bed. Mike sat down on the other bed, facing Rob. "This keeps getting better and better," Mike said with a smile.

"Yes, I know," said Rob. "They seem to stay one step ahead of us."

"One thing is for sure, this is no Caribbean playground," said Mike.

"The military basically runs things down here. They are giving the civilian authorities a hard time, something about who gets what from the merchants who use this as a stopping off place on the way from South America to the States. Whoever controls the government, determines who gets what, and I'm sure they can be bought. We're here as an example of that. Jacobson picked this little place so no one would ask questions, and with the exchange of greenbacks, he got the service of the local military. Jacobson is ex-military, and he likes doing business with military people," Rob continued.

There was a knock on the door. Mike stood up and went to open it. There was Juan. "Mr. Mike, how are you? Is everything comfortable?" he asked.

"Oh, sure," Mike replied. "Come on in."

"No, thank you," Juan said. "Mr. Jacobson would like Mr. Rob to join him in his room."

Rob stood up, and Mike held the door. Rob said, "I'll be back in a few minutes," and he walked down the hall with Juan Pablo.

Juan stopped at Jacobson's door and knocked. Jacobson opened the door. "Come in," he said.

Rob walked in without speaking. "Juan Pablo told me you had a small problem getting fuel," Jacobson said.

"No problem getting fuel," said Rob. "We had a problem getting away after we got the fuel. It seems everyone in this part of the country wants to be on someone else's payroll."

"Yes," said Jacobson. "The drug trade has corrupted everyone. They thought because you were flying an old DC-3, you were on you way south to get a load; and they wanted to be paid off to look the other way. You did the right thing. Now that's in the past," Jacobson continued.

"I thought you were going to be at that airport when we stopped," Rob said.

"No," said Jacobson, "we miscommunicated. We had enough fuel to come on without stopping. Now let's get to the business at hand. I've made arrangements with the local government to allow us free access to and from the airport here at Port-au-Prince. Colonel Chenier will be at your disposal day or night. Juan knows how to communicate with him. Now do you have those charts I gave you back in the Bahamas?"

"No, they are in the room," Rob said.

"Juan, go get the charts," Jacobson said as Juan Pablo was getting up to go to Rob's room.

"Tell Mike they are in the side of my bag," Rob said as Juan hurried out the door.

"The cargo is stored close by the airport," Jacobson said. "What I need is an exact load we can carry on each flight."

"That depends on how far we have to go, and the amount of fuel we will need," Rob answered.

Juan returned with the charts. Jacobson took both charts, looked at one, then the other. He unfolded them and laid one over the edge of the other making them into one large chart covering the Caribbean. "Here is the destination," he said, pointing to Central America. "I will give you the exact coordinates later," Jacobson said. "We'll load the airplane tomorrow morning. Do either of you speak Spanish?" Jacobson asked. Rob shook his head no. "Then Juan will go as your interpreter. He will have a radio to communicate with the ground crew there. When you arrive, everything will be taken care of-the fuel, people to unload the airplane— all that is pre-arranged. Now, I've made arrangements for all of us to dine together in a private dining room. For safety reasons, I expect everyone to stay in the hotel. This is a very volatile situation down here. The civilian authorities and the military are at odds, and we don't want to get in the middle. We've had our food flown into the country, so the hotel will cook something you can enjoy eating."

"I'll have Juan come by later and get your orders for dinner," Jacobson said with a big smile as he stood up, signaling the conclusion of the meeting. "Can you think of anything we've left out? Oh, one other thing, first thing tomorrow morning we'll go for a little ride with Colonel Chenier. He will show us an alternate airport, just in case, you never know what could happen with an unstable government down here."

Rob reached over and folded up the charts. He was uneasy, but he hoped it didn't show. "We'll see you at dinner," said Rob, walking past Juan as he left the room.

Rob eased down the hall to his and Mike's room. He knocked on the door. Mike answered. "What did old Jacobson have to say?" he asked as Rob stepped in the room.

"Not much, we're going to Honduras, a few miles inland from the coast. He'll give us the exact coordinates tomorrow." Rob bent over the bed and spread the two charts out and overlapped them. "This is our route," he said, pointing to the chart, "from here, then over Jamaica, and on over to Honduras, about four to five hours, I'd say, if we have good flying," Rob added.

"So we are going tomorrow," Mike said.

"Yes," Rob said.

"Good, I don't think I can take much of this place," Mike said. "I'm going to take a shower, bath, or something." Mike straightened up, placing his hand at the small of his back with a groan. It had become stiff from leaning over and looking at the charts on the bed. He could do almost anything with the back fusion, a result of a helicopter crash in Nam, but the injury from time to time caused discomfort and pain. He then turned, picked up his bag, and walked into the bathroom, looking for relief in the form of a long, hot shower.

Rob sat for a short time looking at the charts and making some measurements of distance on their route. He then folded the charts and placed them in his bag, turned and looked out the window. There wasn't much to see-some old buildings, and in the distance, an array of small houses on the dim, shadowy landscape. The streets in front of the hotel were very quiet; occasionally a vehicle would pass. Most of the cars and trucks were old and showed decades of use.

Three light taps on the door. Rob recognized the knock and opened it. There stood Juan Pablo with a notepad and a pen. "I'm taking orders for dinner," he said.

"Good," said Rob. "I'll order for both of us. Do we have steak on the menus?" Rob asked.

"Yes," Juan answered.

"Then two steaks with the trimmings. That will take care of us," Rob said.

Juan nodded as he wrote on the pad. "This will be ready in about forty-five minutes. We will eat downstairs in a special dining room. Ask at the desk. They will direct you," he said as he walked away.

Rob stepped back into the room. Mike came out of the bathroom clad only in a towel. "You can have the bathroom," he said with a mischievous smile. "Don't expect too much hot water. It's warm, that's all."

"Okay," said Rob as he closed the bathroom door. Mike was right. Rob finished a tepid shower and toweled off. He got back into his old, soiled jeans.

As Rob emerged from the bathroom, Mike asked, "What are we going to do about our laundry? I'm getting down to repeating, that is, picking out the least dirty ones and wearing them again."

"Remind me when we go to dinner. I'll ask Jacobson. He seems to be managing everything," Rob said as he finished dressing and pulled on his boots. Mike was already dressed.

"Let's go eat," said Mike. "My stomach thinks dat my throat's been cut."

They walked down the stairs and into the lobby. As they entered the lobby, one of the hotel employees was standing at the desk by the main door. He quietly approached and asked, "Are you gentlemen looking for the dining room?"

Rob nodded yes. He pointed to the left to two large carved wooden double doors. He quietly stepped across in front of them and opened one of the doors and held it there as Mike and Rob thanked him and made their entrance. There sat Jacobson and two of his men along with the Colonel from the airport. Jacobson was doing some influence peddling or at least trying as he sat face to face with the Colonel.

He stood up, motioning with his right hand, "Come on over and join us." Rob and Mike maneuvered slowly around the empty chairs and tables over to where the men were on one side of the dining room.

It was an old, but at one time, a semi-elegant place. Now the wear, tear, and time had taken their toll. The tile floors were cracked, and the chair bottoms were worn. Rob noticed Mike was carefully selecting a chair to sit in. The chair bottoms were woven from some type of cane, maybe bamboo. Mike shuffled the chairs around until he was satisfied with one and sat down. Rob glanced at his chair. It appeared to be all right, but the chair beside it was coming apart. Now he understood why Juan had said they had food flown in. At least, there was a small comfort in knowing the food would be safe to eat.

Jacobson spoke as they sat down, "This is Bill and Lewis. I don't think you've been introduced. You have met the Colonel. Bill, Lewis, this is Rob and Mike." All the men ventured slightly from their chairs and exchanged handshakes.

As the introductions were finished, Juan Pablo came from the kitchen where he had been supervising the cooking. "The meals will be served in a few minutes," he said. He stood for a few moments, then returned to the kitchen.

All the men sat making small talk. Mostly, Rob and Mike listened to Jacobson and the Colonel talk. A short time passed, and two of the hotel staff accompanied by Juan Pablo emerged from the kitchen, pushing a cart. Juan stood and directed as the two staff members served the food. There wasn't much talking as everyone ate. The hotel staff members stayed and served the coffee and dessert. The group was mostly coffee drinkers, and only one or two accepted the dessert. As they all finished, the Colonel was the first to leave. Jacobson came over to Rob and Mike after he departed and sat down.

"Gentlemen, we are ready," he said, giving his-as Mike would put it-pep talk. "The Colonel is taking care of all the arrangements on this end, and we have everything covered on the other end. You will leave tomorrow after lunch. You'll need to arrive there no later than two hours before dark. If everything works as we expect, you will rest there and come back the following morning, then return again the next day," he continued.

"How many trips are we talking about?" Mike asked.

"Oh, it depends. How much can you carry per load?" Jacobson answered with a question.

Rob answered, "I'll let you know in the morning. Our gross weight for each single engine is twenty-seven thousand five hundred pounds. I feel we could safely add another two thousand pounds. That will be the max. I'll have to figure everything including fuel. Then we will add cargo until we reach the maximum," Rob added.

"Sounds good," said Jacobson as he stood up. "Juan will get you up around six-thirty. We'll get an early start." He turned and walked away with Bill and Lewis following at his heels.

Rob and Mike sat and drank their coffee, relaxing for a few minutes. When they got this thing rolling, they would be expected to fly everyday. Both men knew that would be a real strain on them and on the DC-3.

"Maybe, we should take two trips, then a day off," said Rob, looking at Mike.

"I think you're right," said Mike. "We'll need time to inspect and do minor repairs to the airplane. That would be only four days," he said, "that, is if three trips will get it done."

"You are thinking the same thing I am," said Rob. "How do they know how many trips when they don't know how much we can carry? Sounds like a little bull's going on," Rob continued. "Jacobson wants to know how much we can carry. I want to know how much he wants flown, the total cargo. We need to have a talk in the morning, first thing."

29 Contra Cargo

Rob and Mike were up and dressed and going over the weight figures of the DC-3 when the knock came at their door. Mike opened it. There stood Juan Pablo and Jacobson.

"I see you are all up and ready," said Jacobson. "Let's go have some coffee and talk about the cargo load."

" Okay, sounds good to me," said Mike as he turned and looked at Rob who was closing up his notepad. Rob nodded.

Disregarding the antiquated elevator, they took the stairs down to the private dining room. There, an electric coffeepot was set up, and coffee was ready. They all filed by and filled one of the white porcelain cups. Jacobson was first, as usual. He walked over and sat at the same tables as the night before.

Rob followed, and as he was sitting down, Jacobson said, "Now, have you got a figure I can give to Bill and Lewis? They will need to know how much to bring in the first load."

"What is our total amount?" Rob asked.

Jacobson sat quietly and didn't answer. He was thinking. "It's much more than we can deliver in three loads, I'm sure," he said. "There is a certain urgency on part of the cargo that needs delivering immediately. That's your concern. If we have room or should I say, weight wise could accommodate more cargo, we will take more. No, there is no way we will deliver all the cargo by air these first three trips, but it's a start. You can carry a total of fifteen thousand pounds in these three trips," he stated. "That's our goal."

"Four thousand five hundred to four thousand seven hundred, that's what we have come up with as a safe load and not overlooking our single engine operating range. We can stretch it a little. We'll handle five thousand but no more," said Rob.

"Good, good," said Jacobson. "After breakfast, we have a meeting with Colonel Chenier, that is, you and me," he looked at Rob across the top of his coffee cup between sips. "He has an alternate airstrip he thinks you should know about."

"Never can be too safe," said Rob. He was wondering what this was all about, this alternate airstrip.

"Juan," Jacobson said, motioning for him with his right hand. Juan was sitting across at another table with Mike, Bill, and Lewis. He came over. "Go to the desk and tell them we will need the van and a driver in forty-five minutes," Jacobson said, pointing toward the front desk.

You'll be leaving early this afternoon and returning tomorrow morning," Jacobson said. "We will begin loading the airplane around nine o'clock. Let's get everything ready," Jacobson continued. "We don't want any problems." Rob nodded his head okay without saying anything. "You will have these rooms until we have finished our mission so leave all your bags and personal items in there. Don't take them with you. This is a private venture," Jacobson added. "You are working for me as a contractor. What I am trying to say is, you are on your own. If you get the job done, I'll pay you. If you don't perform, then well, you understand? I have people I have to answer to."

It all sounds a little like a threat. That was Jacobson's way, strong leadership with a subtle threat. Rob somehow understood. He knew the type of people Jacobson was accustomed to dealing with, and that was the only thing they understood.

Rob and Mike were back in the room, sitting on the side of the bed, talking about the flight when Juan came to the open door. "Mr. Rob, Mr. Mike, the van has arrived. We need to go."

"Thanks," said Rob. Rob picked up a small case from the bed. It held his notepad and the charts. He and Mike followed Juan out the door, pulling it closed behind them.

As they approached the elevator, Mike said, stopping only briefly, "I think I'd rather walk down the stairs."

"Okay," said Juan, following Mike and Rob as they took the stairs down to the lobby where Jacobson, Bill, and Lewis were waiting.

After a routine twenty-minute drive, the blue van rolled into the parking lot behind the large hangar. There was a group of soldiers sitting on the ground beside a large, green military truck. They were watching or waiting for something or someone.

As they unloaded from the van, Jacobson began barking orders. "Juan, you and Mike go over to the airplane and get it ready to fly." Colonel Chenier's man will help you. Bill, you and Lewis know what to do. There's your crew," he said, pointing to the soldiers sprawled on the ground beside the green military truck.

"Rob, Mike, and Juan, come with me," he said, looking at them. With a lurch, he was off down the hall to the Colonel's office. Jacobson tapped on the glass panel in the door leading into the room. The Colonel looked up and motioned for them to come in. The mechanic was sitting quietly in a chair across on the far side of the office.

As they entered, he stood up. The mechanic spoke to the Colonel in a Creole dialect. The Colonel nodded and spoke, "Juan, you and Mike go with him. He will take you over to the plane."

Juan and Mike followed the man through the front door of the office and out into the hangar.

"Gentlemen, be seated," the Colonel said. "I will be through in a minute. He was looking over what appeared to be receipts. Jacobson and Rob sat down. Jacobson was anxious; he was ready to go. The old chair squeaked as he squirmed from side to side. The Colonel looked up. He knew Jacobson wasn't accustomed to having to wait on anyone. The Colonel shuffled a few pieces of paper and placed them in a file, then slid them into an open drawer, stood up and said, "How are you this morning? I am sorry for the delay. We can now go." He stepped across and opened the door leading into the corridor, standing aside as Jacobson and Rob filed past, then he pulled the door closed and shook it to be sure it was locked.

Rob and Jacobson followed the Colonel out the back of the hangar and over to a fairly new Landrover. The Colonel unlocked the door as he and Jacobson got into the front. Rob crawled in the backseat and tried to relax.

The Colonel drove out the back way from the airport and down a small narrow road along the coast to the north. They traveled for approximately forty minutes. As they drove along the coast, the Colonel explained to Rob, "This is an old dirt airstrip once used by smugglers." He said, "It is just across the small inlet," then pointed to an open area across the bay.

The road wound around the bay and into an open field. On one end was the sea; on the other were some small trees. Along one side was the bay, and on the other, there were small scrub bushes and rocks. The airstrip sloped upwards and stopped at the base of a steep hill. Only one way in and one way out. It could be used in an emergency and only in daylight Rob thought.

The Colonel drove slowly from one end to the other. Rob guessed it was at least a half-mile long. "You can never be too safe," the Colonel said. "In the event we have problems at the Port-au-Prince airport, we will use this one."

Jacobson had sat in silence. He let the Colonel and Rob discuss everything. Then he spoke. "What do you think?" he said as he turned in his seat and faced Rob.

"I've seen worse," replied Rob.

"This side of the island is quiet. No one will be here or using this if we need it," the Colonel said, assuring both men. "We've had some problems, but only minor ones," he said. "Our government is in transition, and sometimes, there are misunderstandings."

Rob was thinking. Returning here after going to Honduras? He hoped there wasn't going to be a problem, but he sat quietly on the return trip to the airport. Following the small road around the rear of the airport, they drove into the back entrance. Rounding a sharp corner, they entered into the parking lot behind the hangar. There were Bill, Lewis, and the military men, all sitting in the shade of the green military truck.

As the Colonel drove up, Bill and Lewis approached the Landrover as Colonel Chenier got out, along with Jacobson and Rob. They all met about halfway between the two vehicles in the parking lot.

Jacobson spoke first. "Well, men, how is it going?"

"We filled the list and checked the weight. We have approximately five thousand pounds," Bill said, handing the list back to Jacobson.

"Colonel, let's take the cargo over and load the airplane," Jacobson said, turning and talking directly to Colonel Chenier.

The Colonel spoke briefly to the soldiers in a Creole dialect and walked back over to his Landrover. "I'll need to alert the tower," he said. "Please wait." He walked into the back of the hangar. The men could see him talking on the phone on the wall just inside the door. He spoke briefly, then returned to the Landrover. The Colonel, Rob, Jacobson, and Bill all rode together, and Lewis rode in the military truck. They drove around the end of the runway and along the fence and down a parallel road about a half-mile to the area where the DC-3 was parked. The military truck followed some distance behind.

As they approached, Rob saw Mike, Juan and the Colonel's man sitting under the wing of the airplane. Mike and Juan Pablo stood up as they approached. When they stopped, the Colonel got out of the Landrover and said something to the mechanic, who was still sitting on the ground. He slowly got up and walked over to the Colonel. They talked briefly, then the mechanic walked over to his old pickup truck and got in and drove away toward the hangar.

Rob walked over to Mike and Juan Pablo. The Colonel and Jacobson went to the rear of the military truck as it pulled up. "Rob, we are fueled and ready to go," Mike said.

"All right," Rob said. "You and Juan make sure they load the cargo forward and as near the center of the wings as possible. I don't want a tail heavy load."

Mike nodded and walked over to the cargo door. The front half of the door was open. Mike climbed up the steps and opened the rear half. Juan stood on the ground and pushed the door back against the fuselage of the airplane. The driver cautiously backed the truck up to the door opening. Mike stood to one side and motioned for the driver to back slowly. When he was within a foot, Mike gave a hand signal to stop. The truck came to a quick stop. He stood and looked at the gray boxes. Some had handles; some did not. Slowly, one by one, the soldiers unloaded the truck and loaded the cargo onto the airplane. When Mike was satisfied everything was in its place, he and Juan began placing cargo straps over the boxes and ratcheting them down securely as the truck pulled away.

Rob stuck his head in the door. "How are we doing?" he asked.

"Piece of cake," said Mike. "We're ready to go." It was now a little past ten. They should be leaving around one o'clock. That would put them there two hours before dark.

"Close it up and lock it down," Jacobson said, sticking his head in the door. "We'll go get something to eat. Juan, you better stay here," Jacobson said. "Take this," he said, handing Juan a small hand-held radio, "only use it in an emergency. We don't want anyone to know we have them." He showed Juan another small one he had in his pocket. "We'll bring you something to eat." Juan nodded okay.

Rob and Mike closed the cargo doors and locked them. "Are you going to be okay?" Mike said, looking at Juan Pablo. Juan nodded and smiled, not saying anything.

They rode with the Colonel back to the hangar. When they arrived back, the man in the blue van was sitting in the parking lot. Bill and Lewis were with him. They were eating sandwiches and drinking colas that were delivered from the hotel. "Now, that's service," said Mike as they walked over to the van. It was all laid out neatly, wrapped sandwiches and a cooler with soft drinks.

Mike reached and picked up two sandwiches and a cola. He leaned up against the van.

"Well, men, this is not much, but it beats nothing," Jacobson said as he reached for a sandwich and soda. "Colonel, will you join us?" he said, looking at the Colonel, who was walking toward his Landrover.

"I appreciate the offer," he said, "but my wife is expecting me for lunch. I will return around twelve-thirty and make sure everything goes well for your departure." He smiled and got in the Landrover and drove away.

Sitting in the shade of the van, they made small talk as time passed slowly. Mike drank another cola, but Rob was ready to go. It was now twelve o'clock. They needed to go over to the airplane in the next fifteen minutes and look it over. Oh hell, Mike had looked it over. He was too anxious. He needed to calm down. Jacobson, Bill, and Lewis were standing at the front of the van, talking. Rob was sure they were making plans for the following day.

"It's twelve fifteen," said Mike, looking at his watch. "If we are going to be in the air by one o'clock, we need to be on the move."

Rob nodded. "Grab two of those sandwiches and a cola for Juan."

"How are we getting to the airplane?" Mike asked.

Rob turned and looked at Jacobson. "How are we getting over to the airplane?" he asked.

"He can take us," Jacobson said, looking at the driver of the van. "We need to go to our airplane," he said, looking at the driver. The driver looked a little puzzled. Jacobson pointed across the runway to the airplane on the other side. The driver gestured with his hands and nodded okay. They all loaded up in the van, and the driver was very slow and careful as he drove along the road over to the DC-3.

As Rob, Mike, and Jacobson got out, Bill and Lewis stayed in the van. Mike trotted over and opened the cargo door. Rob was busy draining the sumps and nervously doing a few last minute visual checks beneath the DC-3. Although everything looked good, flying out over water for the next four to five hours was an uncomfortable feeling. Mike was inside the airplane, and Juan was standing just outside the doors talking to Jacobson. They were discussing the hand-held radio Jacobson had given him. Rob moved closer and heard Jacobson telling Juan that the people in Honduras had the same radios and were on the same frequency. Juan shook his head in approval as Jacobson explained every detail to him.

Rob climbed up the crew steps and into the cabin. Juan followed. It was now twelve-forty. Closing the cargo doors, he checked to be assured the latch was securely fastened. Then they climbed up and over the boxes to the cockpit. Mike was already in the right seat, waiting.

"Well, it's now or —," Rob paused.

Mike answered, "Or what? We don't have a choice."

30 Next Stop – Honduras

They started the engines, did all the checks, turned on the radio, and called the tower for taxiing instructions. The tower instructed them to taxi to the north where they would depart on the runway to the south. Releasing the brakes and unlocking the tail wheel, Rob maneuvered the airplane along the taxiway to the north end. All went well as Rob did the run-up. They were given clearance to the runway. They taxied on and lined up, locked the tail wheel, set the flaps, and began the take-off roll. The old DC-3 was loaded. It rolled a considerable distance before the tail came up and then the plane began to lift off in a shallow climb.

"Gear up," said Rob. Mike got the landing gear up and locked. Rob pulled back on the throttles. They did a slow turn to the southwest then a laboring climb up to sixty-five hundred feet, leveled off, allowing the airplane to gain speed, then pulled the throttles back to cruise and set the mixtures. They were on course, heading for Honduras. Setting the autopilot was a little difficult, but after several tries, it stayed coupled. Rob scanned the gauges. Everything seemed good. They were on their way.

They had flown about an hour. Rob felt the plane yaw and the nose swung to the north. He checked the compass. They were going due west. Oh, hell, the autopilot was malfunctioning. He took the controls and turned it off. Now how long had they drifted off course? Not more than ten minutes. He had checked the heading before when Mike had gone back to the cargo bay for a break. Rob looked at the ocean waves. The swells were strong, and by the direction of the waves, the wind was from the south. That was something he needed to take into consideration. In flight planning, they were told there was only light wind at this altitude. If they were on course, he could be seeing Jamaica at any moment. Their plotted course would take them over the southern coast and near Kingston, the capital.

Rob unfolded the chart and looked at it from time to time as he was waiting for Mike to return. Meanwhile, he had to be careful and monitor the exact compass heading. A degree or two off could have caused them to miss their destination by forty to fifty miles, and he needed to possibly make a course correction. When Mike returned, Rob pointed and motioned for him to put his headset on.

"Mike, we've lost our autopilot," Rob said.

"What happened?" Mike said.

"Don't know; it started to drift to the right. We'll have to check our position and heading. The next checkpoint will be Jamaica. Use the DME or Distance Measuring Equipment to find a radio station and get a fix on our position," said Rob.

Mike looked the chart over and dialed in a local frequency. He tuned the DME. "We're seventy-five miles out," he said.

"We should be seeing land at anytime. We'll need to make our course corrections before we have flown over Jamaica. After that, we'll be over the open water for two and one half-hours or more. This is the last navigational aid," Rob said.

Mike nodded as hazy, low mountains of Jamaica appeared on the horizon. They were about twenty miles north of the plotted course. Rob again made a correction.

"By the waves cutting across our nose, I'd say we've got a pretty strong cross wind," Mike said.

Rob nodded his head in agreement as the plane rumbled along the southwest coast of Jamaica and again was out into the open water. Rob had compensated for the crosswinds. Now all they had to do was hold this heading. Dead reckoning was the term- old basic flying. I didn't do much of that back in the States he thought. With all the navigational aids there, all you do is put in the frequency and the way points; everything else is done for you. This was different. Their lives would depend on them getting to the right place and at the right time.

The old bird's performance was excellent. Rob didn't have a problem with the mechanics of the old airplane. It was the old, outdated electronics they were relying on to navigate that brought a swell of tension rolling his stomach into a knot. For the first few hours of their flight, they had avoided bad weather, but now to the northwest dark, blue-gray tropical storm clouds rolled into billowing swells and for short periods of time, faded into soft swirls of powder blue with each lightning flash. The driving rain came in surges as the worn wiper blades streaked the pelting beads from the windshield. Struggling laboriously with the flight controls, the two men tried to maintain a southwesterly heading. They looked out over the nose of the airplane, straining their eyes to see through the rain and gray haze as a vague coastline gradually became visible on the horizon. With only forty-five minutes of daylight left to find a small, dirt airstrip in the green shadowy maze of the Central American jungle, they would have to land the old airplane and drop off their sensitive cargo.

As they passed through the storm, the sun was rapidly setting behind the low mountains as they began to descend. According to the coordinates on the chart, their destination was a seldom-used, small dirt airstrip about twenty miles inland from the coast near the Nicaraguan border. Rob Marshall looked at his old Air Force watch; he nervously scanned all the gauges, especially the fuel; less than one hour was an optimistic estimate, and then they would run out. He pulled a handkerchief from his back pocket and wiped perspiration from his face and brow. Everything seemed okay, but they are sitting on enough arms and explosives to start World War III. They needed to be very careful. Looking out over the nose of the airplane, he watched as the coastline came up slowly. Mike, sitting in the co-pilot seat, took his left hand and carefully adjusted the old, worn headset so the mic would be close to his lips. He took a deep breath, let it out slowly, reached out and carefully pressed the intercom button and spoke to Rob, "You're the boss, but don't you think it's time we talk to the folks at the airstrip and let them know we're here?"

Rob Marshall looked at Mike and nodded yes as he leaned forward and gazed out the windshield as the coastline passed under the airplane. Mike turned in his seat and waved his left arm motioning for Juan Pablo. Juan stood up after sitting for an extended period of time and stretched his lean, five-foot, nine-inch body, took the few steps to the door of the cockpit. Juan Pablo was not wearing a headset so he leaned over close so he could hear what Mike had to say. Mike pointed to the hand-held radio Juan Pablo had in his front shirt pocket and to the ground. Juan Pablo understood. He took the FM radio out, clicked it on, and began to speak into it in Spanish, using a pre-assigned code. A few long seconds passed; there was no reply from the ground; again he called using the assigned code, still no answer! He leaned forward into the cockpit and in a loud voice said, "No one answers."

With less than one hour of fuel, getting dark, and the steamy Honduran jungle coming up in front of them was a foreboding sight. "The airstrip should be here somewhere," Mike said, looking at Rob. "Let's stay a little to the north until we are sure where we are. We don't want to cross the border into Nicaragua and tangle with one of those Russian helicopter gunships. We won't need that airstrip if we do."

Another fifteen minutes went by and still no radio communication from the ground, and still no sign of an airstrip. "Looks like it's going to be a long walk home," Mike joked. He and Rob chuckled nervously as they looked at each other.

There off in the distance was what appeared to be a small brown patch of cleared ground in the middle of the trees and grass. "It could be an airstrip," Juan said. Rob banked the airplane in a slow turn to the south. As they came nearer, the surface appeared to be relatively flat; it could be used for a landing strip if it was all they could find. Rob pulled back on the throttles and slowed the old DC-3 to around ninety-five knots. Slowly the plane began losing altitude, descending into the rapidly approaching twilight and dark jungle. When they were down to about five hundred feet above the ground, Rob added power and leveled off.

Rob looked at Mike. "We're running out of fuel. I don't think we have a choice."

"Let's do it," Mike said with an uncomfortable grin.

Rob flew the old plane down the north side of the field at about three hundred feet above the ground. The shadows were now gone; it was getting dark "This looks more like a plowed field than an airstrip," he said. "It's now or never. We don't have much of a choice with this cargo we're carrying. If we're at the wrong place, they'll probably just shoot us, no questions asked."

To give them better visibility, they circled the plane out to the west and landed to the east so the light from the setting sun was to their backs.

Five hours of flight was culminating in a tense moment of landing in God knows where. Slow it down, slow it down. Now hold it off until the last minute, then bump. Rob felt the main wheels touch down, and then the tail wheel settled to the surface. His technique was right out of a textbook. All the years of flying as a crop-duster, with many landings for every flying hour, had given him the experience to land under any conditions.

They taxied up to the end of the field and then turned around, paused for a minute, then shut the engines down with only twenty minutes of fuel remaining.

Juan went to the back and opened the door. Mike and Rob sat for a short time looking at each other. "Yeah, if we are in the wrong place, they will take us out into that jungle and shoot us, and we'll become another mysterious disappearance for our friends and families to talk about. You know this dirt airstrip in the middle of nowhere isn't exactly a designated port of entry for foreigners coming into Honduras, and we are, by all definitions, foreigners to this country," Mike said with a stoic face and a deep sigh.

Unfastening his seatbelt, Mike, a tall, dark-haired man over six feet, stood up, turned, and leaned over forward, stepped to the door of the cargo compartment, and paused for a moment. "Rob, are you coming?" he questioned, looking back over his shoulder as if he was someone going into the unknown, who for damn sure, wanted some company.

"Yeah, I guess so." Rob in his forty years of rugged living had faced many challenges but could not remember ever letting himself get into such a predicament as this. He had been in scrapes before but never backed into a corner, and he was in a corner of the world he knew very little about.

Mike stuck his head out and looked around. Juan Pablo Ming was out walking around, speaking in Spanish into his hand-held radio; there still was no response to his pleas.

The outline of the jungle was an ominous, gray haze, hiding who knows what dangers. There was only one road, a very narrow seldom used path to the south. It disappeared around a curve into the bushes and tall grass.

Juan started walking toward Rob and Mike as they exited the aircraft, then everyone stopped and listened at the same time. There was a faint noise coming from down the road, and it was coming toward them. They stood in silence as the rustling in the grass became louder.

In the dark shadows, the hazy outline of a horse and rider appeared. The rider was about two hundred feet away when he saw the large airplane and stopped. No one moved at first as the man on the horse sat motionless. Juan Pablo lifted his empty hand in a slight wave. The stranger made no moves as Juan cautiously walked toward him. The rider appeared to be unarmed, but it was hard to tell in the limited light and shadows. Juan walked to within approximately fifty feet of him; the man spoke in a few words that sounded like Spanish to Rob and Mike. Staring at the aircraft and the men for a brief moment, he turned and rode off.

Juan Pablo walked hurriedly back toward Rob and Mike. "What did he say?" Rob asked excitedly.

"I'm not sure," Juan Pablo answered, "something about going to get someone."

"We could be in deep trouble if we're not at the right place, and our contacts are somewhere else waiting for us," Rob said, looking at Mike and Juan Pablo. "From the beginning, they told us that we are on our own. No emergency telephone to call 911 from here."

"What now?' Mike asked Rob.

Rob thought for a minute. "Okay," he said. "Let's do this. Juan Pablo, you be the lookout. Take a flashlight and go over to the other side of that road. If you hear something, signal us with three flashes." Juan turned and trotted across to the road.

They stood quietly and listened. Off in the distance they could hear the faint sounds of engines coming toward them.

Without pausing, each turned on his flashlight and ran toward the tail of the airplane and off into the grass. Out about fifty steps from the airplane was a thick clump of green and brown bushes. They hurried around behind the bushes, turned off their lights and waited.

The engine noises were now much closer. Rob could feel his heart pounding in his throat.

Juan Pablo had backed into the vegetation beside the road and squatted down. The clanking and whining of the engines came closer, and the talking stopped. The vehicles were now getting very close. They were only a few feet from where Juan Pablo was hiding in the tall grass. The procession had now slowed to a snail's pace. As they rounded the curve of the road and came out into the open field, they turned off all their lights. Everything was dead silence except for the low whine of the engine's idling and some low faint talk in Spanish. Suddenly, the talking became much louder; then they heard Juan Pablo calling out their names. He was holding his light up high and flashing it on and off.

"Senor Rob, Senor Mike!" Juan Pablo was now calling in his strong Latin accent. "It's okay." Now all the men were talking out loud and laughing. Rob and Mike walked cautiously around the bushes and out of the tall grass and into the open field. The vehicle began moving forward toward the airplane.

Rob approached the lead vehicle, a four-wheel drive truck. Juan Pablo was walking along beside as it stopped and someone got out.

Juan Pablo spoke first, "Senor Rob, this is Colonel Santini. He was awaiting our arrival."

The Colonel put his hand out and in very bad English said, "Good to meet you, my friend."

"What about fuel?" was Rob's first question as Juan Pablo interpreted. That was their first priority. They needed to get out of this place.

"No problem," the Colonel answered.

Caberallos, the man from Miami, returned and looked the cargo over, gave his approval, and the unloading began with Juan Pablo supervising and Rob looking on to make sure that the aircraft was not damaged in any way.

The original plans were to leave around three a.m. That would put them back at the island between seven and eight a.m. They were advised not to be back before daylight because of all the drug runners and illegal traffic flying in the Caribbean at night. This could pose a particularly hazardous condition, and to explain their presence at night would be very difficult. Timing was stressed.

Everything had gone relatively smoothly except for the surprise packages-five large canvas bags Rob knew were used to transport cocaine- that Caberallos and the Colonel had loaded onto the aircraft after the gray boxes were unloaded. They could not refuse to take the cargo. That wasn't a logical option. Sitting in a foreign country in the middle of a hell-hole jungle with empty pockets except for a Swiss Army knife left them defenseless.

After things had become somewhat quiet, the peace and tranquility had been interrupted by the Contras' announcement that a Russian helicopter gunship, flown by experienced Cuban pilots, was on its way to seek out and destroy them and their DC-3. Narrowly escaping into the night, they were fired on with rockets from the pursuing helicopter. Now out over the gulf, they were safe from the helicopter. Their planned schedule was now off by several hours.

Now the reality of the present grasped Rob when he realized they were out in the ocean in the dark, nervous, tired, and hungry, and on their way back to Haiti with- what appeared to be-drugs. None of this was what they had expected when they had agreed to do the flying for Jacobson.

Mike called on the intercom, "Rob, Rob, Juan Pablo has talked to some-one on the ground."

"I think they got our message," Juan said.

"Let's hope so. We will know in a few hours," Rob said. He tried to relax. They were on their way back. The goods were delivered.

It wasn't a grand slam, but they had made the first run. Rob had to remind himself that this was only the first inning. Maybe the inning wasn't over. It wouldn't be over until they got safely back to Haiti.

The flight was long, and as they passed along the sparsely lit coast of Jamaica, Rob knew they were going to make it back. They were only an hour away from completing the first mission.

Now the time was coming. He would soon know if there was anything in those bags that was illegal. Deep down he knew but didn't want to admit to being a part of something as rotten as hauling drugs. They were doing some-thing Jacobson assured them they wouldn't have to do. Mike had said very little on the return trip. Rob knew how he felt.

Rob changed the frequency on the radio. The needle was moving back and forth; there it was, a faint signal from Haiti. Coming back wasn't as bad as going. All he had to do was find Jamaica, and then Haiti was only a short hop along the way. Rob could see the faint lights of Haiti. Holding his watch up to the instrument lights, he could see it was one-thirty. With a good tail wind, the flight back had taken only four hours. They'd be on the ground in fifteen minutes. His stomach began to knot up as he selected the radio frequency for Haiti, picked up the mic, took a deep breath, then called, "Haiti Tower, this is Douglas one niner-niner eight, over." There was no reply. Rob called again. "Haiti Tower, this in one niner-niner eight, over." Still no reply. There was the rotating beacon on the airport, but no one was in the tower. That could be good, and that could be bad. If they landed and no one noticed, that would be good. If they landed and the military came over, that would be bad. Rob circled to the north and landed to the south. He felt relieved when the wheels touched down. He turned off his landing lights and using the small taxi lights, he maneuvered down the taxiway to the spot where they were originally parked. As they taxied in and started to swing the airplane around, there they were- the Colonel, his mechanic, Bill, and Lewis- all standing beside the old brown truck. Off in the back was the Colonel's Landrover with Jacobson sitting in front with his arm out the window. Rob breathed a sigh of relief. They had received the message. Rob pulled the airplane on around and lined it up with the other airplanes, set the brakes, turned off the radio, and pulled the mixture. Then he sat there looking at Mike.

"Okay, Mike, we can't do a thing about it now, but we'll get our chance, so be calm." Mike was sitting and not speaking. Rob knew he was highly pissed, and there was a rage going on inside.

Juan had the cargo door open, and the men were carrying the bags down the cabin and loading them in the truck. Jacobson was standing in the cabin with his hands on his hips. "Sounds like you had a little excitement," he said.

"Going to a ballgame, going fishing, there's excitement. Being chased by a damn helicopter gunship trying to shoot you down, that's frightening! And no damn amount of money in the world is worth dying for," Mike said.

Jacobson didn't say anything. He knew Mike was pissed, and now wasn't the time to try to reason with him, so Jacobson turned and walked down the step and to the ground. Mike followed with Rob behind. Rob pulled up the steps and tossed them inside the airplane. He closed and locked the door. All the others except Jacobson and the Colonel had driven away, taking the cargo with them in the brown truck.

"We'll give you a ride to the hotel," Jacobson said as Rob turned and finished locking the cargo door. "I know you have got to be exhausted," he said.

Rob spoke, "It wasn't exactly what we expected."

"I know," said Jacobson. "Someone tipped them off about the mission. It won't happen again."

They all rode along in silence back to the hotel. Mike and Rob climbed up the stairs following Jacobson. For a moment, Rob thought he noticed a weakness in Jacobson. He seemed to be concerned about their welfare. No, he thought, the bastard's worried that we won't finish up and get his ass out of a crunch, but maybe, just maybe, he was concerned for their well being. They passed Jacobson as he was unlocking his door.

"See you in the morning," he said. Neither Mike nor Rob acknowledged he had spoken.

They walked on down the hall, and Rob took the key out of his pocket and unlocked the door and went in. He and Mike kicked off their boots and flopped down on the beds. They were relaxed for the first time in about eighteen hours. Too exhausted to undress, the men went to asleep in their clothes.

Later, Rob awoke to a slight sound, rolled up on one elbow, looked over, and saw Mike still asleep. He started to lie back down when there it was again. Someone was knocking at the door. Rob swung his feet over the side of the bed and sat up and rubbed his face. He was having a difficult time waking up. He heard the knock again. He stood up and walked over to the door and opened it. Juan stood poised and asked, "May I come in?"

"Sure," said Rob. Mike was waking up as he entered the room. Mike sat up on the side of the bed as Rob walked into the bathroom and washed his face. Juan Pablo stood in the bathroom door.

"We checked the weather this morning. That tropical storm that was off the coast of South America is now moving along the coast of Central America. It looks like we will be delayed one, maybe two days before we will go back to Honduras," he said.

"Hell, that sounds great to me," Mike said. "I'm not looking forward to the next trip at all. Tell Jacobson we want our money like we agreed," Mike said. "We've earned it, every damn penny."

"Yes, Mike," said Juan Pablo. "I am sure Mr. Jacobson will take care of that and will do it today."

"Good," said Mike, "I need a shower and some food."

"The shower, you must do," said Juan. "I have taken care of the food. It's ready when you are."

"Good," said Mike, stumbling toward the bathroom nearly tripping on Rob who was back from the bathroom, sitting on the side of the bed.

"Juan, we'll need to go to the airplane sometime this morning. There are a few things we need to check on. One is the autopilot. Oh, yeah, check and see if the Colonel's man knows anything about electronics," said Rob.

"I'll do that," Juan said as he turned and walked out of the room, pulling the door closed behind him.

Maybe, just maybe, this was a God sent gift. They could now get the fuel bladder installed on the airplane. Rob needed a plan, one that would let Mike and him work alone on the airplane. They'd need about two hours to do the installation.

Mike came out of the bathroom with his hair wet from showering and a toothbrush in his mouth. "It's yours," he said looking at Rob. As Rob stood up, Mike said, "I need my laundry done."

"Don't tell me, tell Juan Pablo," Rob said, walking into the bathroom. "I don't do laundry."

Rob and Mike ambled slowly down the stairs and across the lobby to the open door of the dining room. Over in their favorite corner sat Jacobson, Bill, and Lewis. "Good morning," said Jacobson as Rob and Mike walked over and sat at a table next to them.

"It looks like we got a little break," said Jacobson. "There's a storm moving along the coast of Central America," he continued.

"Yeah, Juan said something about that," Rob said. "I was about half asleep when he told me. I didn't get any details."

"It should move on across today or tomorrow, then we will be ready to continue our flying. Juan reminded me about the matter of the wire transfer. I'll take care of it today," Jacobson said, looking at Mike.

Mike looked up over his coffee cup that a waitress had just poured.

"Good," Mike said. "That's what keeps us going."

Rob was quiet; he was doing some serious thinking and a little scheming. This was probably the only chance they would have to get the fuel bladders installed, and maybe they'd have time to get the other cargo door, the one with the removable jump door inside. He had a plan. All he needed was to put it in motion.

31 THE DAMAGE WAS DONE

In the old, musty foreboding dining hall, the only things the server had not cleared from the table were the near empty coffee cups the men were drinking from. Mike and Rob sat somewhat alone at the far end of a long table as Jacobson and his men, Bill and Lewis, huddled together at the other end in a subdued but serious conversation.

Rob took the last sip of coffee from the white porcelain cup, set it abruptly on the wood table, turned toward the muffled voices of the trio, and spoke with an elevated but controlled voice. "Mr. Jacobson, we need to go over to the airplane and make some needed repairs," he said.

Jacobson sucked in his breath slowly, then the conversation abruptly ended. Shifting in his chair, he turned toward the two men at the other end of the table and asked with an irritated voice and an intense stare, "What's your problem?"

"The autopilot is malfunctioning," Rob replied.

"Will that ground the airplane?" Jacobson asked.

"No, we can fly it manually."

"Then that's not a problem," said Jacobson, "but I'll have Juan arrange some transportation, and he can go and help you."

"Okay," said Rob. "We'll be up in the room." He and Mike climbed the worn stairs to the room. As they walked in, Rob went into the bathroom and pulled the toilet seat down and then turned on the water in the shower and the sink. Motioning to Mike, he spoke softly, just above a whisper, "We need to get that fuel system installed, and we need the cargo door changed.

I didn't say anything to you, but Jim had a cargo door with a jump door inside that will come out in flight. I think we need it if we are going to get away from these bastards. We will probably need to throw those bags of crap they're putting on the airplane overboard in flight, and the only way is with that door installed. What we need is an accident. The door that is on the DC-3 now needs to be damaged, and we can't do it. Jacobson would be very suspicious if we had anything to do with it. No, we need someone else to accidentally damage the door. Then we'll be in the clear."

Mike sat for a minute, thinking. "I can arrange that," he said.

Rob turned the water off, and the two men walked into the bedroom. Rob sat down on the bedside. Mike lay down and began to plan, "I need some string," he said. Something small, like fishing line, so keep your eyes open."

Rob didn't know why, but he knew Mike. He could be very creative.

Juan knocked on the facing of the open door. "Come in," Mike said.

"Thank you," he said. "The van is waiting to take us to the airplane."

"I'm ready," Mike said as he sat up and swung his feet off the side of the bed then reached and put his cap on. Rob stood up and picked up his small case with the pad and charts. He didn't want to leave it in the room for everyone's eyes. They went downstairs and out to the street and boarded the van.

I see we have a new driver," said Mike, looking at the Colonel's mechanic.

"Yes," Juan said, " he will help us today. We will be using the van and the mechanic. Mr. Jacobson said to utilize his services on the airplane if there are any repairs needed."

Oh great, thought Rob. All we need is a spectator while we install the fuel bladders. He needed a plan to get Juan and the mechanic away from the airplane for at least two hours.

They bumped slowly along the road, through the back gate of the airport, around the building, and over to the airplane. Rob and Mike were the first ones out. Rob unlocked the cargo door and opened the front section and fastened it against the side of the airplane with a small spring catch then pulled it away from the catch. It would not take much for the door to come unfastened. He looked at Mike.

"That's what I'm talking about," Mike said with a smile. Rob understood. All Mike needed was a small piece of line tied to the door and a slight tug. Then the door would swing free. It would appear to have happened on its own.

"We don't have string," Rob said. Mike patted his shirt pocket. Rob knew Mike was prepared. He somehow, somewhere, had found a length of string.

"Where do we start?" Mike asked Rob as Juan and the mechanic walked up from parking the van over away from the plane.

"We need those five gallon cans filled with engine oil. Let Juan and the mechanic do that first," Rob said, as he placed the small crew steps in the door and climbed up into the cabin and handed the two cans to Mike. He took the cans and handed them to Juan Pablo.

"Go see if the Colonel will get these refilled with the same weight oil as was originally in here," Mike said to him, pointing to the writing on the side of the cans.

"All right," Juan said as he turned and motioned for the mechanic to follow him over to the van. They drove away.

"We need to get busy," said Rob. "We can take all the screws and fasteners out of the front floor panel while they are getting the oil. Maybe a little hydraulic fluid in the bottom of the airplane, and we'll have a good reason to pull the floor panel up, looking for a leak."

"I think you have a devious mind, Rob Marshall," Mike said with a smile as he reached for a quart of hydraulic fluid, walked down the cabin, and went out the door.

As he walked around to the bottom of the main fuselage, he poured the fluid on a rag and placed it beneath the area of the cabin between the wings. He cupped his hands over the rag and squeezed the fluid, causing it to run down the bottom of the airplane.

"Oh, an internal leak," he said with a smile. He then poured a small amount on the ground to make it appear to have leaked for some time. He squeezed the rag over the area and picked up the hydraulic can. He walked back to the cargo door. "Mr. Marshall," he said, "you need to look at this. I think we have a hydraulic leak. It's coming from the bottom of the airplane," he said grinning.

"We'll need to pull up the floors and see where it is coming from," Rob said with a smile. "We can't be flying with something that dangerous. You better get the tool box out of the back storage compartment."

Rob and Mike were busy removing the floor panels when Juan Pablo and the mechanic returned.

Juan walked up and stuck his head in the door. "Mr. Mike, where do you want this oil?" he asked. "We have only one five-gallon can. They are getting us another thirty gallons from the supplier. It will be here this afternoon," Juan continued.

"No problem," Mike answered. "It looks like we won't be going anywhere until we get this hydraulic leak repaired."

"You have a problem?" Juan asked.

"Yes, a leak in the hydraulic system, probably a line in the cabin floor. We are pulling up the floor panels now."

"Is there anything we can do to help?" he asked.

"No," said Rob. "We should know something in a few minutes. Then we need you to help find the parts to repair the hydraulic system."

The mechanic walked up and asked in a very strong dialect what the problem was. Juan explained. "These DC-3's are very old. They leak everywhere," the mechanic said. Mike nodded in agreement as he removed the screws from the floor.

Rob and Mike removed all the fasteners and took the floor panels up. Mike had his back to Juan Pablo and the mechanic, who were standing, looking in the door. He took the small can of hydraulic fluid and poured some on the hydraulic lines running along side of the cross structures of the cabin. He then slid the can back up to the fence around the hydraulic system. "We'll need some large wrenches to check the torque on these fittings," Mike said, looking at Rob. The mechanic and Juan came up into the cabin and over to where Mike and Rob were looking at the hydraulic lines.

Rob pointed to the large lines. "We need wrenches to fit those," he said. The mechanic nodded. "I can get them," he said.

"Okay," said Rob. "We will wait here. You and Juan Pablo go, and we will be checking all the other lines under here."

Rob followed them to the door and watched as Juan Pablo and the mechanic drove away. Quickly, he stepped into the aft compartment and picked up the life raft with the fuel bladders then spread it on the floor. Mike walked up as Rob unfastened the flap, opened the cover, pulled the contents out, and rolled them out on the floor. There were two small bladder fuel cells and quick-coupling attachments. Rob pulled out the diagrams enclosed. There were all the instructions, how and where to make the connections. All they needed now was all the plumbing and the layout to install it. Rob removed the hoses and electrical wiring, rolled the package up, and put it back in the bag. They took all the plumbing and lines to the front of the cabin and placed them along the compartment under the floor. Rob ran the electrical lines along the wall and down the side of the fuselage and under the floor. It was all very simple and quick. In ten minutes, they had everything but the fuel bladders in place. All they needed was to make the electrical connections and connect the plumbing to the main tank.

Juan Pablo and the mechanic returned. Mike took the large adjustable wrench and appeared to tighten the lines. "That's it," he said. "The large line was loose," he said as he stood up and handed the wrench back to the mechanic. "We'll run the engines and check the lines later. I'm sure we repaired it," he said, looking at Rob and winking.

"We need the oil," Rob said. "That five gallons will only service one engine. Juan, go with him when he returns the tools and see if they have delivered the oil."

"Yes," he said. "I will get us something for lunch also," Juan said, patting his stomach.

"Sounds like a good idea," Mike said. "I always eat when it is offered; you never know."

Rob watched as the van drove away. Rapidly opening the bag containing the fuel bladders, he removed them along with a roll of tape. On his hands and knees, he moved up to the front of the airplane and began taping all the ribs in the compartment below the floor so the sharp edges would not chafe the fuel bladder. Being very careful, he placed the fuel bladders on each side, connected the fuel line, and put the floor panel back in place. Working hurriedly, they fastened the panel with the screws and then cleaned up the area. The electrical pump was on the left side under the insulation. All they needed was to make a small hole in the side panel and loosen the central panel and connect the fuel line, then make the electrical connections according to the chart; and they would be in business.

As Rob was cleaning up, he noticed Mike was back by the cargo door, doing something.

"All we need is to make two connections, one electrical and the other a fuel line, and we will have our extended fuel, about two hundred fifty to three hundred gallons," said Rob.

Juan and the mechanic returned with the small oil drum. "Where do you want this?" Juan Pablo asked, looking at Rob.

"We'll set it here in the cabin," said Mike.

"It is in the rear of the van," Juan said.

"Okay," Mike said, "back up to the door, and we'll unload it directly into the cabin. That way it will be locked up until we need it."

Juan nodded and walked over to the van where the driver was sitting behind the wheel awaiting instructions. He pointed to the airplane, and the driver nodded. Putting the van in reverse, he slowly started backing toward the cargo door. Juan walked alongside the van, directing the driver. When they were only a few feet away, Mike moved his right foot where a small line was looped to the toe of his boot and the other end was attached to the door. When Mike tugged, the door suddenly swung around. His timing was excellent. The van's rear door was open, and it caught the corner of the cargo door, folding the door with a large crease. Mike threw up his hands, "Stop, stop," he shouted.

Juan, standing on the far side, was pounding on the van. The mechanic stopped abruptly, but the damage was done. The cargo door was severely damaged. As the van pulled forward, Mike jumped down on the ground and with one firm tug, removed the string attached to the door, allowing it to drop from sight. Juan walked around the van and stood looking with a fixed gaze at the crunched door. The driver had now left the van and was standing at the rear. "Well, men," said Mike, "looks like we'll need a door before we do any more flying."

"What's going on?" said Rob as he stepped to the opening of the cargo door.

"We've had a little mishap," said Mike. "The wind blew the door open as they were backing up to unload the oil."

Rob stood looking, trying to look really pissed off. He really wanted to congratulate Mike. Rob stepped down and pushed the door into the closed position. It was useless; the outside bottom half was severely creased, and to repair it would take days. "We need a new door," Rob said. "I think Jim at Superior Air Parts back in Miami has one. Go tell Jacobson to call and see if he does and have him send it down tonight. We'll put it on tomorrow morning, and that way, we can stay on schedule."

Juan stood for a minute, then shifted his gaze from the door to Rob then asked, "What do you want to do with the oil?"

"We'll set it in the airplane," Rob said. Rob and Mike picked up the small drum from the rear of the blue van and set it inside the cargo door of the airplane. Then they tried to close the doors on the rear of the blue van. The right door was sprung; it closed only partially.

"I think it will be all right," said Juan.

Rob and Mike knew Jacobson would be most unhappy when he heard about the door. As Juan and the driver disappeared down the road in the van, Mike reached down in the grass and picked up the length of cord. "You've got a crunched door, sir," Mike said. "It worked easier than I thought."

"Where did you get that cord?" Rob asked.

"Oh, let's just say the blinds in that room don't work so good," Mike said with a laugh.

32 Two for the Price of One

Juan climbed reluctantly up the stairs, then took the few steps to Jacobson's door, paused a moment, took in a breath, and tapped lightly. This was going to be complicated. "Come in," Jacobson said. Juan paused then grabbed the knob with a sweaty palm, pushing the door as he stepped inside. Jacobson was standing with his back to him, looking out the window and talking on the telephone. He finished his conversation, then turned and looked at him. "How's it going?" he asked.

"We have a problem," Juan said. "The cargo door on the airplane was damaged."

"Get it repaired," Jacobson said as he wrinkled up his brow and put both hands on his hips. "Use the Colonel's mechanic."

"I don't think it's that simple," said Juan. "We backed a van into the door and it's crushed."

"What?" Jacobson asked. "How in the hell did you do a stupid thing like that?" he exclaimed, throwing both hands into the air, and turning around.

"It was accidental. The wind blew the door out from the airplane as we were backing up, and it caught on the open door of the van," answered Juan.

Jacobson stopped and composed himself. He really wanted to go into a rage, but years of experience had taught him that only losers lose control. He walked over to the window. "Did that Mike have anything to do with this?" he asked.

"No," said Juan Pablo. "He was standing inside the airplane when it happened. No one is at fault. It just happened."

"Okay, okay, what is the solution? What do we need to do?" he asked as he turned back to face Juan.

"Mr. Marshall said to call Superior Air Parts in Miami. They have used doors," Juan answered.

"I'll get George on the phone and have him go over and get the damn thing and fly it down tonight. How big is it?" Jacobson asked. "Oh, that's not important," he answered himself. "George will make all the arrangements." Jacobson walked over and picked up the telephone. He spoke briefly to the operator and then hung up the phone. "They are putting the call through," he said. "Is the door all we need?"

"I'll ask Rob," Juan said.

"Where are those two?" Jacobson asked.

"They are working on the airplane," he answered.

"You go back over there, and I'll get George to call that Superior Air Parts. He will take care of the details," Jacobson said.

The phone rang. Jacobson picked it up. "Oh, George," he began, "we have an emergency situation. Someone's backed into the cargo door of the DC-3. Which door?" Jacobson asked, looking at Juan. "George wants to know. He says there are two sections on the cargo door."

"Tell him the front one," Juan answered. "The rear one is okay."

"Juan Pablo said the front," Jacobson said. "There's a place called Superior Air Parts or something like that there in Miami. They have one in their inventory." Jacobson turned to Juan. "What is the man's name, the owner?"

"His name is Jim," he answered.

"Did you hear that?" said Jacobson, "Jim," Jacobson repeated. "If you have any problems, call me. We need that door now, not tomorrow. Get it to me. You know where I am so get a move on. Get back to me in two hours and give me a status report." Jacobson hung up the phone. "Okay, let's go take a ride. I want to see that damn door for myself."

"Looks like we have company," said Mike as he stood in the cargo door opening and looked across the ramp. The blue van was making its way over to the DC-3. "Yes, the man himself is coming to take a look."

Rob walked over to the door opening, wiping his greasy, sweaty hand on a paper towel. The van came around the front of the airplane and rolled to a stop by the tail. Jacobson jumped out, walking much faster than his normal deliberate pace, stepped to the side of the airplane and without saying a word looked to the door.

"How did this happen?" he asked.

"Not sure," said Mike. "I was watching from the plane when a gust of wind blew the door into the side of the van as it backed up to unload some engine oil."

"Can we repair it?" asked Jacobson.

"Sure," said Rob as he looked up and threw the wad of paper on the floor,

"In maybe two to three days. What we need is another door. That would be the easiest and quickest way. Pull the bolts out of the hinges and take one off and put another one on. Real simple."

"I've got the replacement door coming," Jacobson staring first at Mike, then at Rob. With clenched fists he used the back of his hand and rubbed the sweaty perspiration from his brow, then turned and went back to the van. Juan came over and handed a brown, paper bag to Mike. "Lunch," he said, then turned and walked toward the blue van.

"Thanks," said Mike. Juan Pablo did a slight head nod in recognition of Mike's thanks. He then closed the door. With a sharp wine the engine came to life, and they drove away.

"That Jacobson is pissed," said Mike. "He wanted to raise hell, but we didn't screw up. His people did; maybe they had a little help," he said, grinning from ear to ear.

Jacobson went up the stairs to his room. What else could go wrong? We've been delayed by a tropical storm; now they have backed the van into the door of the damn DC-3. He was being pushed by his superiors. They had called twice today, checking on the status of the shipment. He was caught in the middle and was being pressured to get this arms shipment finished and cleaned up. Something was going on, but he didn't know what. Now this. All he wanted was to get the job finished and get his ass out of here as soon as possible.

George called Superior Air Parts and asked for Jim. "Sir, you don't know me, but I need to make a purchase. I'm calling on behalf of a friend of yours. His name is Rob. He wants to know if you have a front section of a DC-3 cargo door."

"Yes, I do," said Jim, a little puzzled. The door belonged to Rob; he had bought and paid for it. Evidently this man didn't know that.

"My name is George Garcia, and we need to get that door. Can I send a truck to pick it up now? They could be there in the next thirty minutes. What is the price?"

"Normally, we sell these doors for around a thousand dollars, but since it is for Rob, it'll be eight hundred," Jim said.

"Good," said George. "I'll have someone bring payment with them. Thank you," George said.

"Thank you," Jim said. "Oh, I'll include all the necessary hardware to install the door."

"Good," said George. "It was nice talking to you."

"Likewise," said Jim. "If you need anything, feel free to call."

George called one of his men over, gave him a check, and explained where to go.

The man returned in thirty minutes with the cargo door, wrapped in cardboard and Styrofoam padding for shipping.

Getting out a tape measure, George measured the door. No way, he thought. It wouldn't go in the Navajo. It would take something as big as a King Air with a cargo door to get that thing delivered. He picked up the phone and called a friend in Fort Lauderdale. His plane was available, and they could be down and pick up the door in the next two hours.

George called Jacobson and explained the details, and sat patiently, waiting. It was now two thirty. If they came on now, they could deliver the door to Port-au-Prince before six o'clock, no later than seven.

The flight down was rough. There was a tropical storm off the Mexican coast that was causing a great deal of winds and rain. The further south they got, the better the weather became. By the time they arrived in Haiti, it was very clear. After landing they taxied up to the front of a large, gray hangar where they were directed to park. It was a tight squeeze getting past the door and down the steps on the King air. George climbed off first and was met by a man in uniform, a man with a great deal of rank. The man walked over as George stepped down, putting his hand out.

"I am Colonel Chenier," he said.

"I am George Garcia," George answered.

"Good," the Colonel said, "I was instructed to ask you to place the cargo in the hangar so customs can examine it."

"Sure," said George. "We need some help in getting it off the airplane."

The Colonel with a quick nod walked back to the hangar and returned shortly with a man driving an old pickup truck.

They worked the door from inside the cabin of the King Air, out the door, and loaded it into the back of the pickup. As they were standing beside the truck, with a noisy clamor, a muffled voice, and a fast step, Jacobson, Rob, Mike, and Juan Pablo came around the hangar.

"I see you made it," Jacobson said with a smile as he approached George and shook his hand.

Rob and Mike went over to the truck, pulled the wrapping down, and were examining the door.

"Two for the price of one," Mike said tapping on the smaller jump door inside the larger door.

Jacobson walked over, "Is this what we need?" he asked.

"It'll do," Rob said, pushing his baseball cap up with one hand and using his fingers as a comb, he pushed the shaded gray hair back, then pulled his cap snugly on his head.

"Something's different," Jacobson said.

"It is. This door has a smaller door inside. It's what they call a jump door," Rob continued. "I guess it is the only one he had."

"Will it work?" Jacobson asked.

"Yes," Rob replied.

"Then that's all we need," Jacobson said, as he turned around to talk to

George. "You did good," he said. "Are you staying over or going back tonight?"

"I haven't made any plans," George said. "All I knew for sure was we had to deliver the door, then we'd go from there."

"If you want to stay, we have room. It's not the Hilton; but the food is good, and the rooms are comfortable," Jacobson said.

"On this trip I was only a passenger," George said. "Let me ask the pilot."

The odor of jet aviation fuel hung in the air as George approached the pilot who was watching as the ground crew refueled the King Air. They spoke briefly over the hum from the engine of the fuel truck, and he then returned. "Mr. Jacobson, we need to go back tonight; the weather is getting bad. If we stay over, there is a possibility we could not get home tomorrow."

"Okay, George," Jacobson said. "Again, thanks. We owe you," he said as he turned and headed back to where the others were standing.

"We need to turn in and get an early start tomorrow," Jacobson said, looking at Mike, then Rob. We need this door installed, and I don't want to have any more problems." He stood looking intently at the men as the tropical breeze floated the odors of the fuel into their nostrils.

Both men nodded and watched as Juan and the Colonel's mechanic opened the doors and drove the pickup truck into the hangar then closed the doors, with a rattle and clank, they locked.

They were sitting in the van waiting as Juan Pablo came out the back of the hangar and got in. The driver backed up the van and drove away toward the hotel.

33 The First $60,000

There was a knock on the door at six-thirty. Rob was already up and writing in his notepad. Mike was awake but was still in bed. Rob placed his notepad under a pillow and opened the door.

"Good morning," said Juan.

"Good morning to you," answered Rob.

"I am taking breakfast orders. Is there anything special you want?" he asked.

"No," said Rob. "How about it, Mike? Need anything special this morning?"

"Coffee, toast, bacon, and eggs sounds good," Mike said, sitting up in bed.

"Do you, Mr. Marshall, want the same thing?" Juan asked.

"Sounds good to me," Rob said. "I'm not a big breakfast eater."

"It'll be ready in thirty minutes," Juan Pablo said as he was leaving the room.

Rob and Mike showered, dressed, and walked downstairs to the dining room on the lower floor. Jacobson, Bill and Lewis were all there, sitting in the usual spot.

Jacobson spoke as usual. "Morning," he said. "Looks like a nice morning. We can get some things done today." Mike understood Jacobson's hidden meaning to a nice morning. What he really wanted to say was get that damn door on the airplane and haul the cargo back to the battlefield. Too bad he couldn't go along with us, Mike was thinking. He didn't like the man and didn't trust him at all and it showed.

Rob knew they needed to get the cargo door on the airplane and be sure the jump door worked before they flew this next load back to Honduras.

Breakfast was served. The men sat talking. Rob pulled his chair over beside Jacobson. "Mr. Jacobson," he said, "yesterday, everything was in a turmoil. We didn't get a chance to talk. Did the transfer take place?"

"The transfer?" Jacobson seemed puzzled.

"The wire transfer of funds. We did have an understanding," Rob said.

"Oh, yeah," said Jacobson. "I'm sure it was all set before I left Miami."

"I'd feel much better if I could call my office before we take this next load," Rob said.

"That's no problem," Jacobson said. "We'll go get that door on the plane, and while they are loading the materials, I'll bring you back here and we'll call your office."

"Thank you," Rob said as he stood up and walked the few steps back over to where Mike was sitting.

"Are we ready to go?" Mike asked, picking up his coffee cup and taking the last sip.

"Looks that way," said Rob, leaning over and picking up his cup and finishing it off. "Juan," Rob said, "we'll be in the room when you get ready to go. Oh, we need some laundry taken care of."

"That's no problem," Juan said. "Put it in a bag and set it beside your door before you leave."

"Good," Mike said as they walked out the door, across the lobby to the stairs, and up to the room. Rob wanted to take his notepad and the charts with them to the plane. There were some things only he and Mike should see.

He pulled the pad from under the pillow, slipped it into the small case, and placed the case on the bed. "Mike, don't let me forget this," he said, picking up the small, brown case. Mike nodded.

The blue van came down the narrow road parallel to the taxiway. As it rounded the turn and passed the other parked airplanes, they could see the truck with the replacement cargo door in the back. The mechanic was standing, looking it over as they drove up.

It was a warm, sunshiny morning with a nice, comfortable breeze blowing from the south. They needed to get the door on the airplane and the cargo loaded before the sun got too high in the sky.

"First things first," Rob said as they walked over to the truck. "We'll get the old door off and then install this one. We need to be sure all the latches work properly. We don't want something coming open in the air."

"Yeah, could cause a big problem," said Mike.

The old door was removed without incident. The replacement door was slid into place. The lower hinge was a little different, but with a small adjustment, it went into place. The hinge pins were installed, and with some adjustments, the latch seemed to operate correctly.

"Mr. Marshall, this door is different," Juan said.

"I know," said Rob. "They call this a jump door. They were used in the military to allow paratroopers to parachute from the airplane."

"Then, this door can be removed in-flight," Juan said.

"Yes," Rob answered.

Rob watched as Juan carefully examined the door. "Let's get inside," Rob said to Juan. "We will close it and see if the jump door works."

The large cargo door was closed and latched in place by Rob. He then turned the small handles on the jump door, and it opened inward into the cabin of the airplane. "See?" Rob said. "It's very simple." Rob could see the man pondering the door. He hoped Juan had not become suspicious. Now wasn't the time to think that way, Rob said to himself. I must be positive. He was sure Juan had no reason to think that replacing the door was something they had planned.

Juan walked up to the cabin and looked around. "I see you have finished the repair of the hydraulic leak," he said.

"Yes, all we need to do is run the engines and check the repairs," Rob said.

"We need to finish servicing the engines. I didn't have enough oil yesterday, and in all the excitement when the door got banged, I forgot," said Mike.

"That's not good," said Rob. "Those engines won't run without oil."

"I know," said Mike, "my mistake. I'll take care of it now," he said as he sauntered down the cabin to the rear and picked up one of the oilcans. Using a funnel and with the help of the mechanic, they filled both five-gallon cans with engine oil.

Rob went outside and approached Juan, who was standing beside the truck. "We need to go back to the hotel," Rob said. "Jacobson is arranging a phone call back to my office. I need to talk to Anne for a few minutes."

"The driver took the van and is on an errand. He should return shortly. Then we will all go to the hotel and have an early lunch. When we return, we will load the cargo and then make our departure. Mr. Jacobson will be expecting us," Juan said.

"Sounds good to me," said Rob as he carefully watched him. There seemed to be a noticeable change in his manner. Maybe, they did suspect something. Maybe, just maybe, he and Mike weren't as slick as they thought.

Mike and the mechanic finished servicing the airplane and drained the fuel sumps. Mike came over to Juan and Rob. "I think she's ready to go," Mike said, "but we didn't change the lock out on the door."

"That's not important for now," said Rob. He had a key; one Jim had given him back when he had purchased the door. There were two keys. He took one, and hopefully, Jim still had the other one. If not, it was in someone else's possession. Whose? Rob wasn't sure.

The driver in the blue van picked up the crew at the airport and took them back to the hotel where Jacobson and his two helpers were waiting.

Rob, Mike, and Juan lumbered up the stairs to the second floor. Rob and Juan stopped off at Jacobson's room. Mike went on down the hall to his and Rob's room.

Juan Pablo knocked on the door. "Come in," Jacobson said. Juan walked in, followed by Rob.

"How did it go?" asked Jacobson.

"We have the door replaced, and the airplane is serviced and ready to fly," said Juan Pablo.

Rob didn't speak. He was waiting on Jacobson. He didn't want to appear too anxious. If he did, Jacobson could possibly suspect something wasn't right. He was an expert at that. His was an extra sense, a skill, Rob knew he himself didn't possess.

"Well, Mr. Marshall, it appears we are on our way to completing this mission," Jacobson said.

"I think you are right," said Rob. "Now the financial matter..." It was apparent Jacobson wasn't going to bring it up.

"Oh, yes," said Jacobson, "I called. The matter was taken care of yesterday afternoon. You should have your money in your bank now."

"Good," said Rob, "I would like to confirm the transaction. You know how banks are. They sometimes make mistakes. Do you mind getting my office on the phone?"

Jacobson paused a moment. He wanted to appear offended that Rob questioned him. Rob knew it was only business, and Jacobson wanted to show his authority. The "I'm in charge" attitude.

Jacobson turned and picked up the phone, opened his notebook, and dialed the operator who placed the call as he read out Rob's phone number. He then hung up the phone. "It's not the good, old U.S.A.," he said. "They take their ever-loving time down here. They never get in a hurry. I guess if you had to live in all these conditions, you wouldn't give a damn either."

In a few minutes the phone rang. Jacobson answered it. "Hello," he said. "One moment, please." He extended the phone cord out and handed the phone over to Rob. "Your office," he said.

"Hello," Rob said.

"Well, hello to you, stranger," Anne said. "How's it going?"

"We're okay," Rob said. "How are you doing?"

"I'm doing great. I miss you two. When will you be through and coming home?" Anne asked.

"I'm not sure," Rob said. "Next two or three days, no later than the weekend."

"Good, everything's quiet here. Oh, the bank called fifteen minutes before you did. They have received a wire transfer of sixty thousand dollars."

"Good," said Rob. "Just let the money stay put until I get back. Tell Dan I will see him in a few days."

"Good," said Anne. "I'll call him now. I think he'll feel a little better about things since the money arrived."

"I'll call you about this time tomorrow," Rob said, "so stick by the phone. Oh, call the kids and tell them I'll see them this weekend."

"I sure will," said Anne. "Good to hear from you, and please be careful; those kids need their dad."

"Okay," Rob said, I'll call as soon as I can. Bye."

Rob hung up the phone. He was getting a strange feeling. Maybe it was his imagination, but Jacobson and Juan were both uptight. Something was going on, but what?

"Thanks, Mr. Jacobson," Rob said as he left the room.

34 Easier the Second Time Around

Standing in the front of the cabin by the entrance door to the cockpit, Rob watched Mike at the rear of the airplane supervising as Bill and Lewis, along with four soldiers, were loading the gray boxes of cargo onto the plane. Juan stood just outside of the airplane beside the green military truck, which was backed up to the cargo door opening as the soldiers were busy carrying the last few boxes.

"Mike, you and Juan Pablo go ahead and start strapping all these boxes down. I am going to start the checklist," Rob said.

"How much time do we have?" Mike asked.

"We need to be taxiing out in thirty minutes or so," Rob said, turning and going into the cockpit of the DC-3. He picked up the checklist and began.

The soldiers, along with Bill and Lewis, finished loading the boxes. Then the soldiers stepped down onto the back of the truck from the cabin of the airplane. Bill and Lewis stood in the door looking as Mike and Juan Pablo strapped down the cargo.

"Do you need any help tying this down?" Bill asked.

"No, I don't think so. It's a two-man job, but thanks anyway," Mike said as Bill and Lewis turned and jumped from the cargo opening down to the ground beside the truck then walked around and got into the front as it pulled away. Two of the soldiers did a slight wave as they drove around the tail of the airplane and disappeared.

Juan Pablo and Mike continued strapping the cargo down. As they were doing so, the Colonel and Jacobson drove up in the Colonel's white Land

Rover. They got out and walked over to the cargo door opening and looked in.

"How's it coming?" Jacobson asked.

Juan looked up and said, "Oh, we've got it under control. A few more straps and we will be finished."

"Good. Before you go, I need to see you," Jacobson continued as he turned and disappeared from the opening.

"Go ahead," Mike said. "I'll finish this."

Juan nodded and then walked to the door opening and jumped to the ground. He went over to the front of the Land Rover where Jacobson was waiting. It was apparent that Jacobson was very nervous. They talked for a few minutes, then Juan returned to the airplane.

"Juan Pablo," said Mike, "do you think that the Colonel would be good enough to run us over to the hangar before we takeoff?"

Juan, without saying anything, turned and walked over to where Jacobson and the Colonel were. They talked briefly, then Juan returned.

"Yes, he will take us," he said, "but we must hurry. We need to leave in twenty minutes."

Mike understood what he was saying. They were scheduled to takeoff in the DC-3 for Honduras in twenty minutes.

The Colonel drove rather fast over the narrow road to the hangar, and Mike and Juan Pablo relieved themselves in the restroom. Mike washed his face and hands with the cool water, toweled off as Juan stood patiently by the door.

"Let's go," said Mike as he opened the door and trotted down the hall and out the back door then over to the Land Rover where Jacobson and the Colonel sat waiting.

As the two climbed back into the old DC-3, Rob asked, "Where did you go?"

"I took a much needed break in the restroom if you know what I mean," Mike said.

"Okay, let's go," said Rob. "We've got about ten minutes before we'll be taxiing out."

They finished the checklist, started the engines, and taxied out on schedule. Everything went smoothly. They were airborne. One more flight after this, Rob thought, and I'll be home taking my kids fishing.

As they flew over the sparkling Jamaican coast, it was getting easier. They had an idea of what to expect. They were going to arrive in Honduras before five-thirty, then unload the cargo from the airplane, refuel, and fly back at night. Rob felt much more comfortable with their timing, especially considering the return cargo. He felt sure there would be those bags like before. Arriving back at night without anyone around was much less embarrassing.

Everything was going smoothly as Mike and Rob took turns flying the airplane by hand. The autopilot was out, and in Haiti, no one had the capability to repair it.

When the coastline first became visible, Mike was at the controls, "There she is, boys," he said. "Now, let's be sure we are at the right place," he said as Rob appeared in the cockpit door. Mike handed him the chart. Rob stood looking out over the nose of the airplane while still holding the chart in one hand.

"We need to go a little to the south," he said, pointing to two small peaks to the southwest.

Mike slowly turned the airplane in a shallow bank to the south then flew level toward the small peaks. The coastline passed under the airplane, and then the grassy vegetation with small trees began sloping up into the mountains. Rob said, "I think we are here." He looked down to his left. There was the old field. It appeared to be wet; at least, the color was darker than Rob remembered.

Taking over the controls, Rob was reading the checklist. He slowed the airplane down, and then he made a left turn to a base leg. 'Gear down," he said, "twenty degree flap."

"Gear down and locked," Mike said over the intercom to Rob. "Flaps twenty degrees," Mike continued.

Rob turned the airplane on final. As they approached, Rob said, "Full flaps."

"Full flaps," said Mike.

Rob trimmed the airplane for landing as they made their approach. Off to the southeast, Mike could see some movement. It was the Colonel and his men, who were off in the tall grass, waiting for them.

As the main wheel touched down, the airplane was a little squirrelly; the ground was definitely slick. These tropical storms had dropped a lot of rain. Gradually, the tailwheel settled, and Rob carefully pulled the throttle all the way back. The airplane slowed quickly; it was very obvious the ground was soft.

Rob added extra power to keep the airplane taxiing straight. As he neared the end of the airstrip, he reached down and unlocked the tailwheel, then rode the right brake and added power to its left engine as he maneuvered the airplane on the slippery surface.

As they came to a halt, Rob turned off switches, pulled back on the mixtures, completed the checklist, and then set the brakes.

A short caravan was approaching from the southeast as Mike climbed over the boxes and walked back to the cargo door to help Juan get it open.

This time everyone seemed much more relaxed. They were repeating this for the second time, so it was easier if the attack helicopter stayed away.

Mike opened the front section of the cargo door as Juan jumped down on the ground and pulled it around and up against the side of the airplane. He damn sure wasn't going to damage this one. Mike unlatched the rear half of the door and gently swung it to the rear. As the man named Caberallos was walking toward the airplane, the others were sitting in the vehicles. Some were exchanging words with Juan Pablo; a few waved a greeting. Mike waved back.

Crawling over the boxes, Rob then stood up, and made the last few steps to the rear of the airplane.

"How are we doing?" Caberallos asked, putting his hand up to Mike, who was now squatting in the door opening. The men shook hands as Rob approached, bent over, and also shook Caberallos' hand.

"I guess we can get this unloaded," Rob said, looking at Caberallos. "I don't want to stay here any longer than is absolutely necessary."

"I understand, after what happened last time." Caberallos said, wiping his hand over his brow in a gesture, which said "that was close."

Rob and Mike took the straps off the cargo while Juan Pablo directed the truck as it backed up to the airplane.

"You better go help," said Rob. "I'll do this; we don't have another door."

Mike nodded while he finished loosening a cargo strap and rolled it up as he walked to the rear of the airplane and to the cargo door opening. Juan had positioned himself between the truck and the airplane.

"What are you trying to do?" Mike said, "kill yourself?"

"If I let them damage this airplane, I think Mr. Jacobson would do it for me."

"Well, move," Mike said, motioning with his left hand. Slowly the truck backed into place. The soldiers were unloading before Rob could finish getting the cargo straps off. Caberallos stood in the door and made a note of each box as it was removed. It took about fifteen minutes to unload the cargo.

"What about fuel?" Mike asked Caberallos.

"It's coming," he said. "We didn't want it to be sitting out here in the event we needed to move." Mike thought he understood. Don't set the fuel out in the open. That would be a sure sign that they were coming with the airplane.

Caberallos jumped down from the airplane as the truck pulled away with the cargo. Juan Pablo was over talking with Colonel Santini. Santini waved to Mike as Mike stood in the cargo door opening.

Rob walked up behind Mike. "We need to check out the extended fuel system," he said. "We finished hooking it up when Juan went to get the cargo door ordered, but we never had an opportunity to see if it operates properly."

Mike turned and followed Rob up the cabin of the airplane. They stopped outside of the cockpit. Rob pointed to a new switch. "Left is in, right is out, and in the middle is off," he said. "You can't forget. We have no way of gauging what we are putting into the bladder, so eight to ten gallons per minute is the volume of the bladder pump. When you start fueling the main tanks, I will pump fuel into the bladder tanks for twenty minutes. This should give us close to two hundred gallons. We will transfer it back to the main tanks on the way home. That way, we can check out the system and make sure it all works properly," Rob said.

Mike got the crew steps and hooked them in the door opening. He and Rob stepped down on the rain drenched slippery soil. They trudged through the mud over to the left engine and looked it over. There was mud underneath the wings where the large main tires had thrown it up on landing. Rob went over to the right engine, same thing, but here were no signs of oil leaks. Juan walked up as they stood inspecting the engine.

"Dry," he said, pointing to the bottom of the airplane.

"Oh, yes," said Mike. "We fixed it, no more hydraulic leaks."

"Good," said Juan. "I was a little concerned. As we flew, I kept an eye on the hydraulic pressure."

"That's a good crew member," said Rob. "We all have to work together."

The fuel trailer arrived, and Mike began refueling the airplane. Rob serviced the hydraulic and engine oil.

By now most of the soldiers were gone. Only two stayed behind to help refuel the airplane and to assist the aircrew.

Finishing with the engine oil, Rob went inside the airplane. He could see Mike through the side window out servicing the main tank on the left side of the airplane. "Left in, right out," he repeated as he turned the switch to his left and looked at his watch. Twenty minutes or less, he thought. That old saying about flying entered his mind. "Fuel on the ground and the runway behind you will never do you any good in an emergency." This wasn't an emergency, but it could very well be in the near future.

Rob hung around the cockpit area as Mike did the refueling. He didn't want to be here any longer than was absolutely necessary. The last time they were here, a helicopter gunship just about got them and there was no way it was going to get a second chance. Rob looked at his watch. It had been fifteen minutes. Another five minutes was all he needed to fill the bladder tanks.

Something was moving in the rear of the cabin. Looking over his shoulder, he saw Juan with his catlike motions; you could see him, but you could not hear him. "How are we doing?" he asked Rob, standing in the door of the cockpit. There was a hum of the small fuel pump filling the bladder. Hopefully, Juan wouldn't notice. "Is there anything I can do to help?" he asked.

Looking around, "Yes, there is," Rob said, spying two five-gallon oilcans, sitting in the middle of the cabin. "Store those," pointing to the cans. "Put them in the aft storage compartment behind the curtains," Rob said, pointing to the back of the cabin then glancing at his watch, reading the time, and flipping the switch to the off position.

In a short time, Mike finished refueling the airplane. He came up the crew steps and into the cabin. "Rob," he said, "Mr. Caberallos wants to know if we'll be back tomorrow at approximately the same time."

"Unless something changes," Rob said, "that's the schedule."

Caberallos, who was standing on the ground with his head stuck inside the cargo door opening said, "We'll see you tomorrow."

Rob looked at his watch. It was six thirty-five. "Let's go," he said to Mike. "If we leave now, we can be back by eleven."

"Oh," Caberallos said as he stuck his head back into the airplane, "we have a few other items we need to send with you," as a jeep backed up to the door. He threw six bags about the size of a GI duffel bag into the cabin. Rob and Mike looked at each other. Juan walked over and began moving the bags to the front of the cabin.

Rob and Mike both turned and walked into the cockpit without speaking. Mike was shaking his head. "I thought that was it last time," he said.

"Don't rock the boat," said Rob. "This is not the time or place. We'll have our chance. You need to close the cargo door before you get strapped in," Rob said to Mike.

Mike got up and walked out of the cockpit into the cabin. One of the dark bags was protruding into Mike's path. He kicked it out of his way as he passed. Juan looked up as Mike continued walking to the rear, pulling the crew steps inside and closing the rear section of the door, then the front section. He shook them both to make sure they were securely closed then shuffled back up the cabin. Juan Pablo had moved the bags out of Mike's path. As Mike entered the cockpit, Rob was starting the engines.

Everything went well, and the flight back was uneventful as they landed and then taxied up the taxiway and parked the airplane in the same spot they had left from eleven hours earlier.

Jacobson, the Colonel, Bill, and the mechanic were waiting when they parked. Opening the door, Juan began handing the bags to Bill and the Colonel's mechanic who quickly loaded them onto the back of the truck then drove away. There was a great deal of importance placed on the cargo. The Colonel was always present when they arrived.

As they finished the checklist and got out of their seats, walked down the cabin, and jumped down on the ground, Rob pulled the door closed.

Walking without speaking, they went over to the Colonel's Land Rover. The Colonel and Jacobson were in front, and Rob and Mike climbed into the back. All was quiet on the drive to the hotel. Jacobson was not himself. Something was getting to him. He didn't know what, but something was wrong. Rob sensed it.

Climbing up the stairs and opening the door to their room, "I need a shower," said Mike.

"Me, too," said Rob. "You go first. I think I'll do a little bookkeeping," he said, taking out his pad. Mike knew what Rob was talking about. He was keeping a daily journal of all their activities. Mike wasn't sure why, but it was very detailed.

35 Adios, Senors

"Come in," Jacobson said as Juan knocked on his door. "How are you doing this morning?" he asked Juan Pablo as he entered the room with a pot of coffee.

"Very well, thank you," Juan answered. "I have your coffee," he continued.

"Put it on the dresser and stay until I get out of the bathroom," Jacobson stated as he stepped through the bathroom door. Juan stood patiently waiting as Jacobson finished his shower and came out.

"There are some things going on in my government that have caused me to be greatly concerned," Jacobson said. "Some of the liberals are trying to get our conservative leadership in a smear campaign and have accused the administration of foul play. This could affect us," he continued, "so be prepared to move, and in which direction, I don't know. Keep a close eye on our aircrew. I don't think they know anything about this, and for damn sure, we don't want them talking to some liberal newspaper about what we are doing down here. When we're finished, we will have to weigh all the options," Jacobson said, looking at Juan. "I like that Rob, but Mike is a real son of a bitch who only wants to cause trouble. You understand; we do what we have to do," Jacobson said, watching Juan's face. There was no expression. That was the oriental side. He knew Juan Pablo had become friends with the air crew, and he might, just might, flinch when it was time. He couldn't be sure he could count on him. He needed another option, one that didn't include Juan.

Juan knocked on Rob and Mike's door. "Come in," said Mike.

"Good morning," Juan Pablo said. "I have some coffee." He picked up a tray with a pot of coffee and two cups from the cart he was pushing and brought it into the room and placed it on a table.

"Man, this is great," said Mike. "We have room service, first class."

Juan Pablo stood watching the two men pour the coffee. They were sincerely appreciative of him for bringing the coffee. He had a good feeling inside. "Enjoy your coffee," he said as he was leaving the room. They were really nice people who didn't belong in this, he thought.

"It's great coffee," Mike said, looking at Juan as he walked out of the door. The cart rattled off down the hall. Rob stood up from sitting on the side of the bed and walked over and closed the door. He motioned for Mike to come over closer. "Do you get the feeling we're getting our last rites?" Rob asked.

Mike sat for a moment. "It is a little strange getting room service from him," Mike said. "Now that you think about it."

Rob whispered in Mike's ear. "We need to pump that fuel from the bladder tank into the main tank before we refuel. We didn't do it on the return flight, and with the cargo, we will be over weight on take-off, way over," Rob said. "We're already over by taking the five thousand pounds. That's way over single engine gross weight."

Mike nodded and sat drinking his coffee. It was now a few minutes before seven. If everything went the way they planned, they would not be coming back to Port-au-Prince when they took off today. They would come by here on their way back to Florida. Rob knew they would be stretching it to fly back to Florida all the way from Honduras. They were going to try with the airplane empty and using a cruise setting of about forty-five percent power. If everything was right, they could make it. On the two previous flights, they had checked the fuel used. They usually had a tail wind on the flight back. That left about one and a half hours of usable fuel. That, along with the bladder, which was another two hours, would give them three plus hours of fuel to go from Haiti to Florida. It was a two and one-half hour flight. They had studied the charts. If they flew west of Cuba, they would be over open ocean all the way, and with their lack of navigational equipment, they could possibly get lost. Their only option was to fly back to Jamaica, Haiti, and then on to Florida. Rob had gone over this several times. He and Mike had sat in the bathroom, planning. The big problem was what to do with Juan. He was ever present. They would cross that bridge when they got to it.

"Let's go down to Jacobson's room," said Rob. "There's a little matter of money. We need it transferred to our bank. We did the deed; now we need to be paid."

"That's the only reason I'm here," said Mike.

Both men walked down to Jacobson's room. Rob knocked.

Jacobson answered the door. "Morning, boys," he said in a formal voice.

"What can I do for you?"

"I'd like to talk to my office before we leave on the flight today," Rob said.

With slow deliberate steps, Jacobson walked over to the table and started pouring himself another cup of coffee, picked it up, stood for a moment looking out the window, then turned around, looking directly at the two men. "It appears you boys don't trust me," he said. He paused and then said, "I can't say that I can fault you for that. Sometimes it is a mean world, and we have to live in it. Oh, hell," he said with a smile, gaining his composure. "We'll call from the airport before you leave. We can use the Colonel's office. I know you need your money."

"Thanks," said Rob.

"Don't thank me. I'm only doing what we agreed to do," Jacobson said. "Now go on down and have some breakfast. We'll leave around eight o'clock for the airport."

Everything went smoothly; Rob felt a little too smoothly. He was beginning to feel like a pet pig at a pig roasting. Something was up. Now was the time to be cautious. He didn't feel like Jacobson was going to pat them on the back and say boys, you did a good job, then let them go home after all the secrecy. More than ever, he felt like something was about to happen.

On the drive to the airport, Jacobson said, "We'll talk when you get back tonight. I'll meet you, and get you the final payment. Then you can be on your way home." Somehow, Rob didn't believe him.

The crew loaded the cargo onto the DC-3 while Mike did the refueling. Rob had instructed Mike to leave the left main tank low so he could transfer the fuel from the bladder into it. Then he could come back and check it to be sure the pump was working properly.

"Left is in, right is out," Rob said as he flipped the switch to the right, then looked at his watch. It was twelve before ten. He kept an eye on the left main fuel gauge by turning on the master switch from time to time. The fuel quantity slowly increased. The tank would hold most of the fuel although some would be left in the bladder, less than one hundred gallons.

It was now five minutes past ten. Rob flipped the switch to the off position then went out to the right side where Mike was fueling the airplane and nodded towards the left. Mike nodded that he understood. They pulled the fuel truck around to the left wing. Mike removed the main fuel tank cap. The fuel was within one inch of the top. Their jerry-rigged system was working. Rob watched as Mike finished up and the fuel truck driver was reeling in the hose. "We're all through here," he said smiling.

"Good," said Rob as he approached the two. "Tell the Colonel I'll be over and take care of their fuel bill in a few minutes." Rob walked around to where Juan, Bill, and Lewis were finishing with the cargo.

"It's all loaded," Juan Pablo said.

"Good," Rob answered. "If you and Mike will get it all strapped down, I will go see the Colonel. He wants me to pay these fuel bills before we leave. Oh, where is Jacobson?" Rob asked, looking at Juan.

"He said to tell you he would meet you in the Colonel's office at eleven o'clock," he said.

"Thanks," Rob said. "I'll get the mechanic to drive me over. I'll be back by twelve thirty. We need to leave by one." Juan Pablo nodded. Rob walked over and asked the mechanic for a ride over to the hangar.

"Yes, I can do that," the mechanic said.

Rob stood back as the green military truck drove out and around the front of the airplane, then Rob got into the truck with the mechanic, and they followed the larger military truck down the narrow road to the hangar to the Colonel's office. The mechanic knocked on the steel door.

"Come in," the Colonel said. "Well, Mr. Marshall, I think you're ready to go."

"I am," said Rob. "I need to pay my fuel bill."

"Okay," said the Colonel. "I have it here." He picked up a sheet of paper and handed it to Rob. The fuel bill was written in French, and the money value was in gourde.

Rob looked a minute, then asked, "How much is this in U.S. currency?"

The Colonel laughed. He took out his pencil and did some division as Rob put one foot up in a chair and removed a bundle of one hundred-dollar bills. "That's four thousand, six hundred dollars in U.S. currency for the three refuelings," the Colonel said.

Rob quickly counted out the cash, then returned the balance to his pocket. He pushed the money across the desk to Colonel Chenier. "It's a pleasure doing business with you," the Colonel said as he put his hand out and shook hands, and as Rob walked away, the Colonel said, "Good luck."

"Thanks," Rob said as he hurried out the door with the mechanic following. They rode the short distance around the runway to the far side where the DC-3 was parked. Jacobson was sitting in the van, talking with Juan. Rob walked up to the van as Jacobson opened the door then handed Rob a slip of paper. Rob looked at it for a minute, then he understood. It was a sheet confirming a wire transfer of sixty thousand dollars from the Barclay Bank in Haiti to his bank in Virginia. The money came from Miami, but the transfer was done in Haiti.

"You can go over to the Colonel's office and call if that will make you comfortable," Jacobson said, "but the money is there."

Rob knew Jacobson wasn't that type of man who would go to that much trouble to con someone over sixty thousand dollars.

"Okay," Rob said, "I appreciate it." He looked at Juan. "We need to go."

"Rob," Jacobson said, "Juan Pablo will be staying in Honduras with this shipment. You and the big man will be on your own coming back. Stop in here, and I will have your bags and the balance due you. We'll get it all settled tomorrow. Then you can go home."

Rob shook his hand and walked over to the cargo door opening. Mike was standing inside, watching. "Let's go," Rob said to Mike.

"'I'm ready when you are," Mike replied. The two men climbed over the boxes and into the cockpit. Juan closed the cargo door then followed them over the boxes and sat silently in the small jump seat, watching as the two men started the engines and talked on the radio. The routine was easy as they taxied out and down to the end of the runway, finished their checklist, then began the take-off roll.

"Gear up," said Rob as they broke ground.

"Gear's up," said Mike. The old DC-3 gradually climbed toward the clouds and made the turn to the southwest as they headed for Honduras.

The flight was in virtual silence. From time to time, Mike and Rob talked over the intercom. Both men felt if Jacobson had his way, they would never be allowed to return to the United States. For some reason Juan knew this because he was very quiet and had not talked at all on the flight down.

They found the airstrip and landed. Both men were nervous as they taxied up and stopped. If they were going to do away with them, it would be now; but everything went as usual. They unloaded the cargo, serviced the airplane with fuel, and Rob pumped the two bladders under the floor full as Mike serviced the main tanks.

It was now a little past six. They were standing beside the airplane, talking with Juan as Caberallos drove up in a jeep with three of the usual bags. "This is your last delivery," he said, throwing the bags into the opening of the cargo door.

Juan Pablo looked a little puzzled. Rob noticed that he started to say something to Caberallos but stopped. It was the bags that caused him to react. Something about the bags. Rob's mind was racing. Were these the same as before? He hadn't paid any attention to the bags before now. He didn't want to know. He caught Juan looking at the bags over his shoulder several times as they talked. Was he trying to tell him something?

Rob watched very carefully as the cargo was unloaded so no one would put or store anything on the airplane. Mike kept an eye on the outside of the DC-3. If they let them take off, then they must have put something in the bags. That was the only possibility.

Everyone was leaving with the exception of Juan and Caberallos. They sat and watched as Rob and Mike closed the cargo doors and started the engines. Caberallos was shouting something over the sound of the engines. "Adios, Senors!" the man had said.

36 Tropical Thunder

As they were climbing out Rob said, "Mike, as soon as we get out over the ocean, we are going to dump those bags."

"Let's see what is in them first," Mike said. "It could be money."

"No," said Rob. "I think they planted some type of explosive or something like that." Mike sat for a minute and looked at Rob.

"You think there is something in those bags that explodes?" asked Mike.

"Yes, I do," Rob answered. "It's the only thing that makes sense. Look, we are by ourselves. We are over water, going home. No one will ever know what happened, and those bags are the only way they could get a bomb on the plane without us being suspicious."

The airplane was now crossing over the coastline and getting out over the water. "Mike, go back and take your knife and make a small slit in one of the bags. See what is in there," Rob said over the intercom.

Mike took his seat belt off and went back to the cabin where the three bags were lying. He squatted down and took out his flashlight and began to examine the outer surface of the bags. From his experience in Vietnam, he knew they could be booby-trapped. If he moved or shook them, he could start a trigger mechanism. If Rob was right, they were in a mess. The middle bag somehow looked different. Mike moved his hand carefully over the surface of the bag. Yes, he was right. The middle bag had a rectangular device or something in it about halfway down from the top. Nervously, he stood up and ran back up to the cockpit.

"Keep the plane low." Rob didn't respond. "Level off!" Mike screamed as they were passing through five thousand feet. "We have a problem. There is something in the middle bag. It's different from the others. Maybe it's a bomb with some type of an altitude trigger device. When we get to a certain altitude, bang!" Mike explained.

"Don't say that," Rob said. "What do we do?"

"I don't know," said Mike. "Those sons of bitches are professionals. They blow things up everyday. It's probably some plastique, C-4 or C-6 with a detonation device. They loaded the bags on the airplane, and then waited at the airport until we were airborne so they could push the button and set the device with a remote control. I am going back and make a small cut in the side of the bag," Mike said. "We have got to get it where we can move it. Then we'll throw it overboard."

The three bags were lying in the middle of the cabin, side by side, with one of the cargo straps over all three. Mike took the strap off very carefully. He then took his knife and made a small x incision in the side of the middle bag. He shined his light inside. Yes, there it was, gray plastique but no trigger. The device could be anywhere. The charge was in the middle. The detonator was packed into the plastique, but the trigger device was somewhere else. Mike could see the wire running up through the bag. The trigger device would send a small electrical charge to the detonator, and then the plastique would react and no more Mike, Rob, or airplane.

God, he thought, get me out of this mess. I'll stay home and out of trouble. Get you mind back on the problem, Mike told himself. I've got to concentrate.

With the precision of a surgeon, he slowly cut open the side of the bag. There was something different; the other two bags had locks. This one did not. That was it. The sons of bitches knew their curiosity would get to them, and they would open the bag to see what they were hauling. Meticulously, Mike increased the opening in the side of the bag. There it was, a small black device about the size of a large matchbox, taped to the cover of the bag. Opening it could activate the trigger. How clever! Their curiosity would get the cat.

Mike got up and on trembling legs walked back to the cargo door then opened the jump door inward with a rush of air. He needed to get the middle bag to the door and push it out. He had to keep it flat. If it rolled over or changed positions, that could activate the trigger mechanism and it could go off. Slowly, inch by inch, Mike on his hands and knees worked the bag over to the door. Sweating profusely as he struggled, he lined it up so that the top of the bag with the trigger device would go out the door first. Mike positioned the bag in the opening, stood up, and put his right foot against the bottom of the bag. He took a deep breath and held on to the top of the door with both hands. He then pushed with everything he had in his six-foot four inch, two hundred thirty-pound body. The bag was out the door in a split second. Mike took a deep breath, and then there was a tremendous explosion. The shock waves shook the airplane.

Mike walked back up to the other two bags. The first bag he opened was filled with small bags of sod. With emotion and anger, he picked it up, walked to the door and threw it out, then did the same with the last bag. Straining against the wind, he pushed the jump door back into place and latched it securely. Standing for a few long seconds on shaky legs, he turned and headed back to the cockpit.

"If they heard that, they think they got us," Mike said after he put on his headset and slouched into the right seat.

Rob sat speechless for a moment then said, " They'll know it's not thunder. The bastards tried to kill us." There was a cold, empty feeling. Someone had wanted him dead and had tried to blow up him, his friend, and the airplane. A numbness swept over him. His sense of what was right and wrong was filled with shades of gray. He understood being a part of a disposable world. To these people, life and death had no value. When they were through with you, that was it.

Both men sat quietly for a long time. Their only conscious effort was maintaining the heading of the airplane as they flew.

Mike was the first to speak. "I'd call that a little close," he said over the intercom. He knew Rob was in a state of near shock. Mike was different. He'd seen people die; some were his friends. That was war, or as it was so boldly called by the politicians, peace keeping, which had caused a lot of good men, the best his country had to offer, to die. Now Mike needed to get Rob back to reality. Hell, life was for the living, and they were alive. They had beaten the bastards at their scheme to do them in. He felt good, now that he thought about it. Real good. The sons of bitches had underestimated them. "Rob, let's get this old crate back to Miami and catch a fast jet back home. We will be fishing before the weekend's over," Mike said.

Rob sat dazed. He slowly turned and looked at Mike. "Logic told me they wanted us dead, but in my mind, inside, I could not see how someone could work with you for a week, then when they were through, blow your ass up and go on with their life like you never existed."

"Rob, we need to get back to Miami and catch a fast ride home before they discover we are still here," Mike said. "So let's do it."

"You're right. We'll leave the airplane in Florida and have Jim look after it. Then we'll have someone bring it up later. Do you think that will work?" asked Rob, looking at Mike.

"Sounds great. All we need to do is get to Florida," Mike answered.

37 DEVIL OR THE DEEP BLUE SEA

Both men sat quietly thinking. Rob knew Jacobson had tried to have them killed so they couldn't tell anyone about their last two weeks' activities. When he found out they were alive, he'd try again. They'd spend a lot of time looking back over their shoulders. Yeah, he wanted them dead, or at least, a way of guaranteeing their silence. Rob had one thing going for them, and he had to make it work. He needed to put his plan into motion.

Mike tuned the DME. They were sixty-five miles out from Kingston, Jamaica. The fuel looked good. Rob began to transfer the three hundred gallons from the bladder into the left main tank. He set both fuel selectors to feed from that tank. Rob checked his watch. He should see a small increase in the fuel quantity. The fuel was being transferred faster than the engine could consume it. He let the transfer pump run for twenty-five minutes. The gauge showed approximately eight hundred pounds increase.

Mike changed the DME from Kingston to Port-au-Prince. They were getting closer and closer. "Maybe we should stop and get our bags," Mike said with a smile.

"I don't think so," said Rob. "We'll get some more clothes and a toothbrush when we get home." He smiled for the first time in four hours. He was beginning to relax. "When we get to within fifty miles of Port-au-Prince, we need to turn to a heading of three hundred twenty degrees," Rob said as he looked at the charts. "That will get us close enough to pick up some navigational aids and then on into Florida. We'll land at Opa Locka and call Jim. He'll know what to do with the airplane," Rob said, looking at Mike.

"Sounds like a good plan to me," Mike said. "I'll be glad when we're home. I'll get that old fishing pole and let all those fish know I'm back," he said with a nervous laugh. He knew they weren't out of it, not by a long shot.

They made the turn and were flying to the north-northwest on a three hundred twenty degrees heading. As they passed, they could see the lights of Haiti off to the east. Rob took out his pencil and began to make a few calculations on the fuel. They had another two and one-half hours at least. He began adding up the total gauge by gauge; the old gauges could be inaccurate. He didn't want to think about that. No, it was going to be close, but they were going to make it.

The old airplane shook as it passed through some light showers and turbulence. "That'll keep you awake," Mike said with a nervous laugh. The flashing lightning along with the cockpit lights casts an eerie glow all through the cockpit; and sometimes as the lightning flashed off in the distance, the sky became bright with dancing shadows in the clouds.

"Strange," said Rob. "I never noticed how much you can see when the lightning flashes."

"Me neither," said Mike. "I make it a rule. When lightning is flashing, I'm on the ground. I don't like thunderstorms, especially at night."

"That makes sense except now," Rob said. "We have to go through the edge of some of them. We don't have enough fuel to go around. From those flashes, the thunderstorms are a little off to the west but not by much. They usually move from the west to the east, so we had better strap on our belts and get ready for a bumpy ride." Rob knew that Mike could fly an airplane in bad weather, but he was especially afraid of thunderstorms.

"It's going to be a tough decision," said Mike. "Going through a thunderstorm and busting your ass or going around it and running out of fuel and having to ditch in the ocean. Take your choice-the devil or the deep blue sea," he said with a nervous voice.

Rob was watching the fuel gauges. They were getting low. They had at least another hour of flying, and the weather wasn't helping.

He switched the engines to the outboard fuel tanks. I'll run them dry, he thought; then switch to the inboard mains. He sat with his hands on the fuel selectors and had the boost pumps on. When the engine sputtered, he quickly switched the tanks and hit the boost pump switches to high. Those engines sputtering always made his heart jump. He didn't like doing this, but he needed every drop of fuel that was available in the tanks; and that was the only way.

Mike wasn't saying much. The thunderstorms and the engines sputtering were keeping his butt in a pucker, to say the least.

The closer they got; Rob began to realize they were not going to make it. Looking on his chart, they were nearing Bimini. Then it happened. The right engine began to surge, sputtered, and quit. Rob hit the feather button and pulled the prop lever. One down and one to go. All they could see below them was a misty haze. Slowly they were losing altitude. Rob had to make a decision either to make a controlled ditching into the water with at least one engine, or lose the left engine and have absolutely no control. That was a hell of a decision to make in the dark out over the water at night in the morning haze.

"Look," Mike said, "Look over to the one o'clock position. There it is again. It's a beacon."

"It's for boats," Rob said.

"No, hell no, it's green then white," said Mike. "That's an airport."

The altimeter showed they were below five hundred feet. Rob had turned the airplane toward the beacon and said, "Mike, there it is off the nose of the airplane." In the dark was a light strip of something, running from the east to the west, but there weren't any runway lights. They didn't have time to look on the chart for a radio code to turn them on if it had lights.

"Let's do it," Rob said as he swung the lumbering DC-3 out to the east over the water and made a left turn into the power of the left engine. "Help me on the rudders," he said to Mike. They both pushed the left rudder pedal, and the old bird came around.

"Get the gear," said Rob, as they were only a few hundred feet off the end of the faint gray strip of unknown, running from the beach inland to obscurity.

"Gear down," said Mike. Moments later, the DC-3 hit once, bounced, then settled on the runway. The tailwheel touched, and Rob stood on the brakes then quickly came to a stop in the darkness.

"Well, where are we?" Rob asked.

"On the ground," Mike said with a hallelujah. "We made it and didn't have to swim."

Rob attempted to taxi the airplane with one engine. Unlocking the tailwheel, he had Mike put his head out the window. "I can't see a thing," he said. "Turn on the taxi lights." Rob turned on the lights. "Okay," said Mike. "We need to make a turn to the right, then back to the left."

Rob made the turn to the right off the runway, but that was it. When he attempted to turn to the left into the running engine, he couldn't do it. "This is it," he said.

They were clear of the runway and on a short taxiway to the parking ramp. Rob shut the left engine down and set the brakes. The nose of the airplane and the right wing were out over the ramp.

"Let's go see who's home," said Mike as he pulled off his harness, got out of his seat, headed down the cabin, and opened the cargo door, stopped, stood in the door and looked around. There was only the light from the beacon as it rotated around each time, casting moving shadows. "Looks a little quiet," he said. "I don't think anyone's here."

Rob walked up. They both jumped down on the ground and went around to the front of the airplane. Over across the parking ramp with an outside light burning was a small building. They walked over, and as they neared the light, Rob looked at his watch. It was almost two o'clock. They had flown for over seven hours.

The men stepped up and looked in the window. It was dark. No one was in. The only thing they could do was wait.

Lying on the porch of the small building and waiting, Mike tried to sleep, but the mosquitoes would have no part of that. They were in a feeding frenzy. Both men tried to doze between mosquito attacks but gave up and sat tired, sleepy, and hungry, waiting for morning to come.

38 INVADING THE BAHAMAS

The morning light was beginning to glow in the eastern sky as both men sat up to the noise of a vehicle coming up the shell road to the airport. It stopped at a rusty, metal gate, and a black military man stepped out of a jeep and kicked the gate, pushing it off to the side, then got back in the jeep and drove right past them sitting on the porch. He made a run around the perimeter of the ramp where several small airplanes were parked. As the man drove under the nose of the DC-3, Mike said, "Watch this."

There was a crunching of shell as the soldier slammed on the brakes, sat for a moment, then realized what he had seen. He put the jeep in reverse, backed up, and drove around to the side door of the DC-3, got out and walked up to the opening and called out in a strong Bahamian accent, "Hello, is there anyone in there?"

"Well," said Mike. "I guess its show and tell. Let's go." Both men got up and stumbled reluctantly across the parking ramp toward the DC-3.

The soldier walked around to the front and was standing looking up at the nose of the airplane.

"We're over here," Mike said as they came toward the soldier who was standing with his boots unlaced, his shirt unbuttoned, and his belt unfastened.

"Is this your airplane?" he asked, tucking his shirt into his pants.

"Yes, it is," said Rob.

"What are you doing here?" he asked with a shout while putting both hands over his head. "Where did you come from?" he asked in a loud voice.

"We landed here last night," Mike said.

"Last night?" he said. "I didn't hear you."

"We came in from the east and didn't use any lights," said Rob.

"You must leave, and you must leave now," the soldier said, being very animated. "They will lock me up if they find this airplane here. Start it up. Get it away from here and do it now; and I won't arrest you," he said.

"We can't," Rob said. "We are out of fuel."

"Oh, they are going to think you are drug runners, and they will lock all of us up. They will believe I allowed you to land," he said. "My job is to guard the airport. I left and went to see a friend while I was supposed to be here," he continued. "What do you need? What?"

"We need fuel," Mike said.

"How much?" the soldier asked excitedly.

"Oh, hundred fifty to hundred sixty gallons. Do you have fuel here?" Rob asked.

"Yes, boat fuel. Will that do?" he asked.

Rob and Mike looked at each other. "Yes, that will do," they answered.

"Come on. Let's go. I have a friend who operates the marina. We can get him up. He has those small thirty gallon drums we can use," said the soldier.

The soldier drove the jeep out the front of the airport in a cloud of white shell dust, down several blocks, and over to a marina. He hammered on a door until an older black man came out, putting on his shirt. Rob and Mike stood and watched as they talked. Then the soldier motioned for them to come over. Mike and Rob walked over and followed the two black men around the corner and to a small dock where there was a stack of blue thirty-gallon drums.

"Six of them will be one hundred eighty gallons," the older man said. "How will you be paying?" he asked.

"United States currency," said Rob.

Mike, the soldier, along with Rob, all picked up a drum and walked over to the gas pump. The older man filled the drums and screwed the filler plugs back in. The soldier and Rob began rolling the drums along the dock towards the jeep. Mike followed. They each made two trips.

On the last trip, Rob pulled out four one hundred-dollar bills and handed them to the man. He smiled and folded them and put them in his shirt pocket.

The drums were all stacked in the back of the jeep. They drove carefully along the shell road to the airport. The soldier backed the jeep up under the left wing of the DC-3. Rob got up on the wing. Mike and the soldier handed up the three drums of fuel, then repeated the procedure on the right wing and were pouring in the fuel when the soldier stood up and threw his hands up over his head. "I'm dead," he said. "I'm dead," he said in a strong Bahamian accent.

There, walking up the road toward the airport, were two men in white customs uniforms. They strolled over to the DC-3 where the soldier was up on the wing.

"What have we here?" the senior official asked.

"It's not what you think," the soldier said.

"What am I thinking?" the official asked.

The soldier stopped. He knew there wasn't a thing he could say. His ass was in a bind. He left his post, and someone landed at night.

"The airport is closed from dark until dawn. You do know that," the official said.

"Please step down," the senior official said as the other customs official walked over to the office. Mike and Rob stopped pouring the fuel into the wing tank of the DC-3, climbed down onto the jeep, and then the ground.

"Come with me," the official said as he walked toward the small office. As they neared the office, two more jeeps came flying up the shell drive to the airport. "Those are the defense forces," the customs official said. "I think they should handle this."

"Do they think we are going to invade the country?" Rob asked.

The soldiers all jumped down from the jeeps and surrounded Mike and Rob, pointing their M-16's. "Put your hands up," the captain said. "You are under arrest."

"For what?" Mike asked.

"To begin with, this airport is closed at night. It appears you have used this airport for some illegal activity. I am sure we will find enough evidence to substantiate what we suspect. Now come with us," he said.

The two jeeps rolled through the narrow streets and came to a halt in front of a two story building on a well-established street. There were worn stairs leading to a balcony on the second floor. On the front of the building was a sign announcing Office of the Bahamian Defense Force.

They took Rob and Mike up the outside stairs to the balcony and then into an office with a waiting area. The two men were seated on a small wooden bench. Several of the soldiers stood around them as the captain went into a rear office and used the telephone. He returned shortly and talked to a sergeant who was sitting at a desk with his back to the window along the front of the office. Then he turned to the two men.

"I need some identification," he said.

"No problem," said Rob, pulling out his driver's license, passport, and the visa issued the week before when he had returned from Miami. The captain looked at them, then returned the license and visa to Rob. "And you?' he said, looking at Mike.

Mike handed the captain his driver's license and passport. "I don't have a visa," Mike said. "I wasn't planning to stop off, but we ran out of fuel, and I do appreciate the hospitality you are showing us," Mike continued with a bit of sarcasm.

"Don't get smart with me," the captain said, and a sergeant joined in, "You white Americans think we are just a bunch of dumb n...... down here. Well, we'll show you. We'll lock you up, and by the time we let you go, you'll be old enough to draw your retirement," he said with a loud voice, shaking his fist at Mike.

"Calm down," the captain said, looking at the sergeant. The captain walked back into the rear office. He returned in a few minutes and looked at Mike, "You, Mr. Ricau, will have an opportunity to explain to the magistrate why you are on Bahamian soil without an invitation, or should I say, a visa. You will go with my soldiers. They will show you to the magistrate's office." The soldiers all stood up. Mike looked at Rob. Rob crossed his legs and patted the inside of his leg below his knee. Mike understood. Rob had given him five thousand dollars on the flight down to Honduras. Mike had put it in his boot. Rob was reminding him to use it if he needed to.

Mike stood up and walked out the door and down the stairs. Rob went over to the window and looked out as Mike was going down the street with the soldiers grouped closely around him. Mike stood out. He was a full head taller than all the soldiers. Rob stood watching as they marched off down the street and disappeared around a corner.

Rob eased over to the sergeant at the desk. "Could I possibly use your phone?" he asked. "I think I can clear this matter up with one call."

The sergeant didn't speak. He stood up and strolled back to the captain's office. The captain followed the sergeant up to the front office. He stepped just inside and spoke, "Come with me," he said to Rob.

Rob followed the captain down a narrow hall and into a rear office. "Have a seat," the captain said.

Rob pulled up a chair then sat down, looking around. There on one side was a closet with the door partially open, and inside was a stack of what appeared to be bales of marijuana. Rob stared for a moment. Then regained his composure.

"Now," the captain said as he closed the door to the hall and walked around and sat down behind the desk. "What's this about a phone call?" he asked.

"I think I can clear up this matter of our being here with a phone call," Rob said.

"Who do you want to call?" the captain asked.

"I need to make one call to Miami," Rob said.

The captain turned the old, black telephone around and pushed it across the desk to Rob. Rob pulled out his wallet and removed the piece of paper with Lourdes's phone number and picked up the receiver. The captain gave Rob instructions on the procedure to call to the States. Rob dialed the final digits. The phone on the other end began to ring.

Lourdes answered. "Hello," she said.

"Good morning," Rob replied. There was a long pause.

"I didn't expect to hear from you," she said. "How are things going down there?" she continued.

"We are not down there," Rob said. "We are over in Bimini."

"In Bimini?" she said. "What are you doing there?"

Rob thought for a minute. "We were on our way back after finishing the flying, and we lost some of our fuel to a leaking pump. We couldn't make it all the way back to Miami, so we stopped in here and are having a problem with the local authorities."

"Why didn't you call Jacobson?" she asked.

"Well, that's another problem, Jacobson doesn't know we are here; and we don't want him to know. I need you to call the Bahamian authorities and get us released," Rob said. "We did all the flying, and we want to go home. All I'm asking is this one favor; you owe me," Rob said.

There was a long pause. "I know someone in the Prime Minister's office. I'll make the call, but if Jacobson calls, I'll have to tell him," she said.

"I have no problem with that," Rob said. "Just give us four hours." There was a long pause.

"Okay," she said. "We are now even. I'm getting you out of what I put you into."

"Thanks," Rob said. She didn't reply, only hung up the phone.

Rob sat looking at the captain. "Thanks," he said. The captain didn't say a word. They sat for about fifteen minutes.

The phone rang. The captain answered. "Yes, sir," he said as he stood up. "Yes, sir, I'll do that," he said. "And a good day to you, too, sir." He hung up the phone and looked at Rob. "I don't know who you are, but that was the Prime Minister of the Bahamas. He said to let you go and to give you any help you need. What can I do?' the captain asked.

"I'm tired, sleepy, and hungry. I guess for beginners, you could tell me where I could get something to eat," Rob said.

"That's no problem," the captain said. He picked up the telephone and called. "How does breakfast with eggs, bacon, and some hot coffee sound?" he asked, smiling as he hung up the phone, then walked over to the door, and told the sergeant, "Come in here," he said. The sergeant came down the hall into the office. The captain spoke briefly to him, then the sergeant hurried out. Rob heard the door of the front office close.

In about ten minutes, the sergeant returned with a tray covered with a white cloth. On one side of the tray was a coffeepot. As he entered through the office door, the captain said, "I think we have your breakfast." He arose and took the tray, setting it on the corner of his desk. "Come over here and sit in my chair," he said as he moved the tray to the middle of his desk and uncovered it and began pouring coffee into a large, brown cup.

The smell of fresh coffee and breakfast put a smile on Rob's face. He stood up and walked around the desk and sat down, picked up the cup of coffee and took a sip. "Thank you," he said, looking at the captain then began to hastily eat the bacon and eggs. As he was eating, he heard the pounding of feet on the outside stairs and the rattling of gear as the soldiers returned.

Mike walked to the door of the captain's office. He stood there, filling up the opening. It was apparent he was very emotional. He stood, looking as Rob ate. "Well," he said. "While the judge threatened to throw me in jail for five years, fine me two thousand dollars, then gave me six hours to get off the island, I get back here and find you being waited on like royalty. Looks like you've been sucking up to someone's ass. What the hell is going on?" Mike said as he stepped on into the office. Rob didn't speak; he had his mouth full.

"Would you like some breakfast?" the captain asked. "Now I can't get your money back because it has become public record, but I can get you something to eat and help you get fuel for your airplane," he said with a smile. "I must apologize," he added, "but we didn't know who you were."

Mike stood a minute, then walked over to the desk. He reached down and took a piece of bacon off Rob's plate and ate it. "Yes, I'll have something to eat," he said. "What he's got looks good. I'll have the same."

The captain walked over and sat a cup on the tray, poured some of the coffee from the pot, and handed it to Mike. He then walked out the door and pulled it closed behind him.

"What's going on?" Mike asked.

"I made a call," Rob answered.

"Who did you call?' Mike asked.

"I called Lourdes," Rob said. "She made a call to the Prime Minister's office. She said something about knowing his secretary."

"Then Jacobson will be sitting in Miami waiting when we get there," Mike said.

"No, she said she would give us four hours. What I think we will do is go into Fort Lauderdale Executive. They won't expect that. We can clear customs and then get the hell out and leave the airplane there."

"Okay," said Mike as he pulled up a chair close to the desk and reached over and took one of the pieces of toast off Rob's plate and ate it. "I hope you don't mind, but my stomach is empty. I need to put something in it, and these old boys around here can give you hell, too," he said while eating the toast in two bites.

Mike's breakfast came. They finished eating, and then the captain and two of the soldiers drove them back to the airport.

"Look," said Rob. "The soldier who was here at the airport had nothing to do with us being here. He was only trying to help us when the customs officials came by so don't be too hard on him."

The captain smiled, "He's a good man. He had a problem keeping his pants on if you know what I am saying."

"Sure," said Rob. "He likes the women."

They finished fueling the old DC-3. Rob checked his watch. It was now eight-thirty. They had three hours before Lourdes would locate Jacobson and give him this information. He would like to see the expression on his face when he found out they were still alive. On second thought, maybe not. He hoped he never saw the bastard again.

The soldiers finished pouring the fuel into the airplane fuel tanks. Rob and Mike shook the captain's hand. They climbed into the DC-3 and started the engines. "We'll take it easy on the power," said Rob. "That old boat fuel could be rough on the engines." They taxied out and made their quick run-up. They took off back to the east, then turned slowly back to the west.

39 PLAYING THE ACE OF TRUMPS

Once off the ground, they climbed to twenty-five hundred feet and called Miami Center. It was only a twenty-minute flight to Fort Lauderdale Executive Airport. The center handed them off to Fort Lauderdale approach and then approach to tower. "Lauderdale Executive, this is Douglas November One Niner Niner Eight," Rob said.

"Go ahead, November One Niner Niner Eight," tower replied.

"Lauderdale, we are approximately ten minutes east, inbound for landing," Rob said.

"November One Niner Niner Eight, report five-mile final for runway two-seven," tower responded.

"Roger, Lauderdale Executive," Rob said. To Mike he added, "Looks like we've made it."

"There she is," said Mike, pointing to the west.

"Lauderdale Executive, this is November One Niner Niner Eight. We are on a five-mile final for runway two-seven," Rob said.

"November One Niner Niner Eight, you are cleared to land," tower said.

Rob clicked his mic button then pulled the throttles back, slowing the airplane. "Get the gear," he said to Mike.

Mike watched as the landing gear extended and the indicator lights came on. "Gear down and locked," he said.

They were on a two-mile final. Rob slowed the airplane some more. "Get the flaps," he said on short final. Mike set the flaps to twenty degrees.

"Flaps down," Mike said.

Rob slowed the airplane a little then held it off as it settled on the runway with a thud.

"Great to be back in the good old U.S.A.," said Mike. "I'm not sure I ever want to leave again," he said very seriously.

Rob switched the radio to ground control and was instructed to taxi to customs. They taxied the airplane to the ramp beside customs office and shut it down.

"What are we going to tell these old boys?" Mike asked. "You know they want to know where we've been."

"We've been to the Bahamas to show this airplane to a potential customer," Rob said. "That's all they need to know."

"That we did," said Mike. "That's the simple version. They won't believe the rest, so we'll keep it a secret." He smiled.

Walking into customs and then filling out all the necessary forms, they handed them to an older woman. She turned and spoke to one of the men in the office then turned to Rob and Mike, "I need one of you go out to the plane with him," she said, pointing to a man standing behind her.

"I'll do it," said Rob.

The agent only stuck his head in the open door. Looking at the form he said, "Looks like you boys have been on a vacation."

"You could say that," Rob said.

He then turned and walked back to the office, went in the back door as Rob entered through the front door. The older woman was standing, talking to Mike as Rob walked up. "We need to use a phone," said Rob. The woman pointed down the hall to several blue pay phones hanging on the wall. Rob hurried down the corridor and picked up the first phone and dialed Jim's home.

"Jim," Rob said, "how are you doing?"

"Maybe I should ask you that question," said Jim. "Where are you? No, don't answer that," Jim said. I'm going to give you a number. Call me there in ten minutes."

Rob took the number and looked at his watch then strolled back over to where Mike was now sitting in a chair, reading a Sunday newspaper. "Look at these headlines," he exclaimed. "'Congress Launches Contra Hearings'. I think we need to find a hole to hide in," Mike said. "It looks like Jacobson and his bunch are in the hot-seat, and he's not going to want any witnesses."

Rob took the paper. "Yep, Jacobson's been doing a little house cleaning. We are the trash, only we don't want to get taken out. You know if Jacobson gets a second chance, he won't miss, not twice. We've got to stop him and as soon as possible." Rob walked back over to the phone and dialed the number Jim had given him.

Jim answered. "Have you seen the papers?" he asked.

"Had my first glance five minutes ago," Rob answered.

"Are you involved in that?" Jim asked.

"Up to my eyeballs," said Rob.

"I'm talking on Amy's phone," Jim said. "I wasn't sure if my phone was clear. It could have ears. You two need to be careful. Where are you?" Jim asked.

"We're just up the road at Lauderdale Executive," Rob said.

"Okay," said Jim. "You need to get out of there and now. Take your plane around to Southern Systems and ask for Ken Winstead. He runs the place for a friend of mine. They are a contract maintenance facility. Tell him I sent you; then get someone to take you across to the other side of the airport. On a side street one block west of the airport is a small hotel called the Palms Inn. It's a place airplane people use when they are down here on business. I'll give them a call so they will be expecting you."

"Thanks," said Rob. "I appreciate all you are doing."

"Your friend, that George Garcia, the one who has the charter service at Opa Locka that Jacobson and his people were using, has disappeared. Some people in plain white cars came last night and picked up him and his brother. No one has heard from them since. The rumors are they were a special government team. No one seems to know for sure, so be careful," Jim said. "Real careful."

"Okay," said Rob. "We'll keep looking over our shoulders." Rob hurried back out to where Mike was reading the paper. As Mike looked up, "Let's go," Rob said as he walked by.

Mike could tell Rob was uptight as they boarded the airplane. Mike asked, "What's up?"

"There seems to be a clean-up going on by Jacobson and his bunch. They grabbed George and his brother last night. They aren't leaving any loose ends, and we're dangling out in his face," said Rob.

"Oh, that makes me feel real good," Mike said.

They taxied the airplane around to Southern Systems and parked the airplane beside the hangar then got out and trotted across the ramp to the office. "We're looking for Ken," Rob said.

The man behind the counter pointed to a corner office where a man was talking on the telephone. Rob walked to the open door and stood, nervously waiting for him to get off the phone. Ken hung up. "What can I do for you?" he asked.

"I'm Rob; this is Mike," Rob said.

Ken stood up. "Yes, Jim just called and said you wanted to leave your DC-3 here," he said.

"Will that create a problem?" asked Rob.

"Oh, no," said Ken. "We'll take care of it. I need you to sign some papers authorizing us to service it and put it on tie downs, the usual stuff," he said.

They went over to the service counter. Ken pulled out an order. "I need you to sign here," he said, pointing to the bottom of the page. "We'll do the rest."

Rob scribbled his name, then handed the order back to Ken. "We'll need some transportation. We are going over to the Palm something," Rob said.

"You're talking about the Palms Inn. That's a good place. They'll give you a reasonable rate. It caters to aviation personnel. I'll get someone to drive you over there," he said.

Rob and Mike didn't have as much as a toothbrush or a razor. They walked out the front door of the maintenance office as a blue stationwagon with the company name displayed on the door pulled up, a young Cuban boy driving.

"He'll take you," Ken said, handing Rob a business card. "Call me if you have any questions," he said, closing the door.

As soon as the stationwagon rolled to a stop in front of the hotel, the two men jumped out and thanked the driver. When they approached the front door, they both stopped and looked around to see if they had been followed from the airport. The street was empty except for a black and white cab parked near the corner. They went in the front door and over to the registration where an older, thin man, sporting a dark tan, was behind the desk watching TV.

The man pointed his finger and looked over his reading glasses. "I know who you are," he said. "You're friends of Jim. He said to take good care of you and don't ask any questions. Here," he said, handing them two keys, "the rooms are upstairs, inside," he said, motioning to the staircase across the lobby.

"Thanks," said Mike. "We need some toilet items. All our luggage got lost."

The man fumbled behind the desk and came up with two small plastic bags. "It's not top of the line, but it will do the job," he said, tossing the bags to Mike. "I don't know who you are and don't want to know. Jim wants it that way. We've been friends since the big war," he said with a smile. "If someone asks, I haven't seen you," he said, turning back to the TV behind the desk.

Mike and Rob hurriedly climbed up the stairs to the second floor. The rooms were side by side with an adjoining door. Nervously, they both fumbled with their keys until their doors came open then went inside. Getting the smell of this whole mess off of them was a desperate priority as they showered, shave, and brushed their teeth. For the first time in eight days, they were alone, at least for the moment.

"We need some clean clothes," said Mike.

"I know," said Rob, "But if we can get home, you'll have clothes. We don't need to be parading around here shopping. You never know who's out there looking for us."

"You're right," said Mike with a shrug, "hopefully, in a few more hours we'll be out of this crap and back home."

There was a soft knock on the door. Rob stood up and looked through the peephole. To his relief, there stood his trusted friend, Jim.

Rob cracked the door open cautiously. "Come in," he said.

Jim slipped through the narrow opening. "You boys got your hands full," he said.

"I know," said Rob. "They tried to blow our asses out of the air last night."

"How did they do that?" asked Jim.

"They put a bomb on the airplane," Mike said. "These sons of bitches mean business."

"Okay," said Jim, "We've got to get you out of here, so I've worked something out with a friend of mine who has a Cessna Citation. His crew is going to fly you two home. They'll take you back to your airport, no having to expose yourselves by riding on a commercial airline."

"Good," said Rob, "I need to do something before we go," he said, holding up his small folder with the notepad inside.

"What's that?" Jim asked.

"I need to make a copy of all this and give it to you. If anything happens to Mike, me, or any of our family, I want you to fax all this to the Miami newspaper," Rob said. "I hope you don't mind getting involved."

Jim was slow to answer. "I don't mind, but they know we are good friends. I'd like to make a suggestion; let me give it to someone else. You don't need to know who, but they're someone who will do what's right," Jim added.

"That's good," said Rob. "It may be better if I don't know. Let's do it," he said.

"We can get all of this copied downstairs in the office. Then I'll take you over to the Cessna Citation," Jim said.

Hurrying downstairs, they used the copy machine in the office. Rob placed the folded sheets with all the detailed information, which included each and every name, date, and place in a large envelope, sealed it, and handed it to Jim.

Then Rob thanked the old man behind the desk as they were leaving. Jim took them in his car around to the general aviation terminal and escorted them over to the waiting plane.

"I don't know how to thank you," Rob said, putting out his hand to his old friend.

"Oh, it's nothing," Jim said. "You'd do the same for me."

Rob checked his watch as they boarded the Cessna Citation. It was now noon. Jacobson had known for about thirty minutes that they were still alive. The Cessna Citation taxied out onto the runway, paused while they waited for clearance, and then took off. Mike and Rob both fell asleep as soon as the airplane was airborne. For the last two days, they had virtually gone without sleep.

Rob woke to the sound of the airplane bumping on landing. He looked out. They were back home. Gazing down at his watch, it was a little past three. They had made good time.

Anne came out to meet the Cessna as it landed and the door unfolded. Rob and Mike stepped out and stood up. She ran over to them; Rob hugged her and old Mike picked her up with his strong arms and swung her thin body around in a small circle.

"Damn good to be home," Mike said with a big happy smile.

Rob stuck his head inside the Cessna's door. "Are you going back now, or do you want us to arrange for you a place to stay?" he asked.

"I'm going back, but I do need some fuel," he answered. "Do you have any here?"

"No," said Rob, "but there's a regional airport about fifteen minutes south of here. They'll have jet fuel."

"Okay," the pilot said, "I'll go over there."

"Again, thanks," said Rob. "And tell the owner I said thanks. Send me the bill; here's my card."

"I'll do that," the pilot said as Rob stepped down from the plane, then the pilot closed the cabin door, started the engines, and in no time, had taxied out to the runway and was gone. The three stood and watched as he climbed out and turned to the south.

"Oh, you two don't know how much I've worried about all this," Anne said as they were walking across the ramp towards the office. She stopped. "Where are your bags?" Anne asked.

"That's a long story," said Mike, reaching out and putting his arm around her shoulder. "I'll tell you all about it some day."

As they came through the office door, the phone was ringing. Anne answered it. "It's for you," she said, puzzled. "I think it's that Jacobson." Rob and Mike looked at each other.

"I'll take it in my office," he said as he went into a small corner office then picked up the phone and pressed the flashing button. "Hello," he said.

"What happened to you boys?" Jacobson asked.

"Oh, don't bullshit me. I don't feel like playing games," Rob said. "The bottom line is you sons of bitches tried to kill us, so I'll cut to the chase. Here's how it's all going down. I'm sending you some information. What's your fax number?"

Jacobson gave the number to Rob. It was a Miami area code.

"Okay," said Rob. "I'm sending you a few pages of a daily record that I have been keeping. It has a few names and places you might be interested in. There are several copies, and I have given them to other people who will mail or fax them to all the major newspapers if anything happens to Mike, me, or any of our families."

"Wait, wait," said Jacobson. "We don't need that information being given freely to people who are irresponsible. It could get into the wrong hands."

"No," said Rob. "That's the way it is going to be, so you sons of bitches can now do the sweating. I'm going to fax this to you. By the way, you owe me another sixty thousand dollars. I'll be expecting it the first thing tomorrow morning."

Rob hung up the phone, walked out into the front office, fed the sheet into the fax machine, and dialed the number. He ran three sheets through and waited for the fax machine to finish.

Shortly, the phone rang. Rob picked it up. "Hello," he said.

"If any of this information ever becomes public, I will personally take care of you and your family," Jacobson said. He paused. "That damn money will be there tomorrow." With a click, he hung up the phone.

Rob sat for a few minutes; he had played his only card. He hoped it was the ace of trumps. He felt by Jacobson's reaction that he would leave them alone as long as they remained silent. Struggling out of his chair, he stood up, walked towards Mike who was sitting in the front office, drinking coffee and talking to Anne.

"Well, Mike, old friend, it's settled for now. I think I'll go get my kids and we'll go fishing," he said as he walked past them and out the door.

This text is fictional and any resemblance to any event, person, place or thing is strictly coincidental.